The Journey from Shanghai to Gold Mountain

A novel

Hilarie Gottlieb

Credits:
Edited by Janet Musick
Cover and interior design by Debbi Stocco
Cover art by sanyanwuji/shutterstock.com

ISBN: 978-1-980976-37-0

This book is dedicated
to my wonderful family, friends
and
to my boyfriend, Stephen Bartell,
for all their support.

My deepest gratitude goes to
Professor Eben Wood
for his encouraging words and
his belief that I could write
my first novel.

The floating clouds, the fog, darken the sky.
The moon shines faintly as the insects chirp.
Grief and bitterness entwined are heaven sent.
The sad woman sits alone, behind a curtain.
— Unknown

Table of Contents

Prologue

Pacifica, California, 2018

My name is Susan Jacobs. I'm half-Chinese on my mother's side and I live in Pacifica, California with my husband Robert and our children—Samantha, four, and David, seven.

When I was in high school, I was diagnosed with Hodgkin's Lymphoma, and because of several severe rounds of chemotherapy and stem cell transplants, I became sterile. We made two attempts at in vitro fertilization, without success.

Finally, we decided to adopt a baby from China. The China Center for Adoption Affairs (CCAA) is the Chinese government-run organization for international adoptions. It was very expensive and totally worth it when we adopted our darling baby boy, whom we named David. Three years later, we adopted our little girl, Samantha. The cost was huge, but the rewards were astronomical. There is no way to put into words our joy in these two children. So a Chinese-American Jewish woman and an American Jewish man came to raise two adopted Chinese-Jewish children. Zhang Ling, my great-grandmother, would be so proud that our heritage still remained alive.

I'm a journalist, writing for *C*, California Style Magazine, which is a nationally circulated magazine. *C* showcases California lifestyle through a wide range of lenses. The magazine is a premier ad vehicle, and it reaches the nation's top luxury spenders by offering expert information on trends, styles, and attitudes that reflect how California's rich and famous live and look. It's somewhat of a glamorous position, requiring me to attend various upscale functions, including events such as fashion previews, interviews with celebrities, established designers, and new up-and-coming stylists. My position requires me to travel occasionally, and I have to admit I love it.

Robert is an attorney and he works for O'Brian, Johnson, Graber, and Fine, a mid-sized law firm with their specialty being corporate and securities law. He started his career with Morgan Stanley Smith Barney, the largest wealth management firm in the world. After several years, his growth wasn't what he hoped for and he made the move to the smaller firm. He was close to being offered a partnership. Our jobs afford us a comfortable lifestyle, while Paulette, our wonderful nanny, allows us the freedom we need to pursue our career goals.

We live in a pretty colonial house set back on a gently sloping hill, with two apple trees in our front yard, two recent-model cars in the driveway, and an apricot toy Poodle named Jazzy. Jazzy loves nothing more than to sit on the grass in the sun. If she's lucky, she gets to eat one of the apples that falls from one of the trees. It's funny to watch her struggles since her mouth is much smaller than the apple. It often rolls away from her, and she chases it, occasionally getting her teeth into it. If she gets a tooth-hold, Jazzy is happy for a while, biting off pieces of the sweet fruit.

One wet, windy morning, I awakened with a terrible sore throat and stuffed nose, and not having anything pressing at work that couldn't be rescheduled, I decided to take a well-needed day off. Robert got the kids ready for school, telling me to stay in bed, and that he could manage fine without my help.

"Make sure they wear their slickers. It's pouring out," I yelled down to Robert.

"They're both wearing them," he called back.

A few minutes later, I heard the school bus pull up, and looking out the window, I saw Robert helping my two little loves onto the bus. He must have felt me watching because he looked up, blew me a kiss, and walked over to his car as the school bus pulled away.

Fortunately, I could write from home if I chose to, and I was almost finished with a piece about a young new designer I had recently interviewed in Los Angeles. I called in sick and got back into bed, slept another hour, and when I awakened, I wandered downstairs to make myself a big mug of tea, Jazzy at my heels. Throwing a couple of slices of bread into the toaster while I waited for the kettle to boil, I thought about doing some work on my article, but the deadline wasn't until the following week, and I just didn't have the impetus to sit down and work just then. After putting some peanut butter and raspberry jam on my toast, I thumbed through a past issue of *C* while I ate. Finished, I put the plate and knife in the dishwasher, and grabbing my tea, I went up to the bedroom thinking I'd take a hot shower and get back into bed again. Jazzy would have been only too happy to join me.

The hot water felt good. I could feel the cold coming on as my nose was now running, stuffier than when I got up earlier. Toweling off, I took a couple of cold tablets from the medicine chest and walked back into the bedroom, swallowing them down with some tea.

As I pulled open a drawer in my dresser to grab some clean pajamas, I thought how I'd promised myself to find time to clean out my bottom junk drawer, which was practically exploding. Again, I told myself I would work on the article a little later. The unmade bed looked inviting, but instead, I opened the drawer. I was amazed at how much useless stuff I had accumulated over the past few years. I began to rifle through it and pulled out an old scarf I used to love and a load of receipts for children's clothes that had long ago been passed along to my friends for their children. I found a pair of black leather gloves I had given up for lost, a now-broken hair clip jammed in the back of the drawer, a pair of embroidery scissors, a red scarf, and a travel-sized can of anti-static spray that had also gone missing. At the very bottom was a heavy manila envelope holding a binder of typed pages, as well as my Great-Grandmother Zhang Ling's journal. I had forgotten it was in the drawer.

Sitting down on the floor, I reached up and grabbed my lukewarm mug of tea from the night table, along with the box of tissues, and put them beside me on the floor; Jazzy was happy to join me. With my legs extended in front of me, I leaned my back up against the bed, placed the binder on my lap, and opened it. I was still reading when the school bus pulled up and honked for me to get Sam, who was returning home from her half-day at Pre-K. David would be home later.

When I was sixteen, almost twenty years ago, I came home from school one day, and I recalled that my mother, after she cut me a slice from an apple pie she had just baked that morning and poured me a glass of milk, had strangely begun to talk about my Great-Grandmother Zhang Ling. Mom had spoken of her various times in the past, but today was different. That particular day, as we sat in the kitchen, she with a cup of tea, and me with my pie and milk, she had gotten up from the table and gone into the dining room. When she returned, she was holding a small, brown, leather-bound book, and a manila envelope from which she withdrew a large sheaf of papers, attached with a big clip on the top. She handed it all to me. The book was worn around the edges, and inside, the pages were filled with Chinese characters. In the back were several loose pages that were actually letters, along with some photographs. My grandmother, Yuming, had been the first to inherit this journal. She had understood, and could speak Chinese, but was unable to read the calligraphy, never having learned to write it. So, Mom explained, Yuming must have had the diary and letters translated from the Wu dialect of Shanghai into English. I knew my great-grandmother had come to America from China, and I knew she had a difficult life, but I had never known just how difficult.

Mom explained that Zhang Ling, having already had two husbands, married one more time to a kind, loving man named Song Bao. The couple adopted a son who died young, and later she had given birth to a petite daughter, very much like she herself had been as a baby. They had named her Song Yuming, her given name meaning Jade Brightness. Bao had been a merchant by trade, and it was with him that my great-grandmother happily lived out her remaining years.

When Bao died, Ling had given the journal to Yuming, who was to become my grandmother. Yuming eventually married a man called Dai Wu, and they had a daughter, Min, as well as a son, Je. When Min got married to John Harvey, the first American in our family, she Americanized her name to Mina Dai-Harvey. She became the next beneficiary of these memoirs and was to become my mother.

I remember how Mom had grown wistful then. She had often told me that she was so sorry my grandmother had died before I was old enough to remember her. She had continued her story, telling me how, when she turned sixteen, my grandmother had shared with her these earliest memories of our family, just as she was sharing them now with me. She requested that it be passed on to future daughters at the age of sixteen.

"This journal and these pictures and letters are the most precious thing I will ever give to you, Susan," she said. "Please read the translation, and cherish the book, letters, and photos your great-grandmother valued so much. If you are blessed with a daughter, I hope you will pass them along to her in remembrance of our amazing matriarch, Zhang Ling."

BOOK ONE
Zhang Ling

Chapter One

Shanghai, China, 1920

I am called Zhang Ling. I was born in 1905, just after the turn of the century. I came unexpectedly early, and so was very tiny. When he saw that I was a girl-child, my father was so disappointed that his firstborn wasn't a son, he refused to name me. Because I was small and always happy, my mother called me Ling, which means Little Bird. My father rarely acknowledged me, but I always knew I was my mother's favorite.

All around there was beauty and the trappings that prosperity could offer. Shanghai, known as the "Paris of the East, the New York of the West," glowed with a life of its own. Located at the mouth of the Yangtze River in China, Shanghai was an exciting place to live at this time. It had gone from a fishing village to a great metropolis. By 1921, the city was teeming with wealthy Northern Chinese, British, Americans, Eurasians, White Russians, and even Russian Jews. They were known as "Shanghailanders'. Handsome men and beautiful women spent sinful amounts of money. Eligi-

ble bachelors, their hair slicked back with Brilliantine, wore tight-fitting suits, spending their evenings drinking, and listening to jazz at the various glamorous ballrooms throughout the city. Stunning socialites, on the arms of these men, dressed in slinky, beaded qípáo, (jackets, or dresses with jackets), cheongsams, (also dresses, with frog closures, and high necklines, often made of silk brocade), or the latest French fashions, and danced the night away. Elegant hotels, like the Astor House, were frequented by the myriads of visitors who came to enjoy the excitement and culture of this cosmopolitan city. In the afternoon, couples strolled along The Bund, past the Custom's House, Shanghai Club, and Asia Building, and the many large banking institutions. Many visited the exquisite Yuyuan Garden. It was a glorious place and time.

We rented a house where I lived with my parents, three brothers, and little sister. It was small, just four rooms. There were two bedrooms, a tiny parlor, and a kitchen area. We had a bathroom and indoor plumbing. The furnishings were simple, yet adequate. The kitchen was functional, with a sink, an icebox, and a cook stove. Baba, my father, worked as a rickshaw puller, while Mama was a servant for a wealthy American family. They both left before dawn, never returning before dark. By fifteen years of age, I was finished with school and was now responsible for my siblings, brothers Cheng, Ye, Hu, and little sister Lan, who was only five. The boys attended the nearby Chinese school, but Cheng at thirteen would soon be old enough to leave school to work pulling a rickshaw. My father, only thirty-nine years old, looked like fifty-nine. Stoop-shouldered from the weight of the loaded rickshaws, his skin was brown and wrinkled from the hours spent in the sun. His peaked straw hat did little to protect him from that sun, or for that matter, the wind, rain, and snow.

The rickshaws had iron-shod wooden wheels. Passengers sat on hard seats, and the public rickshaws were painted yellow to differentiate them from the privately owned vehicles. They were a convenient means of travel since they were able to maneuver the winding, narrow streets of Shanghai.

Mama, whose name was Zhang Fang-Xing, toiled long and hard for an American family. The Greenes were American Jews who had settled in Shanghai six years earlier. Mr. Nathan Greene was a banker who worked for the American Oriental Bank of Shanghai. He was a kind, portly gentleman, very often not home. He was a vice president and commanded a great deal of respect in the banking world.

Maxine Greene was a snob; she was a middle-aged matron, puffed up with her own importance, and riding the coattails of her husband's wealth. She adapted quickly to Shanghai, befriending the wives of many of the other ex-patriots living there. Her life was a whirlwind of card parties, afternoon teas, dinners, shopping sprees, and general socializing. A tall, skinny, blonde woman, she possessed a sharp nose, which often matched her sharp tongue. She treated Mama with disdain, sometimes throwing a fit over the slightest wrinkle found on a previously pressed shirtwaist.

Mr. Greene sometimes arrived home quite late, his dinner kept warm by the cook in the huge kitchen. Mama would then have to serve and clean up after the meal, and was finally dismissed long after nightfall. Still, she was lucky to have such a good job.

When the American Oriental Bank of Shanghai made Nathan an offer to relocate, the Greenes made the decision to move; it was too lucrative a deal to turn down. The bank footed the bill for relocation as well as the purchase of a new house, so they had sold their home in Boston and moved into an elegant house in the northeast section of the city known as

Hongkou. Their house was in the *Shikumen* style.

Shikumen houses (literally meaning "stone-framed door") were unique to Shanghai. They were western adaptations of traditional Chinese courtyards. These houses had what were known as stone-hooped doors. Translated from Shanghai dialect, wrapping or bundling was called "hooping." These buildings had long stones as door frames, and wooden planks as doors, each fixed with a huge bronze ring. They reflected a mix of Chinese and foreign architecture. Behind the door, there was a courtyard, and further inside, a parlor. There was a back courtyard, as well. Left and right of the courtyard and parlor were right and left wing rooms. In addition, there was a kitchen. The second story was similar to the one below, but above the kitchen, there was a garret, and above that, a flat roof.

The mansion afforded plenty of space for their family to live in, as well as to entertain. Herbert, their eighteen-year-old son, was enrolled in Fudan University, while Francine, who was fourteen, attended Shanghai American School, known as SAS.

Just after the Great War, several foreign banks set up business in China. Nine of them were from the United States, two from Japan, and one each from France, Italy, and Norway. Of the American banks, the largest was the American Oriental Banking Corporation. The Shanghai branch of the bank was three-fourths American and one-fourth Chinese-owned. Business in Shanghai centered on the import and export of trade goods. Chiang Kai-Shek, the Nationalist leader in control, demanded large amounts of money from the financial world of Shanghai. Most of the bankers and merchants were willing to invest in his army, but this eventually stopped before the decade was over.

Mama tended house for the Greene family, along with two other housemaids, (one of whom lived in), Choi the cook, and his assistant. Maxine was a finicky, difficult perfectionist, and the maids dreaded the one day a month that was her turn to sponsor the Tuesday luncheon and bridge game. Always a demanding woman, the day before these card parties, she ran them all ragged, making them scrub the windows and floors, beat the rugs, and dust every nook and cranny of the mansion. The fine china and crystal had to be washed, lest a single speck be seen on a wine glass, and the silver was to be polished to a satin sheen.

Choi was given the menu, (which rarely changed), several days in advance, and he went to the market early on the morning of the party so as to avail himself of the freshest foods and produce he could find. Often the lunch would begin with borscht, a cold beet soup, and toasted baguettes. A great deal of Russian and French cuisine appeared on many Shanghai tables, paying tribute to the assimilation of the many different peoples who lived in the elegant city. Next, small finger sandwiches of smoked salmon (a Jewish influence) and cucumber were arranged on beautiful porcelain platters, while the finest black Russian caviar glistened in an elegant, footed, heavy lead crystal bowl. The ladies sipped lemonade along with their meal.

When the food was cleared away, some of the women smoked cigarettes from holders, chatting and gossiping, as they finished off their lunch with petits fours and coffee, or a fragrant cup of jasmine tea. The rest of the afternoon was spent playing bridge. By the time the ladies had gone, and Mama and the staff had put things to right, it was time to begin preparations for dinner, with or without Mr. Greene. It was a lucky day for the staff when Mrs. Greene was meeting Mr. Greene to dine out with friends, allowing the maids and the cook some time off from their rigorous jobs.

Mama came home tired each evening, and I was expected

to have the children washed and our evening meal prepared, though that rarely left me much time for myself. Sometimes Baba would arrive first, anxious to wash the day's sweat off in the small bathroom. Baba would clean himself in our small bathtub, and come into the kitchen hungry for his evening meal. We all looked forward to eating our dinner together as a family. My father was a quiet man, but occasionally he would come home and talk about his day. He wore little else other than blue cloth pants and a hat, and so he was barefoot and bare-chested a lot of the time. This was the usual attire for rickshaw pullers. In bad weather, he wore sandals, which were quite expensive. They were made of rubber cut out from car tires. On his head, he wore a conical hat with a flat brim. He also owned a raincoat, which was a sign of a good earner. Baba rented his rickshaw each day. Entrepreneurs rented out the tools of their trade to the pullers.

In Canton, a union had actually been formed to watch out for the pullers. Eventually, this union would exist here, as well.

In Shanghai, when a puller wanted to stop working for the hirer who rented him a rickshaw each day, he had a recognized right to negotiate the payment of a transfer fee from the rickshaw puller who was to be his successor. This was called *dingshoufei* and it prevented the hirers from resorting to hiring new rickshaw pullers in the event of a strike. Fortunately, Baba had rented from the same hirer for several years and never had a problem with the man, which could only have been resolved by striking. *Dingshoufei* certainly gave Baba a considerable advantage. Baba hoped that one day he would be hired to work for one of the many rich businessmen that owned their own rickshaws and maintained a driver. This was the dream of every puller, as there were always more pullers available than there were rickshaws. Sometimes four or five pullers competed for the same *huangbaoche*, as the rickshaws were called. The prospect of unemployment was always a threat, but for now, Baba was safe. Mama had promised Baba that, when the time was right, she would make a suggestion to her employer's wife about Mr. Greene purchasing his own rickshaw and employing a full-time puller. Because they liked her, she might be able to convince them to hire Baba, with his many years of experience.

That night, I put dinner on the table and called everyone to come and eat. We sat on small stools, around our short-legged wooden table. I had made a carp with soy and sugar, as well as a large bowl of boiled *gai-lan*, a delicious kind of greens that Lan loved because she thought it was named after her. We all dipped our chopsticks, bringing the tasty, bitter vegetable to the top of our rice-filled bowls, and into our mouths. Tonight, the last dish was a platter of braised eggplant. I had stewed the vegetable in *Shaoxing* wine, garlic, sugar, and chilies. My family loved this dish because of its perfect combination of saltiness, sweetness, and spice.

Halfway through the meal, Baba started to tell us a story about two women he had picked up in his rickshaw that afternoon. Two female *gweilos,* (a white ghost; a derogatory term for Caucasians in China), one with dark hair, had asked to be taken somewhere to shop. Baba had taught himself a bit of English so that he would be better able to service the customers he picked up around our city. After a while, he had learned to recognize the difference between the various English accents, so he was pretty sure the ladies were American. He continued his story, through mouthfuls of food. He said he had suggested The Bund to the Americans, and they had nodded, climbing up into the red leather seat. The hood was down since it was rarely used unless it was raining or very cold.

Baba continued talking to us, gesturing with his chopsticks, as he described how he had lifted the two long shafts alongside the wheels and began to weave his way through the narrow lanes of traffic. He pulled hard and ran quite swiftly; a fast runner could make good money that way. When they had arrived at their destination, the dark-haired woman had paid him nine-and-a-half *fen* (cents) for pulling them a mile and a half, and gave him an extra *fen* for his tip. They had descended, and he had pulled off into traffic again. After a block or so, he said, he suddenly noticed that one of the women had left her purse on the seat. He quickly returned to the spot where he dropped them off, but he saw no one that looked like them. He hadn't known what to do, but he thought he would be in trouble.

So, he continued his story, pausing to light his after-dinner pipe, he headed for the American Embassy. There, he turned in the woman's purse and was told that the owner had already called twice, and the second time was told her purse had been brought there and that he should wait until she arrived as she wanted to thank him. The purse's owner, a Mrs. Ambrose, was the wife of a wealthy Chicago businessman, and offered a reward of thirty American dollars for the return of her purse. It was an enormous amount of money to us. Baba puffed on his pipe, walking around the small kitchen, acrid smoke drifting around his head. This had been the most he had spoken at one time in a long time. Mama and I had begun to clear the plates as everyone started talking. Cheng wanted to know if Baba had gotten the money. Yes, Baba explained, he had, in American dollars. The *gweilo* had called and arrived at the Embassy not too long after he had let them out of the rickshaw. He had just gotten there when she came in and she was told that the rickshaw puller was there returning her purse. She claimed her purse, thanked him, and pressed money into his hand. He bowed and thanked her for her kind generosity.

It was only after he left that he looked and saw the large amount of money she had given him. He wasn't certain how much it was because she had paid in American dollars. Outside, grateful that his rickshaw was still safe where he had tied it up, he ran into a Chinese restaurant a few doors down and was stunned when he was told the amount of money she had given him. At this point, Baba reached into the waistband of his pants and showed us the bills. Thirty American dollars! There would be prosperity in our home for a long time to come.

My mother got up from the table, and after fetching a bowl of boiled peanuts, she handed Baba a bottle of beer. She had made the nuts in typical Chinese red-braise on her day off. I could smell the aromatic scent of salt, sugar, cinnamon, cloves, and star anise. This time, she had also added a dried chili. They were soft and delicious, and we ate them in celebration of the good karma that had come to our door.

I noticed that, when the children and Baba settled down, Mama went to our small altar in the kitchen. There, I saw her light a stick of incense and bow before the paper effigy of *Zao Jun*, the kitchen god placed near the stove. I watched her move her lips. I knew she was giving thanks for our family's good fortune.

When she had gone off to bed, I opened my pull-out divan, and reaching under the mattress, removed a brown leather book. I had found it a year ago in the garbage at school. Some pages had been torn from it, but the rest were blank and intact. I had taken it home, thinking to start a journal; it would be a diary to write down my thoughts and dreams for the future of my family and me. Writing as often as I could, I already had many entries. Without skipping a line, to conserve paper, I wrote the date and began my entry. I put down Baba's wonderful story, and as my eyes began closing, I ended quickly, and got up to hide the book and shut the small lamp.

The following morning, way before the light of dawn, Baba arose and went to the Jade Temple. He lit incense before both the sitting and the reclining Buddha (the latter representing Buddha's death). Holding his *shu zhu,* (counting beads), he chanted, and then said a prayer:

"May all beings without limit, without end, have a share in the merit just now made, and in whatever other merit I have made; and others, neutral or hostile beings established in the cosmos, the three realms, the four modes of birth, with five, one, or four aggregates—wandering on from realm to realm. If they know of my dedication of merit, may they themselves rejoice, and if they do not know, may the devas inform them, by reason of their rejoicing in my gift of merit. May all beings always live happily free from animosity. May they attain the Serene State, and their radiant hopes be fulfilled."

Chapter Two

Shanghai, 1921

My father, Zhang Pen, was born in Hangzhou, just two hundred kilometers from Shanghai. He and his friend, Li Ching, both orphans, came to Shanghai, seeking their fortunes, when they were in their teens. Baba and Li Ching's parents died in the late 1800s. They succumbed to cholera, or the Black Death. The terrible devastation, (we called it *huolan,* meaning sudden chaos), was rampant in parts of China at this time. Miraculously, Baba and Ching survived. They were both fifteen years old, and by finding daily work on farms, they made their way to Shanghai. Both men had shared a common tragedy, but in Shanghai, good fortune smiled on them when they each obtained jobs pulling for the same rickshaw owner. After a few years of hard work, Baba met and married Mama, and the following year Ching married Meifeng. The men worked long hours to provide for their young brides, both of whom took in other people's wash. They saved their money, and soon they were able to move from their cramped apartments, renting small houses close to one another.

Ching and Meifeng had only one child, a son named Jun.

The two families made a betrothal pact between Jun and I. We were to be married when I reached my sixteenth year and Jun his seventeenth. I would soon be sixteen, and plans were in the making. The Li family still lived just a few streets away from us in the small house they had lived in when they married. Both of our streets were more like alleys and close to Hengshan Lu, known as Avenue Petain.

Jun and I spent a lot of time together, both in and out of school. Often, after we finished our schoolwork and chores, he would come by. We played games with my oldest brother, Cheng, while the younger boys played ball. Little Lan would run around trying to catch the ball when my brothers tossed it to her. When we were younger, Jun and I used to have a favorite game called Catching Seven Pieces. It was played with small inch-square rice bags. We tossed them in the air and tried to see how many we could catch before they dropped. Each turn meant catching one more piece. It was somewhat similar to the game Jacks, without the ball. We played Blind Man, Catch the Dragon's Tail, and Hopping Chicken, too.

I loved Baba's day off when he would sometimes take us to a nearby park to fly our kites. We had made our kite frames out of bamboo wood. After decorating the kites with scraps of colored paper, we glued them to the frames, mine in the shape of a butterfly, and Jun's a dragon. Mrs. Li gave us some fabric scraps, which she had saved for this purpose, for the tails. We held the string tightly in our hands, always fearful that an updraft would grab a kite and hurtle it to the ground. Kite flying was very important in China, and we always loved watching them bobbing and weaving through the sky.

Somehow, Jun and I made it through our childhood still liking each other, which considering my lack of choice regarding a husband, was a good thing. At almost seventeen, his large, almond-shaped eyes were very dark brown, almost black, like his hair, which was thick and straight. A shock of this hair often fell across his left eye, and he unconsciously pushed it back all the time. Jun was a kind young man, a smile often seen on his pleasing face. He, like our fathers, worked hard pulling a rickshaw. We had been friends all our lives, and our wedding was to take place in a few months. I stayed at home, kept house, and cared for my siblings while my mother worked for the small amount of money the Greenes paid her for her hard work.

When Jun and I married, traditionally I would have moved in with his family, becoming the "property" of my new mother-in-law. It was customary for a daughter-in-law to spend the rest of her life in such obeisance, while her husband's mother spent the rest of her life pretending to hate her daughter-in-law. In our case, things were to be different. Mrs. Li, like Mama, worked as a servant, but having no other children, she had no one needing her at home. Were I to leave, there would be no one to run our household and take care of my brothers and young sister, so it had been agreed, though grudgingly by Mrs. Li, that I would remain at home, and Jun would move in with my family. If truth be told, Mrs. Li didn't hate me; if anything, she liked me, and I liked her equally.

I often recorded my feelings for Jun in my diary. I was excited about our upcoming nuptials. The months passed quickly, and soon it was my wedding day. I was dressed in a *cheongsam* of red. Red is the traditional color worn at weddings; it symbolizes good luck. My beautiful, long gown had two slits on the sides and was made of exquisite silk with a phoenix symbol brocaded into the fabric. Jun wore a *qípáo,* also of brocade, with a wingless male dragon to symbolize power. My two closest friends, Lihua and Ming Xiu, also wore *cheongsams*, while Jun's groomsmen wore *qípáos*. We were married at the Buddhist temple, and then the wedding party proceeded to the reception hall, where Baba had arranged a festive celebration.

Chinese wedding ceremonies and celebrations are full of symbolic actions, items, and events. The hall was beautiful; it was decorated with dragons and phoenixes, draped with lucky red ribbons, and each table had centerpieces constructed of red paper flowers, and bright red linens. These are all essential to a Chinese wedding celebration and added to the joyous day. Firecrackers were lit to ward off evil spirits, and our guests signed the red silk guest book. I had never imagined I would ever have a wedding so grand. Baba must have saved for a very long time in order to pay for this, and the money from the lost handbag must have helped.

The menu consisted of the finest food Baba could afford, including roast pig, crab, abalone, and other Shanghainese delicacies. Fruits and vegetables of all types were served. As was traditional, Baba had arranged for a host to be present to entertain the guests and make announcements throughout the evening. We received gifts of money, handed to us in red envelopes. When the reception was over, Jun and I stood at the door of the reception hall and gave thanks to the guests as they departed, handing us the red envelopes of cash. It was the most glamorous, exciting night of my young life. We spent our wedding night at the Astor House, a luxury Jun had saved for. We didn't have the time for the frivolity of a honeymoon. The next morning, we ate an American breakfast and returned home to start our life as a married couple. Now, we had to be frugal with our gift money, as well as Jun's earnings.

We settled into married life. Oftentimes, I caught Jun looking at me out of the corner of his eye. I was slender and diminutive, and like my name, had remained quite delicate. My hair was worn in a thick braid down my back. I knew I was pretty enough though, truthfully, it was of no importance in an arranged marriage. My husband treated me with kindness and consideration.

We slept on my cramped pull-out bed in the parlor. It was a pretty, small room, with a gay flower print on a divan we opened up each evening, my journal buried beneath the mattress, wrapped in a piece of fabric. On the floor was a little woven rug, and a simple lamp sat on a low table.

Mama and Baba slept in one bedroom with Lan, while Cheng, Ye, and Hu shared the other bedroom. We weren't rich, but we weren't poor either. My nights with Jun were warm and passionate, and I hoped I would soon be with child. I was in love with my husband and was certain he reciprocated my feelings.

One warm evening, as we sat in front of our little house, Jun smoked a cigarette, and we talked about our plans. Although a lot of the money Jun earned went toward the household, he was still able to put aside small amounts to save for our future. For a couple of years, we had heard talk about the *Land of Gum Saan*, Gold Mountain, and Jun often spoke of his dream of traveling to San Francisco in America to seek his fortune. I wasn't looking forward to his leaving me, but if the opportunity was as great as it was said, he would send for me, and we might make a good life there.

Chapter Three

Shanghai, 1922

Chinese immigrants made the long, arduous trip by sea in hopes of finding work in this glorious place called Gold Mountain. Stories of the gold rush caused thousands of Chinese men to leave their families and embark on a journey to the new land. Many Chinese emigrants had already gone to California in sailing ships even before the discovery of gold. They had gone there to build the trans-continental railroad. Many able-bodied young men left China to escape overpopulation, famine, drought, and poverty in the hopes of finding their fortune overseas.

Even at its best, the trip from China to California was miserable. The poor were herded into the holds of ships like flocks of sheep, with no sanitation. Their food consisted of rice cooked in water with some pork fat. Water was very scarce. They depended on rain after the initial supply ran out. The Chinese were permitted to come on deck in small numbers when the weather was good, but during heavy wind and waves, they remained in the hold of the ship with almost no light, save the little that came through the openings for air. They were thrown against the sides of the ship and on top of each other. Even during a trip with fair weather, many Chinese emigrants died and were tossed into the sea. Still, they continued to leave home to seek the opportunities they had heard so much about.

The following year, I still wasn't pregnant. Jun and I were very disappointed. We made the decision that he would take our small savings and journey to *Gum Saan* in the hope of making his fortune, and then send for me. My journal bore the brunt of my unhappiness, both over the lack of a pregnancy and Jun's leaving. We could only afford the third-class fee for Jun's trip. The cost was the large amount of thirty American dollars, the same amount which Baba had gotten from the *gweilo*. This bought the most minimal accommodation; it was referred to as steerage because it was actually that part of the ship.

The Chinese Exclusion Act, signed in 1882, was one of the most significant restrictions on free immigration in United States history and made the process extremely difficult. Chinese immigrants were detained and interrogated at Angel Island Immigration Station in San Francisco Bay. U.S. officials hoped to deport as many Chinese people as possible by asking obscure questions about Chinese villages and family histories the immigrants had trouble answering correctly. The men and women were housed separately, detained in barracks between interrogations for weeks, months, and often years.

For women seeking to enter the country, it was a completely different story. Women with a husband or father who was a U.S. citizen stood a chance, and while some were accepted, a large number were deported. Many who were allowed to stay became prostitutes. Even those who had a U.S. citizen to sponsor them could spend years on Angel Island. It was often said that "being a woman is not a way of being a human being.'

It was at this time that Jun made his journey to Gold Mountain on a ship owned by the Pacific Mail Steamship Company.

When the ferry docked at Angel Island in June of 1922, whites were separated from other races, and the Chinese were kept apart from Japanese and other Asians. Most of the Chinese immigrants were males in their teens or twenties, like Li Jun. Soon after his arrival, Jun was taken to his dormitory to await his visit to the hospital for medical examinations. Because of poor health conditions in rural China, some Chinese were infected with parasitic diseases.

Eventually, I received a letter from Jun. He wrote:

Ling,

I have arrived safely. My trip was very difficult. We lived down below in the very bowels of the ship, with little food, water, or even much light. Still, most of us had the will to survive, and we made it to Gum Saan. I am living in a dormitory with many other men, mostly my age. Women live in a separate place. I have been to see doctors to make sure I am well enough to be allowed to live here. The days are long, and the men pass the time gambling, though stakes are small since no one has much money. There are Chinese newspapers, which are sent from San Francisco, and I'm grateful that I can read. We are taken to separate small outdoor recreation yards so we can enjoy some fresh air and the sunshine.

Every week we are brought to the storehouse at the dock so we may select items we need from our baggage. Sometimes, visitors come to help the illiterate people write letters home. One or two come to teach English to those who are interested. I have learned many words from just such a person. Oftentimes, there are fights in the dining hall. Young men cause these disturbances to protest the poor food and general mistreatment. I keep my mouth shut and mind my own business.

I am lonely for home, and I miss you and our family very much. Still, I have come this far, and I can do nothing but pass the days as I wait for my hearing. I have no idea if you will receive this letter, but I will write you again. Those in authority have told us that our letters will be sent home on the steamships.

Your husband,

Jun

How grateful I was to hear from him. At least I knew he had arrived safely and was well. I read Jun's letter to the family, and they were all shocked by how bad the conditions were. Those we knew that had relatives that had traveled to *Gum Saan* had not had any idea that it was so awful. Still, I reasoned, he was in America, and that couldn't be a bad thing. It would only be a matter of time until he could leave the place where he was being detained. Then he would find work and begin to make a new start. I placed Jun's letter under the mattress inside my journal.

A few months later, I received another letter from Jun.

Ling,

Finally, after months, and for whatever happy reason, I have been allowed to leave the Island and enter San Francisco. I was able to keep my small amount of money, so with that, and my small bag of clothes and other belongings, I left there to find a place to live. Hopefully, I will find work, too. I have learned that a lot of single Chinese men live in houses with as many as ten or more in one room. The houses are in Chinatown, in alleyways, filthy and wet, and I know they are overrun with insects and vermin. Still, I needed a place to live, so I have rented in just such a place. There are twelve men sharing a two-room house, and I consider myself lucky to find any accommodation. The food we eat is a pitiful excuse for a meal, mostly rice gruel, and whatever else we can purchase that is cheap. After a few weeks of searching, I was fortunate enough to find a job as a laundryman. Mr. Lim is a kindly man. His wife and family still live back home in China, and he is hoping to send for them this year.

I work very hard. As cheap as rent and food are, there is hardly anything left after paying for that and other small things, such as cigarettes. I make less than forty dollars a month. Still, I manage to put a little bit aside for your trip each week. I miss you, and can't wait until I can send for you. How ironic it seems to me that my Mother and Mother-in-Law are washing and ironing clothes in Shanghai, while I am doing the same on Gold Mountain. My life is defined by the racial exclusion I am subject to, but I know that some Chinese have been allowed to become naturalized citizens, and I hope that eventually, some day, I might be granted such a right.

Please share these words with the family.

Your husband,

Jun

I placed another letter under the mattress.

A year and a half passed, and Jun opened a small laundry. Laundering work had always traditionally been the domain of women, but now men were working in and opening laundries. The small amount of start-up capital, limited language requirements, and desire to be self-employed gave Jun the opportunity to open a tiny shop on a small street in Chinatown. He tried desperately to save the money to send for Ling, but it was not to be. One afternoon (who could say how an accident happens?), Jun caught his hand in the pressing machine. He lost two fingers, and they eventually became gangrenous. Forced to spend time in the hospital after having seen the Chinese doctor to no avail, he had to use almost every penny he had put aside to save for Ling's passage. His friend Wang, who was fortunate enough to have his wife and new son with him, had kindly taken him in after the accident. For several months the American doctors had applied salves and the local Chinese doctor tried his potions, but Jun's fever raced out of control, and soon after the doctor sent him back to the hospital where they had to remove the hand. By then, it was already too late. The infection had spread throughout his body, and within a few more weeks, Jun was dead.

Chapter Four

Shanghai, 1924

At home, things changed for us as well. Hard times fell on our family. Baba was in an accident. One day, while pulling his rickshaw, he was hit by a car, and his back was permanently injured. Though he was not an old man, there was no chance of his ever working again. He often doubled over with pain. With Jun gone and Baba hurt, we would have been in dire straits were it not for my brothers, Cheng and Ye, who were now pulling rickshaws. Between them, they brought in enough money to pay our bills, though there wasn't a lot left over for luxuries. Cheng met a lovely girl; there was no money for an arranged marriage, as was common. He used some of his earnings to take Jiao out on dates. He was a natural dancer, and occasionally they went to one of the hotels for drinks, and to enjoy the music. Times were indeed different for our family.

To make matters worse, Mama became ill, having been diagnosed with a tumor in her stomach. She could no longer work for the Greenes. She was in the hospital for weeks and was finally sent home with a poor prognosis. Nothing could be done, they told us. According to both the Chinese and American doctors, the tumor was too large for surgery. Suddenly, she was in terrible pain, and all sorts of Chinese herbal treatments were tried, as well as acupuncture and cupping. Nothing gave her any relief, and soon she needed to be kept on opiates to help her with her suffering. After more than eight months of this nightmare, Mama died, leaving behind her husband and four children. My journal became a recipient of yet another heartbreaking entry.

Looking for a place to unleash his anger at this terrible turn of fate, Baba made me the recipient of his unhappiness. He ranted and raved, and at times I was afraid he would strike me. He tried to practice the Buddhist way of *Loving Kindness*, seeking to transform life's difficulties into valuable spiritual insights, but to no avail. My older brothers worked, and I stayed at home caring for Baba, Hu, and Lan. Finally, as if enough hadn't befallen our family, a letter arrived from Wang, Jun's friend on Gold Mountain, telling me the terrible circumstances of my new widowhood. The next entry in my journal was a mess; smeared ink ran down the page as tears ran down my face. I poured out my heart on paper, not actually comprehending that Jun wouldn't be sending for me.

One day, several months later, a man presented himself to my father. He introduced himself as Chen Liwei and said he worked as a cook in a local restaurant that catered to the wealthy but he was tired of the poor salary and bad treatment. He told Baba he had seen me in the market numerous times and admired my sweet looks and demure demeanor. He mentioned to Baba that he had saved a nice amount of money, and having inquired and heard I was a widow, wanted the opportunity to court me. He said he hoped that, if things worked out, one day we might marry, and he could take me with him to Gold Mountain. Baba was uncertain, not wanting to lose me. Who would take care of the household if I were to leave? Yet, how could he not afford me this opportunity for a better life? He agreed to let us spend some time to let Mr. Chen get to know me.

Baba presented Chen Liwei's offer to me one afternoon as I was cooking congee. I stirred the thick porridge as he reminded me, in his now cruel way, that I wasn't an innocent virgin anymore. "You are lucky that another man wants to court a widow such as you. Many widows," he said, "often remain alone for the rest of their lives, which you know is a usual Chinese custom." I wasn't an innocent virgin, but I was only nineteen years old and had already experienced a great deal in those short years. I told Baba I would at least meet Mr. Chen.

The first time we met, Mr. Chen came to our home to meet me. He came into the house and Baba and the children stared at him. I felt sorry for the man and embarrassed for myself. We talked about basic things for a while and then he asked Baba if he might call again and perhaps take me for a meal. The following week he took me to an American restaurant; I imagine he thought that would impress me. We ate steaks and our conversation was stilted. I was uncomfortable with Mr. Chen. As we sat at the table, I nervously pulled at the blue fabric of my *cheongsam*—the only good dress I owned other than my red wedding dress. I was unaccustomed to the dressy attire, but I had wanted to make a good impression on Mr. Chen. Throughout the glamorous meal, my only pair of high heels pinched my feet and I looked forward to taking them off and putting on my old brocaded slippers.

Mr. Chen seemed like a nice man. We talked about many things that were changing in Shanghai and in China in general. He was thirty-three years old, ten years younger than Baba. He had already told me he was a widower with no children, which he had said was a great disappointment to him. His wife, along with his daughter, had died in childbirth. Our conversation was pleasant, if not very stimulating. Clearly, he had not gone to school for very long, and it seemed obvious that I was better educated than he.

We spent several months going out for meals, strolling around Shanghai, talking about our lives as we got to know each other better. Liwei wasn't handsome like Jun had been; his face was slightly pockmarked, and sometimes one eye looked off in the wrong direction, but I found him agreeable enough. Frankly, I had had enough of being the family's caregiver and the recipient of Baba's unhappiness.

I considered Liwei's offer. He had made his intent known to me after a little over two months. Eventually, he proposed marriage, having already asked Baba for permission. He spoke of his hopes of traveling with me to *Gum Saan*. Lan was in school now, and Hu was a big boy already; soon he would be able to pull a rickshaw along with my brothers. I wasn't in love with Liwei. I would probably never love him, but I thought that I might grow to care for him someday, so I agreed to marry him and travel with him to make a new life on Gold Mountain. I wrote in my journal my deepest, heartfelt thoughts, as I had soul-searched for the right thing to do.

Shortly after our simple wedding, Liwei and I boarded the S.S. China on our way to our new home. It took twenty-one days to arrive at Angel Island. The trip was terrible. I was seasick most of the time. When we finally arrived at the Angel Island Immigration Station, we were separated and I was interrogated several times. I was frightened and alone, as were many of the other women in the barracks. The children cried a great deal of the time, and it was extremely crowded, but we were decently fed, although I remember Jun saying he wasn't. Perhaps the women and children received better fare.

After several weeks passed, Liwei and I were cleared by the medical department. The officials were finally convinced that we were husband and wife, and so we were allowed to leave. It was soon after that I realized the monstrous mistake that I had made.

We found a small, furnished two-room apartment in Chinatown. It was there that we celebrated our wedding night for the first time. It was nothing like it had been with Jun. Liwei was rough and uncaring, and I learned to submit to his embrace, though I hated it. For the first couple of months, everything was uneventful and pleasant enough. I cooked on a hot plate and tried my best to keep the two rooms clean, but it had been so filthy when we moved in that it was a near impossible feat. We shared a toilet with the other tenants. Liwei left each morning and didn't come home until dark. He told me that, because he had so much experience working in restaurants in Shanghai, it had been easy to find work. I could never have imagined the terrible thing that Liwei had planned for me.

One evening, Liwei sat me down and said, "I have not found work, Ling; there is no work. You will have to earn the money to pay our rent and put food in our mouths."

After that, there was an endless stream of men, while I was held in captivity in our dirty Chinatown rooms. Liwei, my supposedly loving husband, had brought me to Gold Mountain to be a prostitute. Suddenly I was no longer his wife but a slave, alone in a strange land with no money or friends. I wondered how he had known that we both would be allowed to stay but I would never have an answer to that question. I suppose he just took a chance and got lucky. Everywhere there were single men, either bachelors or "married-but-single" men with families back home in China.

The first time I had to prostitute myself, I refused. Liwei brought a man home and told me I was to lie with him or there would be no food for me. I begged him not to make me do this thing, the tears pouring down my cheeks, but he wouldn't listen. The stranger stood there watching as Liwei pulled my cotton jacket over my head and slapped me hard across the face, knocking me to the floor. He told the man, who was young, perhaps in his twenties, that he could have fifteen minutes with me. Money changed hands and he walked out, leaving me with the stranger. I continued crying as the man pushed me down on our bed, pulled my pants from my body, and immediately pushed himself into me. I just lay there, sobbing but not fighting, willing it to be over. When the man finished, he buttoned his pants and left.

Liwei must have been waiting outside as he entered immediately. I threw myself at him, screaming and asking why he had done this to me. He slapped me again, this time pushing me hard and sending me flying across the small room into the wall. I just lay there sobbing, my clothes on the floor, my small naked breasts wet with my tears.

"This is how it is to be, woman," he told me sternly. "You will work on your back and you will have a place to sleep and food to eat. If you try to run away, you will surely be forced to sell yourself on the streets. Better to be here with a roof over your head, I think. Those are your choices."

And so it was. I had no other options. Liwei went out most days. At night I had many men to service. When he left, he locked the door from the outside and it wouldn't open from within. He bolted the windows from the outside as well. He was always there to allow the customers to leave when they knocked as they had been told. I placed my entries in the journal whenever time allowed, hiding it in a small basket that was filled with our dirty laundry. I knew Liwei would never look there.

One day, several months later, he unlocked the door and told me to pack my few things. He paced back and forth, smoking and staring out of the window. His bad eye seemed more askew than ever. I threw my things into a large burlap bag, my diary included. Liwei turned around, asking if I was done, and said "Come, woman," holding tightly to my arm. We left, and he pulled me along for several blocks as I carried my burlap bag. We arrived at what turned out to be a brothel where he brokered me to a man who was a member of a Chinese Tong. We had heard of these organizations in Shanghai and knew they owned brothels and dealt in opium, as well as other illicit practices. I came to Gold Mountain with Chen

Liwei hoping we could find happiness together. Instead, he betrayed me, lured by his greed and desire for easy money.

Thousands of Chinese prostitutes either worked in dark basement "dens" or street-level "cribs'. Because of the Exclusion Act, fewer women than men were allowed to come to Gold Mountain, so the men, whose wives waited back home, turned to prostitutes. These Chinese slaves were far more stigmatized than ordinary prostitutes. The demand was huge, as it was considered taboo to engage in sexual acts between Chinese men and white women. The original Tongs were benevolent protection societies in China and they appeared in America in the late 1870s. Initially, they protected Chinese Americans from lawlessness and discrimination. Eventually, however, a society of organized criminals developed. These Tongs began to fight among themselves, causing violent clashes. They became rich and powerful, acquiring funds from opium, gambling, prostitution, and blackmail.

I worked in such a crib. I was forced to solicit men who passed by. I would sit in the open doorway wearing a short dress that barely covered my breasts on top. When I lured a client, my owner would unlock the pen and draw a curtain; there, I had to service the customer. Whatever service the client wanted, I was forced to perform. There is a slang Chinese term that best describes the creature I had become. I was now known as a "*One Hundred Men's Wife.*"

More than two years of this horror passed. I hardly knew what day it was anymore. When I had a rare moment alone, usually close to dawn, I would quickly write of my life in the journal that always listened. One day, I finally found my moment and escaped. Lee, who ran the brothel during the afternoon, had gotten drunk and fallen asleep. He often did this, but one particular afternoon, he drank a huge amount of bootleg whiskey, and I watched as his head drooped lower and lower until it dropped to the table. He breathed heavily. As he slept, the key to the crib door fell from his hand to the floor. I stared at Lee, massive hate fueling my courage. Deep snores came from his ugly, sparsely-bearded face. Without a moment's hesitation, I snatched the key from the floor, and with only my journal, opened the door. Barefoot, I ran through the streets like a madwoman, not stopping until I couldn't breathe anymore. It was drizzling and the streets were wet.

When I finally stopped running, I looked around, trying to gain my bearings. The only thing I knew was that I was far from the brothel, and it seemed I was no longer in Chinatown. I leaned against a wall, trying to think, panting, and drenched with perspiration. I must have been quite a sight, a young, wet, barefoot Chinese girl in a short, low-cut dress, clutching a brown book to her chest. I saw an American woman approaching me, and I froze with fear. She was a tall, heavyset, middle-aged woman with a sweet face, and was dressed in a modest gray dress. I looked up through wet lashes and saw she wore a dark gray brimmed hat over which she held an umbrella. Strands of wavy, grayish-brown hair escaped from under the hat. On her very large feet, she wore a pair of well-worn black shoes. Small spectacles covered piercingly blue eyes. I took all of this in quickly as she walked straight up to me and asked in Mandarin if I was lost, and could she help. Although we had spoken Wu dialect Chinese in Shanghai, we had studied a little of other dialects in school, including Mandarin and Cantonese. These dialects were spoken all over Shanghai. I was terribly frightened, but I could see the look of concern on her face. I was so overwhelmed by her kindness that I just stood there and started to cry. She put her arm around my shoulder and told me she was Althea Jensen. I was such a lost soul that I allowed her to lead me to the place where I found my safe haven: the San Francisco Presbyterian Mission Home was to be my salvation.

Chapter Five

San Francisco, 1927

Located at 920 Sacramento Street in Chinatown, the San Francisco Presbyterian Mission Home was chartered with rescuing Chinese girls and women from abusive circumstances. Mission workers became adept at protecting rescued girls from writs of habeas corpus, which was a legally sanctioned ploy allowing slave owners to accuse a girl of a crime and have her removed from the Mission Home. The Tong slave owners did not take the loss of their property lightly. The Mission Home and all of its inhabitants were under constant legal and physical assault from the slave owners.

While marriage was a preferred outcome in the eyes of these Mission workers, some of these young women received training for work. Because of resources available for education in the Home, and discrimination against Chinese in the wider society, rescued women often found work as domestics or other service workers. Some were even able to become Chinese language teachers, while a few remained to work as aides or translators at the Mission Home. These last might travel across the country to check in on former residents who had married Chinese men living across the nation who had sought brides at the Mission Home and who had been judged suitable.

The Home was run by Donaldina Cameron who, I was told, had come to volunteer for a year and wound up becoming the superintendent. She advocated for Chinese girls and women throughout her entire life. The Tongs called her *Fahn Quai*, which means foreign devil, or white devil, (similar to *gweilo),* but the girls she rescued affectionately called her *Lo Mo*, or old mother. She had learned the art of rescuing girls. Rescues were often secret night-time raids conducted with axes and sledgehammer-wielding policemen who brought the rescued girls to the Home. Ms. Cameron was a master at finding girls who had been hidden under trap doors and behind false walls.

I met these Chinese women and girls, each with her own terrible story of what she had been subjected to. Some had been beaten, and one was even crippled at the hands of her master. Others, not slaves, but unable to find work, turned to prostitution. We shared our stories and our lives at the Mission Home. I finally started to feel safe, but I was still wary of the Tongs or Liwei showing up. The people at the mission were kind, and they taught me English and mathematics. I also learned about my new faith, Presbyterianism. Eventually, I will find employment or, if I'm lucky, be married to a suitable Christian man. These men come from similar backgrounds of poverty and unhappiness in this new land and so they understand. Because I had separated myself from prostitution, I was considered marriageable, and thus, respectable.

On Gold Mountain, the "Roaring Twenties" were in full swing. Everywhere there was growth and the potential to make money. Businesses were springing up everywhere. People dined out often, dressed in all their finery. Restaurants catered to the wealthy, and even the not-so-wealthy. There were cars and factories spewing out pollution. Washing machines and radios were common in many homes as they became more affordable. The 18th Amendment to the Constitution, which prohibited the manufacture, sale, or transportation of alcohol in America had gone into effect on January 16, 1920. The country was officially "dry" from coast to coast, but while prohibition was the law of the land, in San Francisco, and all over America, speakeasies did business behind closed doors. Liquor found its way into the country via "Rum Fleets" from Europe, and from over the Canadian border. Clandestine distilleries mushroomed in the city, as well as the countryside. Speakeasies flourished as the people drank behind the closed doors and danced the night away.

It was well over a year since I had been found, alone and scared on that street. I learned to speak simple English and could make myself understood. I expected my skills to increase as I persevered. Miss Althea and Miss Donaldina arranged for work for many of the girls and women living at the Mission Home. I was one of the lucky ones. I spoke and wrote in the Wu dialect, and I was reasonably fluent in Cantonese and Mandarin. I also understood and spoke a little of two other lesser-known dialects local to Shanghai. How fortunate I was to have had this education in China. Because of these skills, and with my newly acquired rudimentary English, I was trained to be a switchboard operator at the Chinese Telephone Exchange, located at 743 Washington Street in Chinatown. Both male and female operators were used. I learned the names of nearly fifteen hundred subscribers, as well as their places of residence. In time, I also knew all of the four to five thousand residents of Chinatown. Because names rather than numbers were used, it was my job to know both the addresses and occupations of each subscriber so I could distinguish between two people with the same last name. It was a difficult and challenging job, and I was fortunate to have been offered the position, based on my language skills and a strong recommendation from the Mission Home.

The exchange was located in a three-story tiered pagoda, the first floor of which is occupied by a store which has been redecorated by its owners to be as beautiful as the rest of the building. The entrance is up a long narrow flight of stairs where there is a gaily decorated sign in Chinese letters announcing the presence of the telephone. We Chinese find it one of the most popular of the American inventions. When a person entered the ante-room, someone was waiting to greet the visitor. It was his sole duty to smile and bow, and make everyone feel welcome.

Close to the front door, there was a richly carved teakwood table on which were kept loose tobacco, cigarettes, and tea bowls. A large teapot was kept filled with hot tea of good quality, and this tea and tobacco were served to visitors. This was a symbol of hospitality without which no Chinese business transaction was complete. At the far end of this room, on a very large gold, silver, and red lacquer altar, sat a *joss*, a Chinese idol of considerable size and richness, whose special duty it was to guard and care for the interests of those who sent speech over wires. Many of us believed, to a certain degree, that the presence of a *joss* was not a luxury, but a prime necessity. I was one of those believers.

As part of the facilities, in the very rear, there was a small, neat kitchen, as well as a diminutive dining room and bedroom. The manager of the exchange, Loo Kum Shu, lived there with his assistants, who took turns sleeping there. There was always someone on duty, and the exchange never closed from year's end to year's end.

The front room, which held the switchboard, was the most attractive feature of the place. It was colorfully decorated with dragons and serpents of fantastic hues. Beautiful lanterns, lit by electric lights, hung from the ceiling. It was a contrast of the modern and the antique. Banners in red, yellow and gold hung from the walls, and along one side of the room, there was a row of teakwood chairs with cushions of silk. Near the switchboard were small black stools, like those you saw all over the Chinese quarter.

I was told the switchboard itself was exactly like all those in the other exchanges of the city, except that the operators were Chinese men and women. It was a most intriguing job, and I was grateful to be training for one of the few female operator positions. The telephone, I learned, was an important part of Chinatown life. Chinese people used it a great deal to transact important business. I was told this is the reason there were no party wires, *(a telephone line or circuit shared by two or more subscribers),* but rather each number had its own wire. On my lunch break, I walked around Chinatown saying hello to people and engaging them in small conversations in an attempt to familiarize myself with the names and faces of the people I will soon be servicing on the switchboard.

I worked at the Exchange during the day. In the evenings after the ladies and I ate and cleaned up the kitchen and small dining room, I studied my English and mathematics. On weekdays, we prayed in the Mission chapel, but I looked forward to Sundays when we attended services at the nearby Presbyterian Church. I became Americanized, and I liked it very much. I still believe in the Buddhist traditions in which I was raised, but feel very comfortable with the new faith I am practicing as well. Along with some of the other women at the Home, I participated in Chinatown activities sponsored by our church and the YWCA, (Young Women's Christian Association), which provided help, lodging, and jobs for young women. I also became involved in a civic group called the Square and Circle Club, which was started by a group of teenage Chinese girls. We raised money for flood and famine victims in China by holding a benefit dance. We turned these funds over to the Chinese relief headquarters. It was wonderful to do such good work.

I attended a "hop," as it was called, where American jazz was played by a Chinese orchestra—how very Shanghainese, I thought. That evening, I danced with a nice young Chinese man, wearing my very first American clothes, a hand-me-down party frock and black shoes with laces, provided by the Mission.

I often thought about Baba and the others, and sadness washed over me when I remembered Jun and the life we should have had, but I don't allow myself to linger on these feelings too long. I still write in my journal. Every few months, I send letters home. Baba never replies, (he cannot read, but I am sure my letters are read to him), but I received a short letter from my oldest brother, Cheng, which I stored in the back of my journal along with Jun's letters. He told me that he and a young woman named Jiao were engaged. They met on their own, but the marriage was arranged by Baba and Jiao's parents; they would marry in a few months. He and my two other brothers pull rickshaws, and Lan still attended school.

Cheng wrote that Baba had aged even more since his accident and was still angry and difficult. I was sorry to hear about Baba, but I was elated at the wonderful news of Cheng's upcoming marriage. I made a mental note to send a small gift to Lan when I got my first salary. She loved showing off her gifts to the other girls at school. I often wondered how Mama Li was getting along and planned to ask the next time I wrote. I prayed to Buddha for my family's health and happiness, and prayed again when I attended church each week.

Chapter Six

San Francisco, 1927

Sometimes, it was hard to believe all that happened in just over three years. I had just received a response from the immigration service regarding my application for naturalization. I was to be interviewed in two weeks, and I was excited and nervous. I had a place to live, a job, and I could speak decent, but heavily accented English. I had no idea why I was given this opportunity, but I accepted it and hoped for the best.

I left the Mission Home after some time to make room for another Chinese girl to be rescued by the wonderful women who changed my life. I gave blessings every day that I was not found by Liwei or the Tong owner who bought me. Three of the other rescued ladies and I leased a small, two-bedroom apartment on Pine Street, near Grant Avenue. *(In later years, this area became part of the Chinatown financial district.)* We shared the rent and the cost of food, and generally got along quite well. It was a wonderful time for us all. We finally felt safe and in control of our lives.

Chang-Ma, like me, escaped a life of prostitution and was several years older than the rest of us. She was fortunate to have found a position working for a local shopkeeper. She was a sweet, quiet woman in her thirties. I was never sure exactly how old she was, nor how she had escaped her captors. She refused to discuss her past with us, so we only knew she had been a prostitute who escaped on her own, as I had.

Shen had been kidnapped from *Qingyuan*, a city near Canton in China, *(now called Guangzhou)*. She was brought into the country as the wife of one of the Tong lords, though she served him as a slave instead. She worked long hours, cleaning and cooking, and sexually servicing any man her owner gave her to. He beat her often, and she lived in constant fear that one day she would die at his hand. Her left ankle was broken when he pushed her across a room in anger, and she walked with a limp. She worked in a well-outfitted dry goods store. I often thought how similar our stories were.

Yi, the youngest of us, was a quick learner, and because her parents owned a restaurant in China, she had some skills. After her parents were killed in a robbery at their restaurant, she was sponsored to the U.S. by a cousin who never showed up when she arrived from China, and somehow she was accepted anyway. She came to *Gum Saan* to escape poverty, and wound up working in a crib, a choice she made on her own. She was close to starving when she finally succumbed to the baseness of prostitution. When she escaped from that situation, the owner of a small Chinese restaurant hired her to help order supplies, keep records, and oversee the place. While we all spoke English, Yi had been given a decent education in China, like me. It was very forward thinking of her boss to hire a woman for such an important position. Sometimes Yi would bring home one of the wonderful delicacies served at the restaurant. The pickled jellyfish was my favorite. After work, we prepared our meal, and sat at our table, dipping our chopsticks and sipping tea as we shared our day with one another.

Song Bao, the owner of the dry goods store where Shen

worked, was in his late twenties. He had come to Gold Mountain from another small town near Canton, with the same hopes and dreams as the rest of the emigrants. He was smart and industrious, and after a number of years working in a dry goods store in Chinatown, he became familiar with the business. He lived frugally, saving his money, and eventually sought help from his two brothers in China. He was able to bring in enough merchandise to open a small shop of his own.

The business started slowly, but little by little, more money came in and more merchandise was sent from home. Common items were big sellers. Fans, carved wooden back scratchers, teacups, and teapots were only some of the items that Americans came to Chinatown to buy. Of course, the local Chinese also shopped in his store, coming to purchase *joss*, small braziers, idols, chopsticks, and woks. As his business grew, Song was able to send larger amounts of money home, further including his two brothers in the profit sharing. Fabrics like brocades and other silks began to sell well. Soon he was able to afford to rent a larger store that offered basement storage space and a small living area upstairs. He saved money by living and working on the same premises, and his goal was to eventually own the building.

Song Bao converted to Presbyterianism and took his faith seriously. He became involved with Donaldina and the others at the Mission Home, and was active, along with the police and others, in rescuing female slaves and prostitutes. He was there the night Shen was rescued, so it was not in the least bit strange that he hired her to be his store clerk. In fact, it was Mr. Song who came to the Home one evening with extraordinary news. The police told him a pimp named Chan had been arrested. He told them Liwei had been killed by a Tong slave owner in retribution for two prostitutes he purchased from him that Liwei helped escape so he might sell them himself. Now, though Liwei was dead, once again I lived in fear that the Tong lord would find me.

At the Mission Home, we had shared our stories and gave support to each other. We had all been given a chance at a new life, and we showed our gratitude in word and deed. We prayed together before each meal, reveling in the blessings we received. On Sundays, we got up early, and attended morning services at the local Presbyterian Church, sometimes returning to the Home for lunch with our mentors and the latest group of rescued women. My life was truly a beautiful picture—colored by faith, friendship, and the joyous feeling of acceptance.

While I loved all the ladies, I had developed a close bond with Shen. Often, I would go to her store on my lunch hour. We usually brought our small meals from home, and when the weather was nice, Shen and I would sit on small stools outside the storefront and enjoy our lunchtime together. Sometimes, if there were no customers, Mr. Song would join us, and we reminisced about China and the people we left behind.

Mr. Song's brothers had wives and children, and he was fortunate to have such an established relationship with them. He hoped one day to be able to bring his younger brother, Wing, and eventually Wing's family, to Gold Mountain to help him run the business. His older brother, Fangli, was very comfortable staying where he was and it was a perfect arrangement for them. Wing became proficient at acquiring merchandise to ship overseas and quickly learned how to handle all the necessary paperwork involved in the exportation of these goods. It was a good start for the Songs, and Bao hoped he would be able to continue expanding the business. His wish was that someday the Chinese would be able to own property. He planned to rent another space and open a second shop. He dreamed of importing the beautiful ebony wood furniture inlaid with mother-of-pearl, hand-made rugs, and some pricey porcelain items that Americans appreciated. *"Shouxian di yi jian shiquing"*—first things first, he always said.

I received a letter from Cheng telling me that Baba passed away. I was overcome with grief. Cheng wrote that Baba withered and grew older each year, although he was only in his mid-forties. Cheng felt Baba was never the same after his accident, when he could no longer pull a rickshaw. It was a loss of face not to be able to support his family anymore. I agreed this was probably so. Coupled with Mama's death, it had all become too much for him. Cheng wrote that Baba suffered a fatal heart attack in his sleep. The letter saddened me terribly, and I wished I could travel home to visit my family, but the Immigration Department denied my naturalization papers, which meant I could never leave the U.S. if I hoped to return again. I could re-apply again in a year or two.

Cheng and Jiao had a little girl named Ah-Lam. They enclosed a photograph of the three of them, which must have cost them a lot of money, and I saw a strong resemblance to Mama in the baby's face. The letter went on to say that Ye and Hu still pulled rickshaws, Lan was still in school, and Jiao takes care of the family. He told me he was recommended to a British engineer whose family was living in Shanghai. This gentleman was planning on purchasing his own rickshaw, and so Cheng's name has been passed on as being a trustworthy, hard-working man. I shall pray for such good fortune for my family. I miss them terribly, and God knows when we will meet again. My life is sweet and simple. Work, friends, prayers. I am very content, but still I feel a void, and I am always fearful of being found. Sometimes I look at the photo of my family and my little niece, Ah-Lam, and I feel a stirring. How I would love to have a child of my own. I tell this to my diary.

One particular day, as we sat outside in the bright California sunshine, Mr. Song quietly asked me if I would care to join him for dinner that evening. Shen had gone inside to pour us some tea, and I imagine Mr. Song chose that private moment to talk to me. Shen told me several times that Mr. Song always speaks highly of me. They have developed a great friendship, perhaps by virtue of the important role he played in her rescue. She believes he has started to have "certain feelings" for me, so I was not completely taken aback by his question.

Song Bao is a nice-looking man, tall for a Chinese, and broad-shouldered. His straight hair, which he wears long, falls over his face at times, and it reminds me of how Jun's hair used to do the same. He has a strong faith, and his rescue work with the Mission means a great deal to him. This speaks well of his fine character and integrity. He doesn't judge any of the girls and women he has helped rescue; indeed, he is most supportive. This trait is very endearing to me. I had very little time to think about my answer as I saw Shen coming from the store, carrying a small tray with three teacups on it. I nodded my head, embarrassed, and he quickly mentioned a time that he would call for me. I drank my tea, took my leave, and went back to work. I would tell Shen and the others later when we all returned home from work.

The afternoon was very long, and when it was finally time to leave the Exchange, I was nervous and excited. I thought the streetcar would never come, and by the time I arrived home, I was perspiring greatly. Yi was the first home and I told her about my date with Song Bao. Her eyes sparkled as she began to babble about whether I should dress in traditional Chinese clothing or wear American attire. Mr. Song often dressed in American suits, so I made the decision to wear a simple American dress of a medium blue shade and tan leather shoes. I remembered with regret the blue cheongsam I had worn on my first date with Liwei. I left it behind when I escaped from him.

I owned three American dresses and black and tan shoes. Choosing the tan ones, I quickly hurried to bathe, and when I finished, Shen and Chang-Ma had come home from their day's work. I was the main topic of conversation. Shen was the most excited. She had been expecting this for weeks and voiced her approval. I dressed slowly, and then carefully styled my hair, which waved softly past my shoulders. I parted it in the middle and pulled it back with two precious hair combs loaned to me by Shen. Mr. Bao had given them to her on her last birthday. I rolled two small chignons at the nape of my neck, tucking them in place with several hairpins. A dab of cologne behind my ears, a touch of lip rouge, and my toilette was done. I felt very stylishly American.

When Mr. Song came to call for me, my heart was pounding out of my chest. I entered the parlor and found him sitting stiffly on our divan, looking uncomfortable in his American suit, his hair shiny and slicked back into place. I don't know which of the ladies had let him in. He seemed as nervous as I was. I bid him good evening, and he rose. Just minutes earlier, the women had been chattering in the kitchen as they prepared their evening meal. Suddenly, it was silent, and I knew they were all eavesdropping, hoping to pick up a piece of conversation from us. I disappointed them by picking up my shawl and black purse and leaving immediately.

We descended the two flights of stairs into a warm, muggy San Francisco evening. It felt like rain, I thought. Here we were, two people who, until this moment, were comfortable around each other and were now extremely nervous and at a loss for words. When we reached the street, he offered me his arm, and as I took it, he asked what I would like to eat for dinner. I was embarrassed and answered that whatever he liked would be fine. He was lacking his usual self-assuredness.

"Would you like to eat at the Hang Ah Tea Room? They have wonderful food and I have taken the liberty of making a reservation. They are located on Pagoda Place, and they say the shark's fin soup is very tasty."

"That would be lovely, Mr. Song," I replied, looking down at my shoes, not saying that I didn't know of the fancy restaurant.

"Good, then it is decided, Ling," he said. "May I call you Ling, and will you call me Bao?"

I nodded shyly.

"Shall we walk to the streetcar then?" he continued.

When had we become strangers again? I thought, taking his once-again proffered arm. We walked two blocks and boarded the streetcar that would take us to the restaurant. Hang Ah's, he mentioned, was considered a very fine eatery, and if truth be told, I was as excited about that as he was, never having been there before. I was also excited about getting to know Bao a little better. After we arrived and were seated, Bao made some menu suggestions and ordered, speaking quickly and quietly to the waiter.

We dined on shark's fin soup, a famous and expensive Cantonese dish. (It is said that to "secure" a husband, a Cantonese woman needs to first cook good soup, and though I am not from Canton, Bao is from that region, and I shall have to keep that in mind). After the soup, the waiter served scallops with ginger and garlic, ground pork with salted duck egg, stir-fried bok choy, and steamed white rice. We drank cup after cup of hot, fragrant ooh-long tea. The final decadence was a dessert of pan-fried water chestnut cake, and *bàobīng*, (shaved ices with sweet syrup). As I spooned the cold, delicious treat into my mouth, I thought about how Bao's name was part of the word for ices, and how my sister Lan used to think that *gai-lan* had been named for her. It's funny how one's mind runs away sometimes.

We talked and laughed as we dipped our chopsticks and sipped our tea. After Bao had returned me safely home, I thought how I had thoroughly enjoyed myself, and hoped that Bao had as well.

Things in San Francisco continued changing. "Flappers" abounded, speakeasies still secretly housed glamorous men and women dancing The Charleston, which had been introduced in the Ziegfeld Follies a few years earlier, and the Black Bottom. Other music, such as ragtime, jazz, and the blues were heard everywhere. The streetcars vied for space on the streets, as more and more automobiles appeared. But, despite all this, for those of us living in Chinatown, things remained very much the same.

I often thought about Shanghai, how glamorous it had been when I had lived there and was a young student. I often became terribly sad when I remembered that I had lost both Mama and Baba, though it was unlikely I would ever have seen them again. Three weeks after my dinner date with Bao, he purchased a used Model T Ford. It cost him eighty-five dollars, and he was extremely excited about it. That Sunday, after church, he drove over to the Mission Home, and everyone ran out to see the new machine. Bao showed off his new car and took several of us for short rides around the neighborhood. What a thrill my first car ride was.

Later that week, while lunching with Shen at the shop, Bao stepped out of the store and asked me, right in front of Shen, if I would care to go to the Chinese opera with him on Saturday night.

"I know nothing about opera, Bao," I said shyly, "but I am most happy to accept your kind offer."

"I shall call for you at seven o'clock," he responded.

That evening, I told the other ladies about my plans with Bao, and they all seemed to sense my excitement. Yi teased me, saying that my whole face lit up whenever I said Bao's name.

"It's just that I've never been to the opera, Yi," I protested.

"Yes, Ling, we know that. None of us have either, so you must go and tell us everything about the night. But it is clear that it is not just the opera that has you so excited."

Here I was in San Francisco, about to attend the Chinese opera! I knew I needed something elegant to wear. Shen suggested that I buy a new dress for this special occasion since none of us owned anything appropriate for me to wear to such an event.

The following afternoon, when I left the Telephone Exchange, I took the streetcar to Sook Ang's Dress Shop to buy a new cheongsam. At the shop, Mrs. Sook herself waited on me. I told her that I was going to the Chinese opera on Saturday night and had decided to wear traditional attire. She brought out two dresses for me to try on.

The first, a dark blue brocaded *cheongsam*, was more money than I could afford, but I was ashamed to tell her that. When she showed me the second dress, which was even more expensive, the price no longer mattered. It had cap sleeves and was made of black beaded brocade silk with a mandarin collar and slits on both sides of the skirt. There was a traditional diagonal opening from the neck to the right shoulder, and it had beautiful frog closures to fasten it.

I am not a frivolous woman; I work hard to earn my money. The red dress Baba had bought me for my wedding to Jun was quite beautiful, but this dress took my breath away. I had not taken that dress with me to Gold Mountain because of the memories. I knew I would never wear it again. From that day until this, my life has not been one of glamor or glitter, but I remembered the beautiful women of Shanghai wearing attire like this. I knew I had to try the dress on. Stepping out of the dressing room, I looked at myself in the mirror. My dark eyes glowed, and while I knew I had looked nice on my first date with Bao, this dress made me into a woman I didn't recognize.

"I shall buy it, Mrs. Sook," I heard myself say, knowing I would be strapped for money until my next pay day.

On the streetcar ride home, I planned how I would wear my hair. I would ask Shen if I might borrow her black shawl again, I thought.

The work week dragged by. The ladies and I cooked and kept house, but my mind was often occupied with my plans with Bao. When Saturday finally arrived, I was again nervous and excited. Bao said that, if I wished, we could have a light meal after the opera. I tried to eat a little before I got dressed, but I wasn't hungry, and fortunately, a cup of tea sufficed to calm my jittery nerves. I wanted to make an impression on Bao. He knew everything there was to know about my life, yet I didn't want to be that woman tonight. I wanted to be beautiful and mysterious, like those stunning women I had once admired as a young woman in Shanghai.

I wore my hair down, curling slightly around my shoulders. On my feet, I wore Yi's black shoes, which fortunately fit me and were newer than mine. Around my shoulders, I draped Shen's shawl. I knew my money was well spent when I opened the door and saw the look on Bao's face. I picked up my purse from the table, and we went downstairs.

The Model T was parked in front of the house. After helping me into the car, Bao got into the car, pressed some buttons, got out and then ran around to the front of the car where he cranked it up. I noticed how handsome he looked in his tuxedo, and I wondered if he attended the opera often and with whom. Why else would he own a tuxedo? Maybe he bought it just for tonight. I didn't know, but I was aware that this was a moment of jealousy. I put the thought out of my head.

We drove to the small theater and parked close by. That night I saw a dazzling performance presented by The Nam Chung Music Association, which had just been founded this year. Bao explained to me that this music and the social club's principal activity was the production of Cantonese operas, which were usually staged for such benevolent purposes as fund-raising for charitable or social service organizations. He told me that Cantonese opera, which he loved, has a more than 400-year-old tradition. I sat there mesmerized by the atmosphere, enthralled by the costumes, and totally moved by the music. I was able to follow some of the Cantonese, but Bao whispered the storyline to me as the performance went on. I was surprised to see that the female lead roles were performed by males.

After the performance, we went to a small local restaurant

for a light supper. When Bao took me to my door, he lifted my hand and kissed it, saying he had very much enjoyed the evening. He asked if I would be at church in the morning, and I said that I would. He smiled, turned, and walked down the stairs. My journal entry that evening embodied a different style. There was an air of real hopefulness to my writing.

Several months passed, and Bao and I were going out on a regular basis. How different things were in America, where people were free to court openly by choice. We loved to watch the flickering movies at our favorite nickelodeon on Grand Avenue, visited bookshops and tea houses, and attended church together on Sundays. The ladies grew accustomed to Bao's baritone voice on the telephone, which we proudly added to our home not too long ago. Another group of names has been added to the San Francisco Telephone Exchange—ours!

The weather changed, the warm weather waned, and autumn was in the air. It was almost time for the Mid-Autumn Festival. We Chinese celebrated the Moon Festival, *(Jūng-chāu Jit* in Cantonese, *Zhōngqiū Jié* in Mandarin*),* on the 15th day of the 8th lunar month, which translated to September, or early October in the Gregorian calendar. This was the date when the moon was supposedly at its fullest and roundest. The traditional food of this festival was the mooncake, of which there are many different varieties. Every year, when the festival comes, people go home if possible from every corner of the country, to meet their families and have dinner with them. Because we cannot do this, and since it is such a family-oriented holiday, it was at first a very difficult time. However, Shen, Chang-Ma, Yi, and I agreed that we were a family, and celebrated together as such. Bao, too, was included as part of my new family. All of our blood relations were very far away, and we were lucky to have one another to share this happy time.

The festivities began earlier in the day with a grand parade hosted by the mayor of Chinatown. This year, the holiday was on a Sunday, and none of us but Yi had to work. Her boss asked her to work only a few hours so she could celebrate the holiday later. Several streets of Chinatown were blocked off for the day. Tables were set up all over, and delicious mooncakes were sold everywhere. Yi's boss was one of the sellers. We hoped he would make a lot of money selling his delicious food. We watched as the Lion Dance began with a huge clanging of bells and drums, and we all stepped back to allow the dancers to weave their way down the street. The crowd cheered and children clapped their hands, excited by the music and the long dancing lion. We enjoyed ourselves for an hour or so, and then went inside to prepare our festive meal, and baked the mooncakes to bring downstairs with us after the moon rose. We spent part of the afternoon cooking, and baked several dozen mooncakes to share with our local friends and neighbors, whom we are sure are doing the same. The three types we prepared were made of lotus seed, black bean paste, and red bean paste, but many other kinds will be seen, including those made with dates, nuts, fruits, sesame, ham, Chinese sausage, and green tea. Some mooncakes even contain a salty egg yolk representing the full moon.

Yi came back, and around six o'clock, Bao and two of our Chinese friends from the Mission Home came by to share our feast. It was traditional to eat in a courtyard, waiting for the moon to rise, but our homes are different here on Gold Mountain, and so, lacking a courtyard, we have our dinner, which we prepared earlier, indoors. Dinner is wonderful, both the food and the company. We ate and drank, as we related stories about our families back home. It was a wonderful meal, though quite bittersweet, as we all miss our relatives, whom we know are celebrating the festival in China, and surely missing us, too. Again, my thoughts ran to my parents, but I shook them off; it was Mid-Autumn Festival night, and I would remember them when I worshipped the moon.

Finished with the meal, we all went downstairs to continue the festivities, which would continue late into the night. The moon was high and impossibly huge, and I stood between Yi and Bao and stared up. Straw dragon lanterns were strung up on light poles, and they swayed in the evening breeze. A notable part of this celebration was the carrying of brightly lit lanterns, others placed on towers, and some floating in the air. Worship of the moon was quite the same for Chinese all over. Most people worshipped their ancestors at the same time since it was usually the day when family members returned home. There was no special ritual for moon worship. In a sense, it was meant to show respect, and mooncakes and fruit were served as sacrificial items. The moon, which belongs to the Yin, or negative principle, was associated with the female; therefore, moon worship was performed by women, not by men. We brought a small table downstairs, and we burned paper money and shared our mooncakes with our neighbors, tasting their offerings as well. Women chanted and looked up at the sky. The festival invoked romantic feelings in people, and the young men and women looked around, hoping to meet a special person meant for them. There was a wonderful feeling of connectedness. I felt Bao's eyes on me, and I turned and shyly smiled at him. How splendid a moment it was!

There have been numerous poems about the Mid-Autumn Festival since ancient times, the most famous piece being "*Shui Diao Ge Tou,*" by the Northern Song Dynasty poet, Su Dongpo. Although he lamented by writing:

> *"Men have sorrow and joy, they part or meet again;*
> *the moon may be bright or dim, she may wax or wane.*
> *There has been nothing perfect since the olden days."*
> He further expressed his thoughts:
>
> *"So let us wish that man will live long as he can; though miles apart, we'll share the beauty she displays."*

This he wrote, reflecting on how much those who were far

away from home would like to reunite with their families, and how deeply they missed their hometowns.

By the middle of December, it was unusually cool. The rain came down heavily as I trudged from the streetcar to my apartment. I reached the building, and shutting my Chinese umbrella, which was made of heavily waxed paper with a bamboo handle, I gratefully went up the few steps and unlocked the front door, entering into the building's dry, warm hallway. Today had been a trying day at the Exchange. My immediate boss, Mr. Sing Wee, had some sort of stomach surgery and would be out for a while. His temporary replacement, Mr. Jong Jue, was a very critical man, and though I had never had any problems with him in the past, I sensed he didn't like me, though I didn't know why. He spoke harshly to me in the morning, and I would have to be careful not to incur his ire until Mr. Sing returned. For now, I'm tired and grateful to be home.

I unlocked the apartment door and found only Chang-Ma at home. The others would be home soon. Chang-Ma wore a brightly printed cobbler over her dress and washed rice at the kitchen sink. I greeted her with a smile, hanging my wet coat up on the outside of the closet to dry. I had left my wet umbrella in the hallway.

"How was your day?" she asked.

"Too long. Old Jong will be very trying until Mr. Sing returns. I hope he gets well very soon," I replied. "How was your day, Chang-Ma?"

"Not too busy. Good for me, easy day, but it does not make Mr. Pong happy. Soon it will be Christmas, and business must get better."

"Bao says business has been slow this week, too," I said, I tied an apron around my waist. "It will get better; people need to begin their holiday shopping soon."

In the ice box, there was a piece of pork butt that Yi's boss sent home yesterday. I took that out along with some bok choy and other vegetables. Chang-Ma put the rice up to steam, and we both turned at the sound of the front door. It was Shen. She limped into the parlor, calling out "hello." We spoke as much English as we could at home. It was important for all of us to work on our vocabulary. On Sundays, after church, we dropped by the Mission, and Donaldina or one of the other ladies sat and conversed with us in English, often sending us home with reading assignments. We were all doing very well. By the time Yi arrived, we three had dinner ready, and we all sat down to share our meal and our day

After dinner, I brewed some jasmine tea and decided to do some reading. I was slowly working my way through "A Tale of Two Cities" by Charles Dickens. It was difficult, but I persevered.

After an hour or so, the telephone rang, and Yi answered. It was Bao. Taking the telephone, I said hello, and felt a sense of joy upon hearing his voice. We had been going out for close to a year now, and our relationship was quite serious. I had fallen in love with him. For me, this was a wondrous thing, considering that, other than Jun, I had been badly treated by men. My life of prostitution receded into the past as my happy life with Bao and my dear sisters became my present. I felt sure he loved me, too.

Bao's building was two floors high and he lived on the second floor, utilizing the basement for merchandise storage. He was in the process of opening up another store that he rented several blocks away from the first. The holiday season was important to him financially. The new space was larger than the first store and allowed him more room to accommodate the furniture and other large items his brothers would ship from China. Plans were made for his younger brother Wing to move to *Gum Saan* next year, temporarily leaving behind his wife and two children. Bao would hire someone to work in the first store as Shen, whom he trusted implicitly, would work in the new store. He would need a helper for Shen in that store and divide his time between the two. He was a very smart merchant, and I hoped that business continued to be bountiful. Oh, I was so proud of him, I thought to myself, as he asked me what I would like to do this coming weekend.

Later in the week, I received a letter from Cheng. He wrote that everyone was well. Jiao, my sister-in-law, was expecting a baby in the spring. My brothers were doing well, and my sister Lan was growing up. Cheng said she was very smart, and that the teacher said wonderful things about her. I was happy to hear that, and I prayed for them all at our Presbyterian church on Sunday.

Chinese women were going to college now, and I hoped Lan would have that opportunity. I decided to visit the Buddhist temple, to light *joss*, burn paper money, and say prayers for my sister-in-law Jiao, that she would have a healthy and comfortable pregnancy. My brother was a wonderful man who took on the care of his family after Baba died. He told me Mama Li had moved away to live with her sister's family. I missed them very much, and, as always, I wondered if I would ever see any of them again. And so another letter was placed in the back of my book.

At the Mission Home, Donaldina, Althea, and the others who helped run the Home were over-extended. There was no end to the number of girls being rescued. Bao was there for many of the raids. Last week, Althea asked me if I would be interested in helping some of the ladies learn some simple English. How flattered I was, since I am still learning myself. I attended church on Sunday, spent a brief time at the Buddhist temple, as I planned, and then took the streetcar to Sacramento Street.

At the Mission, Althea introduced me to a young woman named Ma Da-Wei, explaining that she had been kidnapped and brought to Gold Mountain from a town not very far away from Shanghai. All they knew about her was that she had been sold into prostitution, and forced to work in one of the cribs. She had been rescued by the police when they staged an early morning raid. She had given birth to a baby boy several months ago, and she would never know who the child's father was. When the police raided the crib, Da-Wei was fortunate enough to be rescued along with her baby. Many of the prostitutes became pregnant, but the brothel owners were only too happy to raise the offspring sired by the customers. For these brothel owners, it was a small amount of time to wait, and then these children would provide free or cheap labor in just a few years. I always said prayers of thanks that I had not become pregnant either by Liwei or the men I had been forced to sleep with, but I had also not been able to conceive with Jun.

It was late in the afternoon, and one of the ladies brewed some tea, bringing us a pot and two cups as I sat down with Da-Wei in the parlor to see if she would be willing to talk to me. Many of the young girls and women found it very difficult to talk about their experiences, and I could surely sympathize with them. Althea hoped that perhaps I could make her feel a bit more comfortable. Da-Wei's son slept alongside us in a small cradle lined with a blanket. I sat quietly sipping my tea, saying nothing. She didn't touch hers, but looked down at the sleeping baby and then at her hands in her lap. She was sweet-looking, with a slender face, and very high cheekbones. Her lips were shaped like a rosebud, and I imagined that when she smiled, she was very pretty. I waited, hoping she would start a conversation with me, but she was not forthcoming. I finished my cup of tea and poured myself another.

"Won't you drink your tea, Da-Wei?" I asked.

"Thank you, Mrs. Chen, I shall," she responded in a muted tone, finally picking up the cup but not raising her eyes.

I gazed at her for a moment, then spoke gently. "I want you to know that I am one of the many 'One Hundred Men's Wives' that passed through this Mission Home, just like you, and please, will you call me Ling?"

She nodded, just barely moving her head.

"Miss Althea tells me you lived in Wenzhou," I said, speaking in the Wu dialect. "I am from Shanghai, and so we were almost neighbors in China, though I am a bit older than you, Da-Wei. I know your town is close to the water, and a great deal of shipping is done from there."

Da-Wei took a sip of her tea at last, though it must have been cold, and hesitatingly began to speak. "I was taken from off the street one afternoon as I was returning home from a girlfriend's house. We had done our homework together, and when it had grown almost dark, my friend's mama said I should hurry home before my family worried about me. I left and was suddenly grabbed by two men who pushed me into a car." A tear slid down her cheek, and she wiped at it with her hand. "They kept me in a house for three days, fed me sparingly, and then I found myself on a ship, on my way to Gold Mountain. Shortly after I arrived, I was cleared through Angel Island because of the man I had traveled with who had papers showing me to be his wife. I was held captive and pregnant until the night of the raid."

The baby suddenly awoke, cried out, and immediately went back to sleep. Da-Wei sighed and finally raised her eyes to mine. "I love my baby very much, Mrs. Chen, but I don't know how I will be able to take care of him." (She didn't call me Ling, and how I hated being called Mrs. Chen).

"Don't worry, Da-Wei, you are safe now, and you and your son will be cared for. You must learn some English and then find a job. The American ladies will teach you, and if you like, I can help you a bit when I visit on Sundays. You must call me Ling. The name Chen brings me bad memories."

Da-Wei started to cry, and the sound re-awakened the baby, who also began to cry. Picking him up from his little cradle, she unbuttoned her blouse and put her son to her breast.

"I call him Ming," she told me. Tears spilled down her cheeks as the baby suckled. I didn't know what to say, so I said nothing.

The following week, Bao and I went to Hang Ah's for dinner. It was one of our favorite places to eat. When we arrived at my home, we parked near my building. He put his arm around me, and I laid my head on his shoulder and sighed. We sat like that for several moments, neither of us talking.

"Ling," he said in a quiet voice, "surely you must know that I have fallen in love with you, and I hope you feel the same toward me. I could not speak to your brother in person for his blessing as he is so far away in Shanghai, and I didn't know how to contact him. I would like you to be my wife if you will have me."

I saw him fumble for something in his jacket pocket. Withdrawing a ring box, he snapped it open, and inside was a beautiful, traditional American diamond engagement ring. "I thought to kneel in the restaurant and ask you then, but perhaps that would have embarrassed you, so here I am hoping you will say yes and become my wife."

"Yes, Bao, yes, I will marry you," I replied, feeling my eyes growing wet. "I love you, too."

He took me in his arms, and I knew that, finally, I would have the love and the life that I had waited for.

"We shall marry soon. Let us make plans for the New Year if that is agreeable to you," he stated.

We hurried upstairs to tell the women. Shen was out having dinner with her new beau, but Yi and Chang-Ma were home and became ecstatic over our news. Later that night, I drew out my journal and wrote words of such joy that I could barely imagine they were written by me, but they were; they were words of hope for a wonderful future.

CHAPTER SEVEN

SAN FRANCISCO, 1928

We decided to marry shortly after the Chinese New Year. Because neither of us had parents or blood relatives living in America, we thought we would have a Chinese-American wedding, paying attention to Chinese tradition, yet recognizing that we were now Americans. It was to be the start of our lives as modern Chinese living in America. We were married by Pastor Johnson at the Presbyterian Church on a cool, early February afternoon. I wore a simple ivory lace, western-style knee-length dress and an ivory, small-brimmed hat with a short veil and a red silk rose attached at the side. The rose was to honor our Chinese tradition of a bride wearing red for her wedding. Bao wore his black tuxedo with a red rose pinned to the lapel.

The ceremony was lovely, and all our friends were there. There were Chinese friends and customers of Bao's, as well as several of his American long-time customers. Of course, my dear friends were there, too, as well as Donaldina and Althea along with several others from the Mission. From there, we continued on to the banquet, which was held in a beautiful

Chinese reception hall in Chinatown. The color red was incorporated into the décor. For Chinese, red represented joy and happiness and was considered good luck for the couple. There were red and white flowers on the tables, red and white place cards, and red banners with calligraphy hanging all around the room.

We adhered to the tradition of the tea ceremony, honoring our Chinese friends, and remembering our families that were far away. I changed into a traditional red *cheongsam* for the tea ceremony and afterwards back into my ivory dress. I remembered how recently I had worn a red dress similar to this one when I married Jun. It seemed a lifetime ago.

The banquet was wonderful. We served a combination of American and Chinese dishes, starting with shark's fin soup that Bao liked so much. I had wanted American food served so the wedding could be different from the one I remembered when I had married Jun in Shanghai. Along with the soup, there was the choice of a fresh green salad with tomatoes, cucumbers, and red onions topped with a spicy vinaigrette dressing. There were delicious entrees of rare prime ribs of beef served in generous portions, along with potatoes, green beans, and gravy. Also served were platters of sea bass made with ginger, garlic, and onions, which is symbolically offered to bring a couple wealth. Whole pigeons were served according to Chinese tradition to ensure a peaceful marriage. Lotus seeds, symbolizing fertility, were incorporated into a delicious dessert. The wedding cake was large, beautiful, and traditionally American, right down to the Chinese bride and groom figurines placed on top of the three layers. Gifts of red envelopes, as well as other gifts, were offered in keeping with both Chinese and American traditions.

After the wedding, we went back to Bao's apartment over the store. In the morning, we planned to leave for Los Angeles to spend a few days. Shen reassured us she would be able to oversee the stores so that we could enjoy a short honeymoon.

Bao knew she could be trusted to turn over every penny when we returned.

Because I had no mama to care for me, Althea and Donaldina presented me with a gift earlier in the week. I opened the package and blushed. I was ashamed when I saw what they had bought me, but they would have none of my modesty. I was to forget the past, they said, and move on to a happy life with Bao. It was a beautiful silk ivory-toned peignoir set to wear on my wedding night, and so traditionally American!

That night at Bao's apartment, I excused myself and went into the bedroom to change. He waited in the small parlor. Undressing, I could only see myself from the waist up in the small mirror. I unpinned my hair, brushing it through with Bao's hairbrush that I found sitting on the dresser. We had moved my belongings from the apartment, but I hadn't unpacked yet. I looked at my reflection and wondered if I could be the woman that Bao wanted. I said a small prayer, hoping that my past could be washed away in the arms of a good man who loved me.

I changed into the lovely gown and robe, and taking one last look in the mirror, I shut off the light and walked down the small hallway to the parlor where Bao waited. I was barefoot, and he didn't hear me approach. He sat with his back to me, and as I reached him, I placed my hand on his shoulder. He stood and turned to me, his eyes warm and tender. I had never felt more loved as he enfolded me in his arms, and picking me up, carried me to his bed. Bao and I had never made love. His kisses had been sweet and respectful. Because of my past, he didn't want to make love to me until we were married. He had courted me as if I was a young virgin, never once making me remember the sordidness of my life.

My wedding night with Bao was wonderful. I was far from a blushing bride, and I'm sure he was aware of how nervous I was. My fear was that he would judge me, knowing that I had been with many men. Only one, Jun, had actually made love to me. Now I offered myself to Bao to be his for the rest of our lives. There had been more men than I cared to count, but this was different. I was no longer the "One Hundred Men's Wife". Not since Jun had I loved a man and wanted to give myself to him. I had made peace with myself over my poor judgment regarding Liwei. The past was to remain in the past.

As Bao placed me on the bed, I slipped the robe and gown off. I was not innocent, and would not play that role. I was in bed with my husband, the man I loved dearly, and all I wanted was to feel his mouth on mine, and his hands on my body, washing away the memories of my past.

Chapter Eight

San Francisco, 1929

Ming crawled after me into the kitchen. He was fourteen months old, and crawling since he was seven months old. Now he was pulling himself up and cruising around on every piece of furniture. He would be walking soon. I wanted to start cleaning the chicken for dinner, but it was impossible to ignore Ming. He reached up and pulled on the hem of my skirt. I bent down and picked him up.

"What a handful you are, Ming. You are such a big boy already. Soon you will be walking."

He looked at me, cocking his head as if to say, of course I will. I gave him a Zwieback cookie, a hard, toasted type of biscuit originally from Germany. He was teething terribly, and it was common for babies to scrape these tasty cookies on their aching gums. Four little white prongs protruded in his mouth, and I knew the new ones cutting through hurt him a great deal. Putting him back down on the kitchen floor, I reached into a cabinet and retrieved a Chinese herbal mix that was used to ease a baby's teething pain. I gave him a toy to try to keep him amused while I washed my hands and rubbed some on his gums. I washed my hands once more and resumed preparing the chicken.

Ming was Da-Wei's little boy; well, that wasn't exactly true, he was Bao's and mine now. A great deal had happened in such a short period. Da-Wei and I had become friends. She had continued living at the Mission Home, and after a few months, a job was found for her. She worked as a waitress at a local Chinese restaurant, leaving Ming in the care of the residents of the Mission, who were only too happy to help. Four months earlier, Da-Wei had not come home from work. Several hours had elapsed, and finally, the police were called. When he was questioned, the restaurant owner said that Da-Wei had left at her usual time.

The case was investigated for several weeks, but there were no leads. No one knew anything about yet another woman who had once been a prostitute and was now missing. It was nothing unusual. It was thought that most likely she had been found by her Tong lord. She was just one of hundreds. Eventually, the search was discontinued.

Ordinarily, Ming would have been placed in an orphanage, but under the circumstances, with the mother being one of our women, the baby continued to live at the Home, the kindly ladies overseeing the care of him and hoping against hope that Da-Wei would be found.

Bao and I had been married for over a year and were trying to have a baby of our own. I realized I might not be able to conceive. I had not become pregnant at any point in my life. We had talked it over and decided that, if Donaldina and Althea agreed, we might be foster parents to little Ming until such time as Da-Wei returned to claim her little boy. Placing him in a child care institution would have been a terrible option. No one knew what had befallen her. Had she run away, been killed, or been kidnapped? There were no answers to those questions and so, after a great deal of thought, we decided I would quit my job at the telephone exchange, and if the women at the Mission acquiesced, we would bring Ming home to live with us.

On Tuesday, October 29th, 1930, called Black Tuesday, the stock market crashed, plunging America into an economic nightmare. The Great Depression had begun. It was worldwide, but it hit California like a ton of bricks. The population had boomed. The Bay area had grown and prospered, and suddenly, almost overnight, the mood darkened. Businesses that had been expanding had to cut back. People were laid off, couldn't pay their bills, and couldn't find new jobs. Those at the bottom of the economy felt it first. There were strikes and terrible, bloody riots.

Chinatown was crowded, overflowing with out-of-work people living in dilapidated tenements. Its schools, hospitals, nightlife, and, of course, the telephone service continued to be separate as always. Chinese-Americans lived in America, yet also in a world apart. Hundreds of people were out of work but tried to help one another. There was grinding poverty and fear. We still lived on the second floor of Bao's building, but things had changed a great deal. Bao was forced to give up not only his second store but any thoughts of his brother traveling to America. We were very fortunate to have the money, in the beginning, to run our business, but as the months passed, the monthly bills became harder and harder to pay. Of course, we no longer had my paycheck, and while I had earned a small salary, it had still supplemented our income.

Up until now, Bao's stores had been doing well, and there had been no warning, no way to know what was coming, not for anyone. We continued to do business, mostly dealing in simple staples, but our trade declined tremendously. How fortunate we were to be selling items that people needed, rather than desired. Few were interested in beautiful brocade and silk fabrics, as no one could afford such luxuries. People were making do with what they owned or buying inexpensive ready-made clothing. We could no longer focus on bigger-priced items such as furniture. Other than necessities, such as pots and pillows, people weren't spending money fixing up their homes.

Times were difficult, but we eked out a living and somehow got by. The ladies at the Mission Home were having a difficult time; donations were no longer as forthcoming as they had been in the past. They might not have been able to stay open had it not been for the government's subsidy. My "sisters" were just managing, having taken two other ladies from the Home into the apartment to help split the bills.

One evening, after I finished washing the supper dishes, Bao and I sat down to talk over a cup of jasmine tea. It was almost Chinese New Year, only two weeks away, and we were discussing the scaled-down party we were planning. We had decided to hold it at our place, regardless of the difficult times. It was an important event in everyone's lives, and even the Depression wasn't going to stop us from celebrating this year. The New Year has been celebrated every spring for over five thousand years in China. In past years, we had all been generous with the amount of money we spent on presents, decorations, food, and clothing. This year we all had to be very frugal.

The first thing I had to do was clean the store and apartment in order to "sweep away" any ill-fortune and make way for good incoming luck. We would cover the windows and doors with red paper cut-outs with sayings such as "good fortune," "happiness," "wealth," and "longevity." We sold these items in the store and hoped people would come to buy because, despite the lack of money, to us Chinese, this was as important as food. Just like the Autumn Festival, on the Eve of Chinese New Year, supper is a feast held with families.

"It will be a simple meal, Bao. I have spoken with the

ladies already, and they have said they will all cook and bring food to share at our place. The meal won't be the fancy banquet that we have had in the past, but we will all be together, and that's all that matters."

Ming was sitting on the floor next to the table, playing with some blocks. I watched him pick up a red one in one hand, and a yellow one in the other. He did this very carefully, examining each one in turn, and then placing them down on the floor, and picking up two more. He was a beautiful, happy child, with high cheekbones like his mother, and a lovely head of dark hair.

"We will have a wonderful time. What we eat is of no importance, as long as we are all together; better times are coming, I'm sure," Bao said.

Unfortunately, better times were a long way off, but we had no way of knowing that. It was just the beginning, and things would get a lot worse before they got better. Still, we were optimistic and grateful to have each other and little Ming. After we finished our tea, I took the cups to the sink and washed them, after which I scooped up the baby and took him into the bathroom for his bath. As the tub filled with suds made from Ivory Flakes, I undressed the happy child, wondering for the millionth time what had happened to his mother. Would we ever know? I sat Ming in the foamy, warm bath, and he splashed happily as I lathered his sweet, soft body and washed his hair. Then I dried him off with a towel, and powdered and diapered him. Holding the boy with his still damp hair, I warmed his bedtime bottle and tested the formula on the inside of my wrist. Ming struggled in my arms, tired from his bath, and craving his bottle.

"Here, Ming, little plum," I crooned, sitting down with him as he thirstily began sucking. I looked down at the beautiful boy in my arms, and my heart turned over. I loved him more than I could express. Every Sunday I prayed that Da-Wei would be found, but we all knew in our hearts that it was unlikely. Yet, with each week that passed, I didn't give up hope and wondered if she would show up at the Home and claim her little son. I prayed for God to forgive me for my feelings of confusion. I felt such love for someone else's child, yet I truly hoped Da-Wei was alive and safe and would return for her baby. I tried not to dwell on how great the loss would be to me if that happened. My diary bore the brunt of my confusion. As the baby drank, these insidious thoughts entered my head, unbidden, as always. I watched his little mouth pulling on the nipple, and made myself think about the firecrackers we would set off outside after New Year's dinner, and the sweet desserts we would eat. It was a time to forget grudges, and wish peace and happiness for everyone. I knew that, during these hard times, it would be difficult for some to celebrate with true reconciliation in their hearts. Many were angry, hungry, and filled with hate as this New Year approached.

Ming had fallen asleep on his bottle, and I nudged him a bit. He started sucking again, finishing a little more, but fell right back to sleep. Getting up, I carried him into our small bedroom and settled him in his crib. Although the crib had been donated to the Mission, Bao had refused to accept it as a gift, making Donaldina and Althea accept money from us. We knew how badly they needed it, and while they protested at first, they had given in and taken our offering. We returned the cradle they had originally given us so that another baby could make use of it.

I watched Ming put his thumb in his mouth, and my heart turned over. Leaving the door slightly open, I went into the parlor to listen to the radio with Bao. The radio had become an essential part of the country's daily life. We listened to the news every evening after supper. Also, there were music shows presenting everything from opera and classical concerts, to lively swing music performances. We enjoyed the Rudy Vallee Show and laughed at the comedy of Eddie Cantor. We were very proud of our ever-increasing ability to understand English as well as we did. All over America, the radio was an important connection to the country and the rest of the world.

It was New Year's Eve. It seemed that there was a bit more spring in the steps of the people as they hurried off to their jobs, happy to have one to go to. Mothers, with children in tow, were rushing them to school, knowing that there were cooking and cleaning tasks to be done at home. Bao had gone downstairs early to do some work in the store before opening for the day.

I was feeding Ming his *congee* when the telephone rang. It was Althea, calling to say good morning, and acknowledging that she had remembered it was Chinese New Year. "Hello, dear, how are you and the family today?"

"Fine, thank you, Althea. How are things at the Home this morning?" I asked.

"We are overcrowded and short of funds as always. What could possibly have changed?" she laughed.

Althea was my savior. Where would I be today had she not found me that day on the street? I didn't allow myself to think back to those days. Today was hard enough.

"I was wondering if you needed any help with your cooking today," Althea said. "I could have Soo-Lee or one of the other girls stop by to help you. Some of the ladies are cooking here, as well."

"How kind you always are, Althea. I shall finish cooking later," I said, "after I put Ming down for his late-morning nap. I did some preparing last night. The others ladies cooked last night, too. We shall all have a lovely meal together later this evening. I really do appreciate your asking. Thank you so much."

"You are welcome, Ling, dear," she told me. "If you change your mind, just call me later. I want to wish you and Bao, and the others, a very happy New Year. Oh, and please give the boy a kiss for me. Will I be seeing you on Sunday?"

"Yes, Althea, I'll see you at church, and thanks for calling," I said, hanging up the phone.

Althea was almost like the dear mother I had lost. I sighed, noticing the mess Ming had made while I had been on the phone. He was feeding himself. I had lost my concentration during the phone call, and now his high chair tray, another donation from the Home, had more *congee* on it than was left in the bowl. I wiped the gooey porridge out of his hair and finished feeding him. I would bathe him later, before the company came.

When he finished his meal, I sat down on the floor with him and his toy train. It, too, was a gift from the Mission, newly purchased along with other toys before the horrible day hit us. It was his favorite toy. I wanted to spend some time with him before I began to cook for the festive dinner, so we played for about fifteen minutes. I laughed as he ran his car along the top of my leg, making huffing noises as he did so.

"Are you the train conductor, Ming? Make the choo-choo sound again," I said.

He stood up and shakily walked to the divan. He was only walking a couple of weeks and was unsteady on his chubby little legs. It was really quite funny to see. He overcompensated for his bad balance by spreading his legs apart. He ran the train up the front of the divan and across the seat, little gobs of saliva leaving his mouth as he tried to make the train noises. He was teething terribly, poor baby. Within a minute or so, he grew tired of the game and toddled over to his scanty toy box. Picking up two blocks, last week's favorites yet again, he brought them over to me, placed them on the floor, and went back to search for more. I showed him the letters on the blocks Bao had bought him months ago. He tried to repeat the letters as I said them to him. He had a small English vocabulary, and we worked with him often to teach him to speak English. We played for another ten minutes or so, and then I began straightening up the parlor, keeping my eye on him as I did.

Soon everything was dusted and neat as a pin, and I could see he was getting tired. It was almost four o'clock and I decided to put him down for his afternoon nap, then I could start cooking. Tonight he would be up later than usual and I wanted him to be in a happy mood. I changed his diaper and laid him in his crib. It was made up with pastel-colored sheets and a matching blanket, both illustrated with little green-and-yellow bunnies; this was yet another hand me down. He started to cry, not wanting to sleep just yet. I made him a half bottle of apple juice, and seeing it, he took it from me and stopped crying.

While Ming napped, I prepared for the evening's events. I would have to clean the bedroom using the carpet sweeper after Ming's nap. I hoped he would sleep for a while so I would have time for everything. I had coordinated the cooking with the other ladies—Shen, Chang-Ma, Yi, Sang-Li, and Ping-Wa, who now all lived together. It was a rather tight fit in my old apartment, but times were tough and they made the best of it, happy to have a place to call home. Sang-Li and Ping-Wa had stories similar to the rest of us, and they were both fortunate enough to have jobs. Fortunately, many of the richer families still maintained some of their household staff, though the ladies figured their jobs were tenuous.

We had decided I would cook the chickens. Everyone liked my recipe. It is traditional to serve the whole chicken during the holiday as it symbolizes family togetherness. Yesterday, after Bao came upstairs from the store, I went out and bought three whole chickens, (freshly killed and plucked at the market). The cost was dear, but it couldn't be helped; it was New Year's Eve! I kept them in our ice box overnight. Refrigerators had just appeared on the scene, but not many could be found in Chinatown.

I seasoned the chickens inside and out with just salt and pepper, then I stuffed them with ginger, scallions, and basil. I also added some of the fragrant items to the water in a huge pot I used to cook the chickens, along with more salt and pepper. I submerged the chickens completely in the liquid and covered the pot, letting it simmer for about thirty minutes, after which I added carrots, covered the pot again, and removed it from the heat. This I let stand for about an hour, never lifting the lid off the pot so the heat wouldn't dissipate. Thus the chickens would not overcook; that was the secret. Later, the chickens would be presented on a bed of rice, not cut until it was time to eat, and they would be extremely tender.

While the chickens cooked, I did some cleaning. Though I had already cleaned most of the apartment and store, I would have to sweep the store again and the basement, as well. There was a great deal to do, including *sycee* to cook.

My friends were preparing other traditional New Year's dishes. Noodles were served to represent long life; an old superstition says that it's bad luck to cut them, so they were served long, in delicious oyster sauce, to be wrapped around and around our chopsticks. Ping-Wa would bring those. Clams and spring rolls were served to symbolize wealth. I made clam *sycee*, a Shanghainese dish, with clams steamed with ginger, soy sauce, onions, rice wine, and cornstarch. Afterward, the shucked clams were chopped up and added to the mixture, which was then stuffed back into the clam shells, then they were fried in hot oil in a wok. The clams resemble gold or silver bullion (*sycee*), which was originally used as currency in China. Spring rolls are eaten because they look like long, gold bars.

Yi, who had been working for a while in a restaurant, had shown a tremendous interest in cooking and had learned a great deal from the chef. She would prepare the spring rolls. We could not afford shrimp or lobster, they were way too costly, but there would be sweet, sticky rice cakes to symbolize a rich, sweet life, layered to represent rising abundance for the coming year, and the round shape signifying family reunion. Chang-Ma and Sang-Li were making traditional lettuce wraps, filled with turkey and bean sprouts marinated in hoisin sauce.

There would be pomelos because the Chinese word sounds like the word for "to have', and tangerines and oranges as well, the words for each sounding like "luck" and "wealth'.

Fish plays a large role in the celebration, too. The word for fish, *yu,* sounds like the words for both "wish" and "abundance." On New Year's Eve, it is customary to serve a fish, such as a carp, at the end of the evening meal, symbolizing a wish for abundance in the coming year. For added symbolism, the fish was served whole with the head and tail attached, symbolizing a good beginning and ending for the coming year. The ladies were also making coconut pudding and apricot sweet-and-sour cakes for dessert. None of these ingredients were terribly costly, but the meal would be traditional and delicious.

Ming slept for about two and a half hours, and I got a lot accomplished. I had just about finished cleaning the house, except the bedroom where he slept, in order to sweep away any ill-fortune and to make way for incoming good luck. The ladies, and many other Chinese, would be doing the same at their homes. When I heard Ming cry out from his crib, I went and got him, put him in a clean diaper again, and let him play with his toys for a bit. I would give him something to eat, quickly bathe and dress him, and then bring him down to the store so I could sweep and dust a bit there. Then Shen, Bao, and I would hang the red-colored paper decorations in the store windows.

The day before, Bao and I had put some on our windows upstairs. One said "good fortune" and another said "happiness". Later tonight, after we had eaten, we would go downstairs to enjoy the noisy firecrackers, and then go back upstairs to exchange the small gifts we have for one another, then eat our dessert. The holiday would continue for sixteen more days, ending with the Lantern Festival on the last day. This would be a time to reconcile, forget grudges, and wish peace and happiness for everyone. Times were difficult, and it would be nice to come together and celebrate tonight, forgetting if only for a while, the problems plaguing all of us.

The rest of the afternoon passed quickly as I finished preparing my share of the dinner feast. I fed and bathed Ming and we went downstairs. Shen helped me clean and hang the red paper signs of good fortune. Bao closed the store a little early and watched Ming while I went upstairs to bathe and get dressed before our company came. He also wanted Shen to have some time to finish her cooking and change her clothes at home.

I sat in the bathtub, soaping my hair and thinking about my family back home in Shanghai. I knew that Jiao would prepare a similar meal for my brothers and sister, the baby, her parents, and her brother. Days like this I missed them terribly. It had been so many years, and again I wondered when we would ever meet again. I had prayed for them in church the previous Sunday, and just for good luck, again visited the Buddhist temple.

I finished washing, and after rinsing my hair, I toweled it dry and hurried into our bedroom to get dressed for the festive evening ahead. I heard Bao giving Ming a Zweiback to teethe on until the company came, and I was happy he had thought to do so. What a good man he was. Many men wanted nothing to do with "women's work', and would never even consider helping their wives.

I wore a simple, inexpensive beige cheongsam, embroidered with butterflies. I pulled my damp hair into a bun and placed two small, golden butterfly clips above each ear to hold the wisps from escaping. These barrettes and other hair accessories were big sellers in the store. Because of the Depression, women wore what they had, and made do with simple, unadorned hair pins. I went inside to rescue Bao and let him have some time to wash up and get ready for our guests. Soon after, the doorbell rang, and the ladies arrived, arms laden with packages and containers of food.

"Gong Xi Fa Cai!" I exclaimed as I had so long ago in Shanghai. "Happy New Year! Come in, everyone!"

"Gong Hay Fat Choy" Bao shouted in Cantonese.

"Let me take some of that from you," I said, and Bao came to help. We placed the food in the kitchen, and the red-wrapped presents in the parlor next to ours, all to be opened later.

Yi brought her boyfriend Soo Wing with her. They had been dating for about five months, having met at the restaurant she worked in. Mr. Soo had been eating there for a long time but had started sitting at one of Yi's tables whenever he dropped by for a meal. A long-time bachelor, he had taken a liking to Yi's petite, delicate beauty, and her friendly demeanor. He found himself there more often than he could afford, but he decided the pleasure he experienced when she served him and they chatted outweighed the extra expense. Finally, after several weeks, he had gathered up the gumption to ask Yi if he could take her out for a meal, and she agreed. He was a pleasant-faced man in his late thirties who made it clear he was very much hoping to find a wife and settle down. He owned a laundry, (as had Jun), and despite the troubled economy, his services were still needed, though many now did their own washing. Still, he got by. We all liked Wing very much and knew that Yi hoped for a proposal. Soon it would be a new year, hopefully a better one.

Wing and Bao settled down to chat in the parlor, while the ladies and I proceeded to the kitchen to warm up and finish preparing the food. We chatted as we worked in my small kitchen, placing the dishes on the table I had set. It was cramped, but we managed. The men offered to eat in the parlor, as there was so little room at the table. The tantalizing smells filled our apartment. Finally, all was ready and we sat down to our New Year's Eve feast. There was much laughter and gaiety as we ate.

The men walked back and forth refilling their plates as

the ladies placed different foods on the table. Our chopsticks clicked as we rolled noodles, while Bao carved up the tasty chickens I had prepared. We dipped Yi's spring rolls into the various sauces placed on the table. At last, I brought out the delicious *sycee* I had prepared according to my family's traditional recipe from back home. We enjoyed the meal, dipping our chopsticks again and again. Ming happily mushed around his noodles on his high chair tray and ate the tiny pieces of chicken and spring roll I cut up for him.

It was a wonderful meal for us all. We spent a long time at the table, talking and reminiscing about our families and sharing stories about life back home in China. By nine o'clock, everything was cleaned up, and it was time to go downstairs and walk the few streets to where we could hear the firecrackers being set off. Many of our neighbors were there, too.

"*Gong Xi Fa Cai,*" I called out in Wu dialect over the noise of the firecrackers. Some said, "*Xin Nian Kuai Le*" in Mandarin, while yet others yelled out "*Gong Hay Fat Choy*" in Cantonese.

Little Ming began to cry. I took him from Bao's arms and tried to soothe him. The loud noises scared him, but he soon calmed down, looking all around him at the many people filling the streets, talking, laughing and wishing Happy New Year to each other, be they strangers or friends. We spent about half an hour outdoors and then decided to go back for dessert. We walked the short blocks back to the store, trekking up the stairs to open our gifts and have tea and sweets to complete the evening's festivities. The coconut pudding and the sweet-and-sour apricot cakes earned high praise.

After dessert, we opened the red paper-wrapped presents we had brought for one another. The presents were but small tokens of our love and affection for one another. We exchanged fans, hair decorations, a fountain pen from Bao and me to Wang, and other small items. Ming received several new toys, and he could barely hold his head up as we opened his gifts. I put him to bed and came back to spend more time with my wonderful "family'. The evening ended on a high note; everyone had forgotten, at least for a little while, the trials and tribulations that plagued us. My diary held only happy words that night.

Chapter Nine

Near San Francisco, 1930

Robert Mason owned a cattle ranch located in an area just southeast of San Francisco proper. Cattle, chicken, and various kinds of crop farms populated what would eventually become McLaren Park. Surrounding it were areas that would become Excelsior, Portola, and Visitacion Valley. Robert and his wife Wanda, along with their three children, lived in a modest house and maintained a small ranch, raising beef cattle. They made a comfortable living with about one hundred thirty acres of land, and between seventy to seventy-five head of cattle. Robert worked the ranch along with several hired hands, one of whom lived in a small cottage on the property. Others came in daily, rotating so there were always plenty of workers.

When the Depression hit, Robert's business began to slack off. He was forced to lay off several of his workers. It hurt him to have to do it, knowing the men had families, but he just couldn't afford to pay the salaries. He and Wanda sat down one evening and talked late into the night. People didn't have money to buy beef and were resorting to eating a lot more chicken, fish and goat, not to mention eliminating meat from their diets in general several days a week. It was a difficult situation at best. They made the decision they would devote twelve acres to raising crops their family could sell and live on. They would plant basic garden produce: tomatoes, carrots, lettuce, bell peppers, cucumbers, and cabbage. They hoped the crops would help supplement their meager income from the cattle.

One afternoon, while Mason was riding through his produce acreage, his ranch hand, Jack DeSarno called out to him, visibly upset. "Robert, you have to see this."

Mason rode over to the area where DeSarno was sitting astride his horse. It was immediately apparent what he had discovered. His digging had uncovered a body part, a leg or arm perhaps, buried there in the soil where they had been planting tomatoes. The rest of the body was clearly there.

"My God," Robert exclaimed, "what have you found? We have to get back to the house and phone the police immediately."

A day later, Althea read in the newspaper that a body had been uncovered in a field owned by a cattle rancher. The article stated that a worker planting crops made the discovery. The body, though partially decomposed, was possibly identifiable because of a red birthmark on the woman's shoulder. Althea contacted the local police, knowing that Da-Wei had had just such a mark. It seemed quite certain that this was her body. While we could never be positive, it seemed certain that this was how Da-Wei met her demise. We would never know the details. The police had many cases of Chinese prostitutes found dead, and more often than not, the cases were quickly dropped.

It seemed that Ming was to be Bao's and mine forever. After the police finished their investigation, and the coroner released the body, a funeral was held, which the Mission Home paid for. We had been allowed to bury the body in the Chinese cemetery since no else came to claim it. I prayed for

Da-Wei's soul, both at the Presbyterian Church and the Buddhist temple, and told her that her baby boy would always be loved and cared for. I told of my deepest feelings that night, praying again as I wrote in my journal, tears hitting the pages and smearing some of the words. How many pages had smeared words on them, I thought.

Meanwhile, life continued in Chinatown. The weather was mild, and spring buds were on all the trees. I took Ming for a walk in his carriage, hoping he would fall asleep in the beautiful sunshine. Stopping at a small market stand in the street, I bought two several-days-old apples, planning that, while Ming napped, I would sit on a bench in the local park and enjoy one. Finding an empty bench, I sat and looked around me. Old men were comfortably seated at small tables playing Mah Jongg, the ivory tiles clicking, while two mothers with young children were sitting together chatting.

A woman, perhaps in her mid-twenties, sat down alongside me on the bench, a small baby in the carriage she was wheeling. She smiled at me and asked me how old my child was. I replied he was sixteen months old and politely inquired about her child. She told me her name was Din Fan, and that her little girl had just turned one a few weeks ago. I introduced myself to her, and we struck up a conversation. I offered her my other apple, which she initially refused. Apples weren't expensive but times were hard. I encouraged her and finally, she accepted the apple with thanks.

We sat eating them side by side while the babies slept. She told me she was married to a very nice man who had worked in a fish store but recently lost his job. Their small savings was dwindling, and soon they would be in serious trouble if he didn't find work. She wanted to seek a job cleaning in one of the homes of the wealthy Americans who still had help, but her husband, old-fashioned Chinese that he was, didn't want his wife to work, nor would he stay home and take care of the baby. Still, she continued, they had no family, but if there was someone to watch the child, she was sure she could find work, and then her husband would have no choice. Otherwise, they would soon be on the streets. It was a common story, and could easily become ours. I liked Fan; she was sweet and personable. We finished our apples and just sat companionably in silence until Ming awoke from his nap.

I had brought a small, red ball with me. I checked Ming and found that his diaper needed changing. I did so, placing the soiled one in the metal garbage pail a few feet away. He had had his bottle of milk earlier, so I offered him one of water, but he only wanted to get out of his carriage and walk around the park. I lifted him out, and taking the little ball with me, started pushing the carriage and walking with the toddler to the grassy area in front of our bench. Fan said goodbye, hoping we'd meet again since we both often spent time sitting in the park as our babies napped. I looked back and waved. Ming took the ball out of my hand, and threw it in his best overhand. It landed just in front of us, and I laughed as he tried to run for it, falling down in the grass.

Later, at home, I gave Ming some left-over chicken and some bok choy, which I broke up into tiny pieces for his lunch. I ate some of the food, too, thinking as we both chewed. Bao came up to eat lunch, leaving Shen to run things for the short amount of time. There were fewer customers by the day. Ming was tired from his earlier outing, and I put him down for his afternoon nap. After Bao left, I continued thinking as I did a little straightening up of our place, returning Ming's scattered toys to his toy box. What if I watched Fan's baby while she worked? Hopefully, she could find some sort of work, perhaps as a maid, as she had suggested. I could charge her a small fee to take care of her little girl every day she worked. I would be home taking care of Ming anyway. Up until now, Bao had managed to continue employing Shen. But, if things got any worse, he would have to let her go, and I would bring Ming with me to work in the store. This was something none of us wanted to face. What would Shen do? Still, for now, I was home and thought, how much harder could two babies be? This would mutually benefit both our families. I would have to discuss this idea with Bao later, and if he agreed, I would have to hope I ran into Fan at the park again.

That evening, after dinner, I broached the subject with Bao. He actually liked the idea but said that he would have to interview the family very carefully before he would agree. He wondered, though, if I would ever see Fan again. My plan was to go to the park tomorrow, around the same time as I had that afternoon.

Late the next morning, with the weather being mild and sunny, I headed off to the park, finding the same bench I had sat on with Fan yesterday. I stayed there for quite a while. I played ball with Ming, changed him, gave him a bottle, and let him nap a bit. In my constant effort to improve myself, I had brought the San Francisco Chronicle with me, as well as two apples again, but Fan didn't show up. Not being faint of heart, I went home and planned to go every day that wasn't raining until I found her. The following day it rained, but a day later, I was rewarded when I spotted Fan strolling down the path, wheeling her baby in her carriage. I called out to her and hearing her name, Fan looked in my direction and waved. She came and sat with me, and didn't want to take the apple I offered. I cajoled her into taking it, and she finally did, thanking me over and over.

"It is nothing," I said.

We sat enjoying the fruit companionably as I presented my idea to her. She was excited but didn't think her husband would allow it. Still, I had sowed the seeds of an idea in her head. We arranged to meet after the weekend, same time, same place.

The following week, Fan and I met again. We really enjoyed each other's company, and we introduced the children to each other. We let them sit on the grass, rolling the little red ball between them. I watched them laugh and play in the sunshine and hoped things would work out. Fan had broached the subject to her husband, and he had been vehemently against the idea. He was sticking to his old beliefs that a man provided for his family while his wife stayed home, taking care of the house and children. She had patiently explained that this was not China, and even in China, women worked if there was someone to take care of their children. It was 1930, for heaven's sake! Besides, he had not been able to find work, so she told him it was time to let her try.

I offered to talk to Sang-Li and Ping-Wa. Perhaps each could ask her employer if they had any friends who might need domestic help. Maybe if Fan found a position, her husband would be more welcoming to the idea. On the other hand, it might make him very angry. I certainly didn't want to come between a husband and wife. When I said this to Fan, she told me she would take total responsibility for this plan.

It turned out that Ping-Wa's mistress had a wealthy friend that could use extra help. Some of the rich Americans had been able to continue their lifestyles, though in a lesser way. Fan and I had exchanged telephone numbers the previous week, though she didn't know how much longer they would be able to afford the phone. After speaking to Ping-Wa, I ran to call Fan and tell her the news. At first, Ping-Wa had been uncertain about vouching for Fan since I barely knew her, and she didn't know her at all. But I explained what a lovely woman she was, and understanding that this would help Bao and me as well, she agreed to help. She told her mistress about Fan and that she had had experience with domestic work in China. A few days later, she told me the woman was willing to meet with her.

Ping-Wa's mistress kindly set up an interview. Fan was hired and told she could start the following week. The big problem was how would she break this news to her husband? There was no way but to tell him the truth and deal with his ire. When we met again, she told me she had finally convinced her husband to meet us. I invited Fan and her husband to bring the baby and come for tea and dessert one evening so we could get to know each other. They came the following night, and Bao and I liked the man a great deal. He seemed mild-mannered, but old fashioned in his ways, and while strong-minded, was still a reasonable sort. After meeting us and asking some questions, (after all, it worked both ways), he was finally convinced this was something they had to do. He, too, had finally gotten an offer of work at a small pajama factory, and while it paid poorly, it was something. Fan was to be paid five dollars a day for a six-day week, and I would receive twelve dollars a week to watch her baby girl, May-Lee. Our arrangement was agreed upon over sticky buns and tea.

May-Lee was a sweet little girl with a pleasant disposition. They had only met once, but now she fell in love with Ming immediately, and though not yet walking, she crawled around after him all day long, sometimes pulling herself up on the divan. I asked Althea to keep an eye out for a used high chair that May-Lee could use. The babies shared the crib at naptime. They also had to share the carriage when I took them to the park. It wasn't easy, but we managed. All in all, it helped provide some small income to offset our financial woes.

One Saturday night, Althea kindly volunteered to watch Ming so we could attend Yi and Wing's wedding. It was small, simple and beautiful, with a classic meal served at the restaurant where Yi worked and they had met. Both the bride and groom wore traditional Chinese wedding attire. The groom, like so many of us, had no family in America. In China, there was only a sister, her husband, and two nieces. When we got home we thanked Althea for watching Ming. He was asleep, and she said she hadn't had a bit of trouble with him. Bao drove her back to the Home while I got undressed and ready for bed. What a lovely time we had at the wedding, I told my diary.

Chapter Ten

San Francisco, 1932

Eleven months passed, and another New Year's celebration came and went. A lot happened this year. Ming was two and a half years old and was still a happy, delightfully clever little boy. Perhaps I was a bit prejudiced, though. Little May-Lee, Fan's daughter, would turn two in a few months. She had developed a very different disposition than when she was younger. In just a few months, she became difficult and willful, often hitting Ming and sometimes throwing toys. Along with Ming and May-Lee, I found two more children to watch. One was a three-year-old girl belonging to a single Chinese mother who worked in a beauty salon. She had styled hair in China, and fortunately was able to apply this skill in San Francisco.

The other child was a boy, almost four, whose father worked hard as a day laborer on local farms, such as the one where Da-Wei's body was discovered, and the mother worked as a cook in the home of a wealthy family. Their son would start school in the fall, and I would lose that income. Our house was turning into a nursery! Three high chairs sat in the parlor, with one crib in our bedroom and another in the hallway between the parlor and the kitchen. All the furniture was used and had been located by our wonderful friends at the Home. We were crowded and happy. The store was holding on, and I was bringing in some money.

My sister-in-law Jiao had another baby. She gave birth to a little boy, and I was glad to hear that my brothers and sister were well. Soon Lan would be leaving school to find work. Times were very hard in Shanghai, but all the men in our family were working and they were getting by. Bao got his hands on a camera, which he borrowed from a friend who bought it before times became so bad. Wang took two pictures for us. Cameras were manufactured by Eastman-Kodak, and few people we knew could afford one. We sent a photograph to my family in China; the other I placed in a frame brought upstairs from our store. It was a black-and-white photograph, capturing us in a moment of extreme happiness despite the hard times.

The following week, Ming caught a cold that lingered on for almost three weeks. When his fever and cough wouldn't abate, I had to take him to see a doctor despite the cost. He thought Ming had bronchitis or even pneumonia. X-rays were just starting to be used to diagnose lung problems, and after his cough continued for weeks longer, the doctor recommended an X-ray of his chest. We paid the large bill to find out that Ming had tuberculosis. It was a terrible diagnosis. This was just more bad news my poor journal had to endure on my behalf.

According to the doctor, Ming might have had the bacteria in his system for many months, and only now had it made its presence known. Tuberculosis was highly contagious, and it was a cause of tremendous concern to us. Ming had come into contact with so many people, especially the children I watched, and there was nothing anyone could do to prevent the spread of the disease. Because of this, we had no choice but to send our little boy to the San Francisco Hospital that had a wing that housed only tuberculosis patients. We were devastated.

Our lives changed drastically. I could no longer care for the other children and had to tell everyone who came into contact with Ming that they been exposed to tuberculosis. I didn't fear for myself, but was horrified at the havoc this disease might wreak on all our dear friends and the children who had been in contact with Ming.

Ming was placed in a special wing in the hospital. After taking the case history, the doctors made the assumption that Da-Wei, Ming's mother, must have been carrying the tuberculosis bacteria, and had infected him. Initially, his treatment was primarily supportive. He was kept in isolation, made to rest, and was well fed. The doctors talked about the possibility of surgically collapsing the infected lung so that it could "rest" and heal. After a month, there was little change in his symptoms. He continued to cough up phlegm-laced blood and burned with fever at times, so the procedure was performed.

What a terrible time we had as we watched our little boy being wheeled away to have surgery to collapse his lung. After the surgery, another treatment was used that involved placing him out of doors so he was exposed to sunlight. Doctors believed that large amounts of Vitamin D from the sun were helpful in the treatment. Ultraviolet sunlamps were used when the weather was unfavorable. We visited Ming as often as they allowed us, taking precautions to wear a cap, gown, and mask whenever either of us entered the isolation area. It was awful to see our little boy in such a horrible state. He had been a chubby little boy and now was a skinny, sickly one.

Bao's business was now doing very poorly, and I had lost the income I had gotten from watching the children. We struggled to keep up with our bills. Fortunately, the hospital accepted Ming as a charity patient, as most of the other patients were as well. We knew how difficult it was to keep these tuberculosis wards funded, but we barely had enough money to keep afloat.

In July of 1932, when we least expected it, something happened that should have been joyful, but instead wound up being a very difficult situation. I was almost twenty-seven years old and had never had a child. Throughout my marriage to Jun, my time with Liwei, the men who had me when I was a prostitute, and my marriage to Bao, I had never conceived. Suddenly, at this most trying time, I found myself pregnant. Bao and I had both been tested for the tuberculosis bacteria and were found to be clean, so at least there was no worry of infecting the baby. But how, I wondered, were we ever going to be able to afford a baby when we were barely getting by? How could I possibly stay away from Ming in order to protect the baby growing in my womb? My journal entries were rife with my confused thoughts.

In 1933, the Twenty-First Amendment to the Constitution was passed, repealing Prohibition. The Democratic president, Franklin Delano Roosevelt, enacted a series of programs, passed by Congress, during his first term. Economic conditions were terrible at the time. The staggering numbers of unemployed clearly illustrated the major impact the Depression had on the unemployment rates in San Francisco. As a result, unemployment relief aid and the agencies who distributed it were an important part of survival for the citizens of San Francisco.

These programs were called The New Deal. Actually, there were two New Deals. The First New Deal, as it was called, was instituted from 1933-34. The Second New Deal, from 1935-38, was more liberal and more controversial. A commissary system was used, where families had the choice of having boxes of food sent to them, or they were able to go to a "groceteria" to choose their own food. Milk was delivered to their homes, while a supplemental check was given to families for fresh meat and bread. These items they were able to buy at regular retail groceries. The WPA (Works Progress Administration), a national works program, made the federal government by far the largest single employer in the nation. In addition, the Social Security act was implemented. Second New Deal policies allowed some women in Chinatown to be eligible for assistance and training. Chinese women, and some men as well, left San Francisco and returned home to China to use these new skills and education on behalf of the people of China.

BOOK TWO
Song Yuming

CHAPTER ONE

SAN FRANCISCO, CALIFORNIA, 1941

The Great Depression was beginning to level off. Sadly, my parents were in the middle of their own great depression. My brother Ming, who had been adopted by my parents, had been in a hospital suffering from tuberculosis. He had been ill for a while and was very young when he died. I grew up in the shadow of all this sadness. We lived in Chinatown, in an apartment over my father's dry goods store. My parents had been struggling for years, and they had only just started to make a living again. I grew up happy enough, as youngsters do. I played with neighborhood children, started school when I was five, and hardly realized how difficult life was for my parents.

> *America was still in a crisis. One-quarter of all wage earners were unemployed. President Hoover had done little to alleviate things. He had referred to the times as a "Passing incident in our national lives." In 1932, a new president was elected. Franklin Delano Roosevelt resolved to use the power of the federal government to make life better for all Americans. His New Deal was*

to play an important role in the government. While it didn't end the Depression, it did provide an unprecedented escape from the poverty and struggle of the American people. It also served to restore confidence. Roosevelt had declared in his inaugural address, "The only thing we have to fear is fear itself."

Within the first one hundred days, Roosevelt and Congress passed many new laws, such as the Glass-Steagall Banking Bill, the Home Owners' Loan Act, the Tennessee Valley Authority Act, and the National Industrial Recovery Act. By June, Roosevelt and Congress had passed fifteen major laws.

United Auto Workers started a sit-down strike at the General Motors plant in Flint, Michigan. It lasted forty-four days. By 1937, eight million workers joined unions. A World's Fair, called "A Century of Progress International Exposition," took place in Chicago from 1933-1934. The theme was technological innovation. The motto was "Science Finds, Industry Applies, Man Conforms." There was a Sky Ride, a transporter bridge on which one could ride from one side of the fair to the other. During this time, people had little money, but most had radios, and listening was free. Comedies were popular as a way for listeners to be distracted from their day-to-day struggles. "Amos 'n' Andy," soap operas, and sporting events were popular, as was swing music. Bandleaders like Benny Goodman and Fletcher Henderson were popular with the young people at ballrooms and dance halls throughout the country. Musicals and gangster pictures were popular as another form of escape.

At this time, the Republic of China and the Empire of Japan had been at war for two years, and on Septem-

ber 1, 1939, with the invasion of Poland by Germany, and other declarations of war on Germany by France and the British Commonwealth, World War II began. Early on in the second Sino-Japanese war, the Japanese scored major victories in Shanghai and captured the capital of Nanking. China was ruled by communists, and the Japanese were unable to defeat their forces. On December 7, 1941, the Japanese attacked Pearl Harbor, and the following day, the United States declared war on Japan. This stimulated American industry, and suddenly the Great Depression ended.

I was a young girl, and totally unaware of anything other than my immediate surroundings. When America entered the war, life continued to be very hard. My father was thirty-six years old and my mother, at thirty-eight, looked older than her years.

President Roosevelt established the Selective Service System as an independent agency that was responsible for identifying and inducting young men into the military. In 1940, national peacetime conscription was instituted, requiring registration by all men between twenty-one and forty-five years of age for one year's service by a national lottery. After Pearl Harbor, it was further amended, extending the term of service to the duration of the war plus six months, and required the registration of all men eighteen to sixty-four years of age. In the draft of World War II, fifty million men from eighteen to forty-five were registered, thirty-six million classified, and ten million inducted.

With America in the war, my father registered with the Selective Service as required. America entered the war in December, 1941, and while I was too young at the age of eight to understand much about it, I knew my parents were upset when they sat talking about it at night after dinner while I did my homework.

My father's business was growing again, and though we still lived upstairs from the store, he again rented another storefront in Chinatown and hired two young Chinese men to work for him, and he went back and forth to supervise. Shen continued to work in the first store and had become a dear friend and trustworthy employee. Sometimes, when they thought I was asleep, I sat on the floor behind the door of the dark bedroom that they left ajar. I heard them talking about war and Mama's family. Mama said Shanghai had been destroyed, but I was young and easily able to be distracted from the seriousness around me. So, for me, life continued to be the same. I went to school not too far from my home, but outside of the Chinatown area, since my local school was too overcrowded. This was a big deal, as Chinese hadn't been welcome in American schools before this. I enjoyed playing with all the different children who didn't seem to care if I was Chinese.

While nothing seemed different to me, things were very different. So far, Baba hadn't been called up to serve. Many of the young men had gone overseas to fight the war. Women stepped up and took over the jobs, replacing the men. Mama went back to work as a telephone operator. Baba picked me up after school and I did my homework in the store until Mama got through with work and brought me upstairs. It was a lot more modern now than in her days at the Chinatown Telephone Exchange. About half of American homes had telephones. We had gotten our phone before I was born, and it didn't seem different to me.

Prior to the war, very few people made long distance calls, but now, because of the war, people wanted to call overseas. Mama worked for Bell Telephone, and every call went through a live, long distance operator who connected callers to the numbers they requested. Mama explained to me how she used to have all the names and telephone numbers memorized in the Chinatown exchange.

In 1945, the war finally ended. My father was never called to serve. Thousands of young American men had fought overseas and never came home. I studied all about the war in school. I learned that China had become an ally of ours against Japan, and things in Chinatown, and for Chinese in America in general, changed. Our people had stood side by side with the Americans wearing the same uniform under the American flag. We all felt the difference in the attitude of other Americans. Many flocked to Chinatown to shop in our stores and eat in our restaurants.

I was proud to be a young Chinese-American. Chinese people on the home front were offered jobs that were previously closed to them. I was in fifth grade and learned about how, in 1943, President Roosevelt had signed the repeal of the Chinese Exclusion Act. We Chinese knew all about racism and discrimination. Still, I learned how things were starting to change for the better for my people. My father explained to me that Chinese immigrants were finally allowed to become citizens and to own property. He purchased the building we lived in, which he had wanted to do for many years. There was a large mortgage, but we were doing well again. He continued to rent the second building, hoping that one day he could buy that one, too. Both my mother and father applied for American citizenship again.

I felt more of the change in attitudes in school. My two best friends, Dai Xiao, and Dai Wu, were brother and sister, and we spent a lot of our time together. They lived in the building two doors down from us, also above their father's business. They owned a restaurant, and business was excellent. Dai Wu, who was a year older than me, teased me a lot, always saying he wondered where my wavy hair had come from since my parents had such straight hair. I wondered too, since I was a natural-born child, unlike my adopted brother, Ming, had been. One day Wu went too far, saying that he bet that I was adopted like my brother. After that, I thought about it all the time. Every time I brushed my dark, wavy hair, I wondered if my parents had told the truth. How did I get that hair?

One particular evening, as I lay on the living room floor doing homework, notebook and textbooks all around me, I broached the subject to my father. My mother was in the kitchen brewing some after-dinner tea, as was her habit. My father was catching up on the day's newspaper.

"Baba," I asked, "am I really your daughter?"

"What do you mean, Yuming?" he asked, looking up from his paper. He was smoking a cigarette, his hand halfway to his mouth, the smoke curling into the air, as his straight, uncooperative hair fell over his face. "I don't think I understand the question."

My mother walked in just then, carrying two cups of tea.

"Do you want some milk and apricot cakes, Yuming?" she asked, putting the cups on the lamp table alongside the divan. "There are still some left from the batch I baked over the weekend." She stopped halfway to the kitchen, turning around as I repeated the question again.

"Am I really your daughter?"

"Why, yes, yes of course you are, darling," Mama replied. "You know you are. Your brother Ming, who was our adopted child, was so ill when I was pregnant and gave birth to you. Why on earth do you ask this?"

"How do I have such wavy hair? You both have straight hair."

"Oh, Yuming, those things happen sometimes. Baba's mother had wavy hair, and so did my Baba. My sister, Lan, has wavy hair, too. She had little, black curls when she was born. I don't understand what has made you so upset to start questioning us about this."

I didn't want to tell them that Wu had been teasing me. I felt better now, sure that my parents had told me the truth, and that Wu was only playing. Besides, his family had lived next to mine for several years and surely his parents had seen my mother pregnant with me. Still, it was very mean of him. The next day at school, I avoided Wu during recess. I was a bit standoffish with Xiao, too, though she had done nothing. When she asked me what was wrong, I finally told her as the bell rang to signal the end of recess.

"I'm going to ask my Mama," she said.

"No, don't," I pleaded. "Please leave it alone. My Mama explained it all to me. My relatives had wavy hair, too. I'm just so angry with your brother. I never want to speak to him again!" But, of course, I spoke to him again. We three continued to be great friends through junior high school and into high school.

Mama continued working as a telephone operator, and Baba was doing business with China, importing merchandise that was costlier and very much desired in America. In the second store, which had a huge basement, he sold, among other things, expensive lacquer-wood furniture, with dragons of mother-of-pearl inlay. Things had settled down in China, at last, so Baba's brother, Wang, had begun scouting out resources where he purchased and arranged to ship the new merchandise. He learned about customs policies for these shipments. Their third brother decided he didn't want to be involved in the family business. People in America now wanted to buy luxury items, and it was a good, working relationship for my uncle and father. Chinese merchandise, which had been boycotted by Americans, was suddenly desirable. So, with the economy returned to a certain normalcy, we began to prosper.

Chapter Two

San Francisco, 1946

Now in high school, I was an excellent student, and my self-confidence was finally improved. I was still small and slender like my mother. My wavy hair, which had caused me so much stress a few years ago, was long and shiny, and I wore it in a ponytail. My eyes weren't as dark as my mother's or father's, and they were slightly rounder. I had a medium complexion, with a small beauty mark just below the corner of my right eye. Now, if only my breasts would grow.

Xiao was still my best friend, (I saw much less of Wu since he was not really interested in girls), and we had a whole clique of girls we hung around with. I had gotten a phonograph for my last birthday, which was a very big deal for the time, but my parents wanted to do something special for me to make up for the lean years. The girls and I would lie on the floor in the living room listening to my small collection of 78 vinyl records. Sometimes my family joined us. We played records of "Night and Day" and "I've Got a Crush on You" over and over. Mama especially loved Dinah Shore, while my Baba was crazy about the smooth style of Perry Como. We wore just-below-the-knee full skirts that were the style, and Mama hosted a Tupperware party, which was a clever way of selling these brand new, handy plastic containers in one's own home. Our lives were simple and finally normal. Baba's stores were thriving, and Mama left the telephone company and took over Shen's job, seeing to the management of the men who worked on the selling floor, as well as the men who worked in packing and receiving. They had branched out, now selling American-made furniture, among other items. The imports were still a major part of the business.

Shen, who had worked for Baba, and been instrumental in his meeting Mama, had married a wonderful man who worked in the food supply industry and had moved to a city in northern California. They had two daughters, and it was nice that the families kept in touch. They often spoke about getting together, but somehow it never happened. Shen, who had a limp caused by a broken ankle inflicted when she was a slave in Chinatown years ago, now had a hard time walking, and had resorted to using a cane.

Mama kept in touch with the other women she had shared her first apartment with. Chang-Ma, who had been older than the rest of them, had never married but seemed to be happy living in a small apartment in Chinatown. Yi, who worked in a Chinese restaurant when they had met, was happily married to Wing. He was a kind man, and they had a son. Mama and Yi saw each other occasionally as they didn't live too far from each other. I had met her once, two or three years earlier. She told me they always reminisced about how Yi would bring home a delicious treat from the restaurant from time to time, and how Mama would borrow her black shawl and shoes when she had a date with Baba. It was lovely that she still kept in touch with her original roommates; sadly, they had all lost touch with the Mission Home, which still existed, but not in the same way as they had known it.

School years and summer vacations passed so quickly.

My freshman year ended, and my sophomore year flew by as well. I was in my third year of high school, and for some time had been thinking about my future career. While it was common that only boys went to college, my parents had made it clear that they hoped I would go to college, too. I had no disagreement with them, as I wanted to very badly. It was a big deal to be the first in our family to do so. One evening, while Baba was working late in the store taking inventory, Mama asked me if I had a few minutes to sit with her, as there was something she wanted to show me.

"Of course," I replied. She was in the living room, and as I sat down on the couch alongside her, I noticed several items on the coffee table.

"Yuming," she began, "this is a journal that I began writing many years ago. She handed me a brown, worn, leather book. You have always known parts of my life, but not all, and not about this diary. I began it when I still lived in Shanghai. I found an empty book in the trash at school, and I just started writing in it whenever I had the time. I have kept it hidden all these years. Only your father has seen it. It tells the story of my life up to now—my thoughts, dreams, hopes, disappointments, and incredible moments of happiness. You are almost seventeen, and soon I hope you will be a college girl.

"I have written the journal in my native tongue, the Wu dialect of Shanghai," she said turning the pages. "I shall have it translated so you may understand it. In the back are various letters, from Jun, my first husband whom I've told you about, and letters and a couple of pictures from my family—which is also your family—back home in China. My dearest hope is that, when you are grown and married, you will have a daughter you can pass this journal to when she is around sixteen years of age. This is my story. This is a legacy I hope to start through you so that future women of the Zhang family heritage can read this diary when they are your age and understand where they came from, and how they came to be who they are."

Mama had the journal translated, with the letters, as well. I read it several times, never able to believe the details of the life Mama had lived.

Chapter Three

San Francisco, 1950

On June 30, 1950, President Harry S. Truman authorized U.S. forces to enter yet another war, the war in Korea. The end of World War II brought peace and prosperity to America, but a state of tension between the Soviet Union and the United States began to escalate. The United States feared the Soviet Union intended to force communism on other nations, and because of this, America's foreign policy became centered on trying to contain the spread of communism both at home and abroad. While the Truman Doctrine, Marshall Plan, and the Berlin Airlift suggested that the United States had great concern over the spread of communism in Europe, America's policy of containment extended to Asia as well. Indeed, Asia proved to be the site of the first major battle waged in the name of containment—the Korean War.

At this time, the Korea Peninsula was divided between a Soviet-backed government in the north, and an

American-backed government in the south. Korea's division had come at the end of World War II. The United States, fearful that the Soviets would seize the entire peninsula from the north, moved its troops into the south. Korea had been under Japan's control since 1910. Japanese troops surrendered to the Russians in the north and to the Americans in the south. To avoid making a long-term decision regarding Korea's future, the United States and the Soviet Union agreed to divide Korea temporarily along the 38th parallel, a latitudinal line that bisected the country.

My senior year was a whirl of classes and great fun with my large circle of friends, especially Xiao and Wu. At the end of my junior year, we had started looking at colleges. My parents wanted me to attend a local school. As modern as they had become, they still liked the idea of me being close to home, so I applied to several local colleges and universities and was offered admission to two, University of the Pacific and San Francisco State University. We visited both schools, and I finally decided on San Francisco State University. Mama and Baba were so proud of me. Xiao, too, had applied, and been accepted there. I was planning to enter their Humanities program, with thoughts of becoming a teacher. Xiao entered their college of Ethnic Studies, which was one of very few in the country at the time.

The previous year, Wu had been granted and accepted a scholarship to Stanford University's business program. Even though Wu was always an exceptional student, this still came as wonderful news to everyone. It was beyond anything his parents could have imagined. The school was located in Stanford, near Palo Alto, and though it was only about thirty-five miles from San Francisco, Wu lived on campus, lucky enough to find work waiting tables at a local Chinese restaurant on weekends. His experience in the family business served him in good stead. It cost the Dai family a great deal of money to send Wu to this school, but the honor he bestowed upon them far outweighed the expense. Fortunately, Wu's scholarship provided the family some savings, and they were forward-minded enough to allow Xiao the same opportunity, though she would live at home. Surely the fact that I was going to college helped her parents make that decision. Our families had been close for years and I was certain they had discussed this. It was a very exciting time.

Wu, at age 18, was required to register for the draft. A lottery system was used, and men twenty years old and up would be called first, according to their month of birth. Wu continued to go to school, as college students were deferred from serving, and while many young men went to school to avoid this, Wu wasn't one of them. He was elated about attending college, but nevertheless, he felt remorse about not serving his country.

Chapter Four

San Francisco, 1955

The armistice agreement was signed on July 27, 1953. The troops had returned, and our country settled down. Wu graduated from Stanford, and Xiao and I did the same from our school a year after him. My college graduation was a grand affair and a source of pride for my parents. After the ceremony, we had a festive lunch at Golden Dynasty, the Dai family restaurant.

During my last year of college, Wu and I realized that our friendship of so many years had turned into love, and we knew we would spend our lives together. Several months later, unbeknown to me, Wu approached Baba and asked him for permission to marry me. One evening, as we sat on a bench under a street light in Golden Gate Park, Wu, who had not been himself all evening, turned to me and said, "Yuming, I have known you forever, and have come to love you very much. If you feel the same about me, will you marry me? Your Baba has given his blessing."

Throwing myself into his arms, I responded, "Yes, Wu, I will be your wife. I don't think I can remember when I didn't love you." I hesitated for a moment, then laughed. "Well, maybe when you teased me about my wavy hair!"

Wu drew a box from his jacket pocket, opening it for me to see a tiny diamond ring, which he slid onto my finger. I imagine he had been saving money from his small salary and tips at the restaurant. He picked me up off the ground and swung me around and around until I was dizzy and begged him to put me down. What a day it was! I was the first member of my family to have graduated from college, and now I was engaged to be married to Wu.

A short time later, I began sending my resume out to local elementary schools and initially had little response. After three months, I was feeling despondent. Then I received an invitation to be interviewed, and was fortunate enough to be offered a position teaching first grade in the Richmond District, a suburb in the northwest part of San Francisco. While there was a Chinese enclave in the area, it was not Chinatown. The school, though multiracial, consisted of predominately white students, along with some Asian, Negro, and Hispanic children. Some spoke no English at all, but they assimilated well, as young children do. Things were changing, and Chinese-Americans who were newly college-educated were entering white workplaces, schools, suburbs, and professional and civic organizations.

After graduating from college, Wu resumed working for his father, taking over the actual running of the restaurant with his new knowledge in business management. His father was proud of him and agreed with the innovations he suggested. They applied for and were granted a liquor license, which brought in a different clientele. Along with traditional American drinks, such as martinis and Manhattans, customers enjoyed sweet frozen drinks, garnished with little paper umbrellas, as well as Tsingtao, the most popular Chinese beer. The restaurant even served sake, a Japanese alcoholic drink made from fermented rice, traditionally drunk warm or cold in small porcelain cups. The patrons loved it. The newly added bar, long and sleek in the front of the restaurant, was always busy, and Wu's suggestions were a wonderful way to increase the restaurant's income and patronage.

We set a wedding date for June 15, 1955, and began planning. We wanted some time to work and put money aside for our future. We were becoming more and more Americanized, and we decided our wedding would be less Chinese than American. We arranged to be married in the same Presbyterian Church as our parents. Our long-time pastor had passed away, and we liked the new minister, Pastor Alvin Henks, very much. Our reception would be held at the St. Francis Hotel. An American band would play, and the meal would be mostly American fare with selections of Chinese specialties, both Shanghainese and Cantonese, to pay tribute to both of our heritages.

The months dragged by as we worked to save money to establish our lives, but before we knew it, it was time to send out wedding invitations that we had ordered months before. I went shopping for my bridal gown with Mama, Mrs. Dai, and Xiao. The first two shopping trips yielded nothing, but on our third try, at a popular bridal shop, I found the perfect dress. White, with a scooped neckline, three-quarter length sleeves and bodice of lace, it had a full-length chiffon skirt over layers of crinoline. The dress was simple and elegant. It showed off my slender waist, and the long veil was the perfect accessory to complete the look. A pearl-encrusted comb secured the veil in place. White satin pumps completed the outfit. I protested that it was all too costly, but Mama said that when she saw the look on my face as I stood in front of the salon's mirror, she knew that this was my gown at any cost.

I selected Xiao to be my maid of honor, and after she tried on a few dresses, we all agreed that a simple, blush pink A-line dress was the perfect complement to my gown. She looked slender and beautiful. My mother found her dress that day as well, but Mrs. Dai didn't find anything that suited her. Mama had chosen a slimming cocktail length lace dress with a short jacket. The ensemble was a darker shade of pink than Xiao's. Mama looked stunning in it, slim and attractive. There were no shoes to her liking, so she would have to keep looking. The following week, Mrs. Dai found her perfect dress at I. Magnin, a popular, elegant department store. Also dark pink, it was a simple knee-length sheath made of taffeta, with three-quarter length sleeves and a scooped neckline. Mama and Mrs. Dai found perfect shoes, as did Xiao. They all chose satin pumps that would be dyed to match the dresses.

After months of planning, our wedding day finally arrived, sunny and warm. It was a fairy-tale day, starting with the beautiful, simple ceremony in our church with Mama and Baba, our friends, colleagues, and close neighbors there to celebrate our joy. Later, at the reception, Wu and I danced our first dance as a married couple to the popular love song, "Till There Was You." It was written for the play "The Music Man," and we enjoyed its beautiful, simple sentiment. As we circled the dance floor, everyone we loved watched us, me in my beautiful gown, and Wu in his elegant tuxedo.

We began our married life in an apartment close to Golden Gate Park. It was a small, cozy, one-bedroom place, with a nice-sized living room, a fairly modern kitchen with popularly colored green appliances, and an attached dinette. The bathroom was tiny, but large enough for two. Waiting a bit until we married had allowed us to put some money together, and we were able to furnish the apartment inexpensively, but stylishly.

The restaurant was doing well, and our savings allowed Wu to give his father enough money for a small down payment toward becoming a half-owner in the business. We would continue making payments. His Baba was happy to relinquish more responsibilities to Wu. We couldn't believe how busy the restaurant was. We had a large lunch business and an even larger dinner trade. On the weekends, people called to make reservations to ensure a table for dinner.

The kitchen employed a head chef and three assistants, while the dining room was covered by four servers running from kitchen to table as quickly as they could to provide the best service to our loyal customers. We offered a menu of predominately Cantonese dishes because these were the ones the Americans seemed to be most comfortable with. Still, in keeping with our tradition, several Shanghainese specialties made their way onto our menu. At any given time, one could see both Americans and Chinese dining in our restaurant. Apart from the responsibilities of ordering food and supplies, Wu kept the books, supervised the staff, and was general manager, while his Baba, whom the guests knew well, presided over the front of the house, smiling and collecting cash as the satisfied customers left patting their bellies.

Chapter Five

San Francisco, 1956

At the very end of the year, I became pregnant. I had morning sickness in the beginning, but it passed soon enough and I was happy to be able to go to work every day. Wu and I spent many an evening imagining what our little one would look like. He, of course, hoped for a boy to carry on the Dai name, and I dreamed of a sweet little girl. I took up knitting, and when the dinner dishes were done, I planned lessons for my class and then worked on the little hats and booties that Mrs. Klein, our next door neighbor, taught me to knit. She was a lovely lady, widowed for many years, with a whole slew of children and grandchildren that came to visit her often. She was always ringing our bell whenever she baked her rugelach, a delicious Jewish pastry, filled with nuts, fruit, or chocolate. I would open the door, and find Mrs. Klein in her housedress and apron holding a plateful of her decadent treats and a skein of yarn she "just happened" to find in her closet.

I worked until I was quite far along in the pregnancy, but stopped about two weeks before my due date. One evening, as I was putting away the dinner dishes, my water broke. Wu called my doctor, and after a few hours, we set off for the hospital. Our little girl was born the next day, a week early, and perfect. We named her Min, so close to my little brother Ming's name. But, while the names sounded alike, they had very different meanings. Ming translated to shining, bright, or clear, while Min meant clever, or sharp. She was a sweet, happy baby, and I arranged with my school to take a maternity leave for three months. I decided to push my luck and asked my principal if I might take the rest of the year off, without pay and without losing my job for the following school year. Fortunately, he liked me a great deal and was able to get someone to cover for me.

Min was smart, just as her name suggested, and did everything earlier than many babies. When she was just past eleven months of age, I was folding laundry when she walked alone for the first time. She had been walking around the room holding onto the furniture for a few weeks, but this time, she finally let go, and just walked across the room, although hesitatingly. She laughed when she reached me, and I picked her up, and hugging her tightly, ran to the phone to call Wu at the restaurant. He wasn't in the least bit surprised when I told him, and when I called Mama, neither was she.

"She takes after you, Yuming," Mama told me. "You were young when you walked and talked. She'll be talking soon, I bet." Mama was right. After Min started walking, there was no stopping her. She learned word after word and had a mouthful of teeth by sixteen months. Our lives were simple and I returned to work. Wu's mother and Mama were happy to babysit.

We made friends with several couples in our neighborhood and enjoyed seeing them on weekends. I still considered Xiao my best friend. I also kept in touch with several of my closest college friends, who were getting married and having babies too.

> *A great many changes occurred in America during this time. The Immigration and Naturalization Act had removed racial and ethnic barriers to becoming a U.S. citizen, but racial segregation came to the forefront. Dwight D. Eisenhower was the president. Men wore gray flannel suits, and women wore dresses that had narrow waists, along with high-heeled shoes. Dr. Jonas Salk discovered the polio vaccine, and Elvis Presley swiveled his hips on TV as teenagers sighed and swooned. It was the start of rock and roll.*

We bought a TV and a new car. We were the perfect young American couple. But, in the middle of our happiness, things suddenly changed. My father-in-law passed away from a massive heart attack, leaving the restaurant to Wu. Mama Dai was left well provided for financially, but she was never the same after her loss. She withdrew into herself. Baba Dai had had a warning heart attack the year before, but when he had this second one, the doctors could do nothing to save him. We missed him terribly, especially little Min, who had adored her *YeYe*.

Grandparents play very important roles in Chinese families, and so we had always spent a lot of time with our parents. Now, we tried to see Wu's mother as often as she allowed us. We didn't speak a lot of Chinese at home anymore, so my parents and Wu's mother felt it was their responsibility to see to it that Min learned some Chinese, as well as something of our traditions. She learned some Shanghainese from my mother and Cantonese from Wu's mother. We hired a nanny to watch Min during the day as it was too much for my mother and Mama Dai couldn't do it anymore. This allowed me to go back to work. Chunhua, the new nanny, was eighteen years old, had just finished high school, and had gotten a used car from her family as a graduation gift. She was sweet and quiet and Min took to her immediately.

We made a decision to redo the restaurant by updating its look to fit the modern times we lived in. We took out a small bank loan and had new carpeting put in, re-did the booths in a vibrant, bright red, and updated parts of the kitchen to allow for faster, more efficient storing and cooking of food. New stylish light fixtures hung over the tables, while gold and red dragons cavorted on the back wall. Live lobsters, crabs, eels, and various fish, swam in beautiful tanks along the front wall, allowing passers-by to see them through the glass window. The business was good, but with the new look, we could barely accommodate our patrons. Wu hired another cook for our already crowded kitchen.

When Min was two years old, I became pregnant again. I didn't have morning sickness, but I was exhausted all the time and needed to rest a lot. Chunhua watched Min during the week and I continued teaching. A few weeks later, I suffered a miscarriage.

The doctor said, "It wasn't meant to be."

I became severely depressed. Wu, our parents, and friends tried everything to cheer me up. While my body healed, my mind didn't. I continued working, but I was just going through the motions. Mama spent more time with us than she did with Baba. Months passed, and Min continued to grow and learn. She was speaking in short, but intelligible sentences. She was a beautiful little girl, with fat, rosy cheeks, and a toothsome smile. She had wavy hair, like mine, the very waves Wu had teased me about years ago. One afternoon, after Chunhua left, she climbed onto my bed and handed me her hairbrush.

"Will you brush my hair, Mama?" she asked.

My mother had come by the apartment earlier, and I heard her doing something in the kitchen. I remembered I hadn't eaten since my light lunch at school, and even though she made me tea and a sandwich when I got home, I hadn't eaten it. Looking at my little girl, something suddenly snapped inside of me, and I took the little pink brush from her hand and began running it through her hair. It was silky, almost black, and it curled around the brush in soft waves. I remembered how long ago I had wondered where my wavy hair came from. It seemed like a recurring theme.

I got up from my bed, and opening a small box on my dresser, took out elastics and two pink barrettes to catch the wisps. We sat on the bed together as I made two pigtails for her. This was the moment I came out of my depression. It was over, and I was suddenly aware that I was starting to feel human again. Taking Min by her little hand, I walked with her into the kitchen. Mama looked up as we came in. "Mama, I'm hungry. Do you think I could have that sandwich you made for me earlier?"

"Min hungry, too, *Nai Nai*," Min told my mother.

Mama retrieved the sandwich from the refrigerator, and since Min had already eaten the lunch that Chunhua made for her, she poured her a cup of milk and brought her a shortbread cookie. She began to make tea for us as I took a bite of my sandwich. I finished eating, and instead of Mama doing it after Min finished her snack, I put her in her crib for a nap, kissing her on top of her sweet little head. "Mama loves you very much, sweetheart," I told her.

The next day was Saturday, and I had asked Min if she would like to go to the park to play tomorrow. "You can bring Julia," I said. Julia was a stuffed, pink bunny Min slept with, and dragged around wherever she went.

"Yes, Mama," my sweet girl replied, yawning.

I went back into the kitchen, and walking over to Mama, I hugged her, thanking her for all her help. "Go home, Mama," I said. "Baba will be missing you by now."

That evening, as Wu was watching television in the living room, I took out my mother's diary, and lying in bed, began to read it. For the past few nights, I had been re-reading it, remembering again all that my mother survived. The next morning, having finished Mama's journal, I knew I would continue to get better, and our lives would begin to regain some of the normalcy we enjoyed prior to my miscarriage.

Several weeks later, Xiao announced that she was engaged to be married. What wonderful news that was. She had been going out with a terrific American man named Matthew Danners for close to a year. Mrs. Dai had never been totally happy with the relationship. She knew that Matt, as everyone called him, was a wonderful man, but she had expected that Xiao would marry a Chinese man. Still, Matt was a smart, kind, attractive young man who, coincidentally, like Wu, had attended Stanford University, and had graduated two years prior to him. He was an engineer, working for the brand new company, Westinghouse Electric, located in Palo Alto, and was planning to continue his studies in the engineering graduate program at night.

We liked Matt very much, and prior to my miscarriage, we had spent a great deal of time socializing with them. Now that I was feeling better, I was able to throw myself into the wedding plans of my sister-in-law and best friend, just as she had done for me. They set a wedding date for the end of the year. Mrs. Dai reconciled herself to the marriage, and gave herself a chance to get to know Matt. Besides being a terrific person, Matt clearly loved Xiao very much.

Matt's company was involved in the new technology of semiconductors. When he tried to talk to me about it, I was lost in a world of strange terms and difficult explanations. It was cutting edge, exciting work, even though he was just a ground-level employee. Wu had considered going back to Stanford for his Master's in Business Administration, but my depression had precluded his pursuing it at that moment. Still, we could use the money the degree would allow him to earn, and now, with our lives stabilized once more, he began to do some research into the programs being offered. Like Matt, Wu too would have to attend at night. That September both Wu and Matt went back to school to take advanced degrees in their respective studies. It was a long drive from our area to Palo Alto, close to thirty miles each way, but both felt it was worth the trip two nights a week to attend a school as prestigious as Stanford. They worked out their programs so they could take turns sharing the driving.

Xiao and Matt got married a few months later, and in December, I happily announced that I was pregnant again. We had already outgrown our one-bedroom apartment near Golden Gate Park, and with this wonderful news, it was time for us to purchase a house. We needed to live in an area that was a reasonable commute to the restaurant, families, and friends, but not too far from Stanford. The newlyweds had also decided to buy a house, but for the time being, they were staying with Mrs. Dai, who had at first been reluctant but then seemed to be doing a lot better, and now actually seemed to enjoy Matt's company. If anything, it helped pull her out of her malaise a bit.

We did our research, and with some areas in mind, began looking at properties that were halfway between Palo Alto and San Francisco. Although Wu would finish school in a couple of years, it was also important to find a location where the schools were highly rated. Min would be in school before we knew it. Matt worked in Palo Alto, so he and Xiao were also looking in that neighborhood. Wu and I looked in Burlingame, but felt it was a little too suburban an area for us. Xiao and Matt, however, loved it there, and after seeing several houses, found just what they were looking for and could afford.

We continued searching, spending every weekend with realtors, driving from town to town. Just when we were abandoning hope of finding something in the right location that we could afford, we found it. Our very first house was located in Daly City. I would still be able to go to work at my school, and Chunhua, who had a car, was willing to make the daily drive. It was about a twenty-minute drive to the restaurant. It wasn't as close as we wanted, but otherwise it was perfect.

We had looked at many properties, and when we saw this one, we knew we had found our new home. It was a small, three-bedroom house on a block of similar houses, in a good school district. There were things that needed re-doing, but for now, it was just right for our little family of three, soon to be four. Our long-term plans were to eventually open another restaurant, still maintaining the San Francisco Chinatown location, which continued to be the wonderful means of support that allowed us to buy this new house.

Chapter Six

Daly City, California, 1960

We were living in our new house for just over two years and had settled into a happy life in Daly City. Our son, Je, had been born not long after the move.

> *The decade of the '60s was a very turbulent time filled with political changes, war, civil unrest, and the emergence of a new counterculture, the Hippies. The country was going through a metamorphosis, experiencing things it had never encountered before. John F. Kennedy was president. America trusted him to turn things around after coming through the post-war era of the 1950s. He managed to keep America out of nuclear war and attempted to alleviate increasing racial tension in the South. Tragically, his life was cut short when, on November 22, 1963, Lee Harvey Oswald shot and killed him in Dallas, Texas. The assassination was a defining moment in the formation of the rising counterculture of the Hippies. Lyndon B. Johnson, vice president at the time, stepped in to fill the position of*

president, and in 1964, ran for and was elected president. Things were looking good in America, but there was political upheaval in a small country called Viet Nam. While the Hippies called for peace, America entered the war to defend itself and the rest of the world against Communism. Still, racial unrest continued. Martin Luther King Jr., who fought for civil rights for African-Americans, and political activist Malcolm X, were killed. In 1968, Senator Robert Kennedy, brother of President John Kennedy was also assassinated.

The youth of San Francisco, mostly children of middle-class families, believed that people were lying to them, and their rebellion, via drug use, long hair, marches, free love, and psychedelic music was their way of protesting both the war in Viet Nam, and in general, adult society. Folk music and acid rock became the norm. Haight-Ashbury, a neighborhood in San Francisco, was the focal point for the Hippies. They adhered to the slogan "Make love, not war." Finally, the war between North and South Viet Nam ended, and American troops exited in 1973. There was a great loss of life, and ultimately the country accepted the loss of the war as well. Over 58,000 Americans lost their lives in what was considered an ultimate failure.

Je was a difficult, colicky baby. Fortunately, Min was a bright, happy little girl, who gave me very little trouble, allowing me to focus on Je, who gave us a run for our money. For some time, we lived in a daily madhouse. Je cried constantly, and despite various medications, nothing calmed him. I'd stopped nursing him. Our pediatrician suggested that I do that so I could hand the bottle to our nanny and get outside for some time of my own every day.

My nerves were frazzled, and by the time Wu returned

home from his long day at the restaurant, he walked into a house of upheaval and crying. Thank heavens he was finished with his Master's degree. Je was always screaming, Min was clamoring for her dinner, and as for me, I was completely overwhelmed. I could rarely get a meal on the table as I needed to hold Je constantly. I felt awful about how much I was neglecting Min. This continued for some time. Wu and I began fighting a great deal. The lack of sleep, and not enough time for myself, had taken a terrible toll on me, and our marriage had suffered.

Je finally got through the colic and became a happy little baby, but it seemed like it was too late. Wu and I just weren't getting along. We argued about the littlest things, and love-making barely existed in our lives. He started coming home later and later.

A year went by, and we hired a full-time nanny to live with us. She was a lovely young woman named Ana, but despite this additional help, things barely changed. We were sorry to see Chunhua go, but two children were too much for her at her young age, and we needed full-time help at this point.

Wu and I became more and more estranged. One night Wu didn't walk in until close to midnight. Then, he began coming home late several nights a week, and while I said nothing, I wondered where he was during the time after the restaurant closed until he came home. Owning the restaurant was a long, hard day's work since Baba Dai passed away. Although the manager was an honest, trustworthy man who had been with us for several years, Wu was reluctant to leave him alone to close up in the evenings. The business generated large amounts of cash, and while we trusted the manager, Wu made it his business to close out the register every evening.

Still, I couldn't imagine it would keep him there so late. I didn't say anything the evening he walked in at midnight, but I knew something was really wrong. When it happened again, I confronted Wu. That particular night, Ana had put the children down early, and while Je had reawakened, she finally got him to quiet down and go back to sleep. I watched TV for a while, and then went to bed. I was asleep when I heard Wu come into our bedroom.

Looking at the clock I asked, "Where have you been, Wu? It's past midnight."

"I got caught up in paperwork, Yuming. I'm very tired and I need to get to sleep," he said.

I said nothing further, but when Wu slipped into bed, I moved all the way to the outside of the bed. I lay there thinking as I listened to his breathing grow even. Wu and I hadn't made love in months.

Wu continued to stay out late many nights a week. We grew further and further apart. I thought about discussing it with Mama, or Xiao, but I was too embarrassed. Things continued like this for some time. Outside, we made a pretense of being a happy couple. At home, we barely spoke unless we had to. We spent time with our parents and socialized with our friends.

One Saturday afternoon, Xiao, who was six months pregnant, invited me to meet her for lunch. I left the children with Ana. Wu had gone to the restaurant. We agreed to meet at one of our favorite places. Xiao, who had changed her major and graduated with a degree in social work, worked at the Mills-Peninsula Medical Center in Burlingame. Xiao was waiting for me when I arrived. Slipping into the booth, I noticed how wonderful she looked.

"Xiao, you are positively glowing," I said.

"I feel great, Yuming," she told me, "but I must have gained a hundred pounds already."

"You don't want to do that," I responded. "Your doctor will kill you, and besides, it will take forever to get back to yourself after the baby is born."

"I know, I know, but I'm hungry all the time. I'm dying for a cheeseburger and fries." She smiled at me guiltily.

The waitress came over, and we ordered lunch. Xiao got her burger, and I asked for a Cobb salad. We chatted about my children and her job, but suddenly, I was overwhelmed by the need to confide my unhappiness in someone.

"Xiao, I need to talk to you," I said. "Something is very wrong. I haven't said anything, but Wu has been coming home late… very late, for quite some time now. He had no patience for Je's crying when he had the colic. I told you that, but that was a while ago. His lateness had been sporadic, but now, he's late all the time."

"Oh, Yuming, I'm sure it's just that the restaurant is so busy. It's grown into such a large business," Xiao said, taking a big bite out of her burger.

I watched a blob of ketchup drip onto her maternity top. "Xiao, wipe your top, you got ketchup on it," I told her.

"He must have a lot of work," she answered, looking down, then dipping her napkin into the water and rubbing the red spot on her shirt. "C'mon, maybe it's just too much for one person to handle the books alone. Maybe you should consider finding a reputable accountant to use all year around, rather than just when you file taxes."

"It's a good idea, Xiao, but somehow, in my heart, I know it's more than just the business."

The next morning, I quietly asked Wu if he would consider hiring an accountant on a full-time basis. He said he'd consider it and headed off to the bathroom to shower. I put it aside for a few more weeks.

The following week was Thanksgiving, and we planned to be with Mama and Baba for the holiday. The restaurant was open, and Wu trusted the manager to run things for the afternoon, but he planned to take over in the evening so the man could go home to his family. It was amazing how many people went out to eat on Thanksgiving, even for Chinese food. Mama Bao joined us, as always, as well as Xiao and Matt.

We had a wonderful time. Je was happily running wild, while Ana chased him. Min played with some of the toys she kept at my parent's house. The ladies were busy in the kitchen, while the men watched television, and enjoyed a Tsingtao beer and some snacks we had put out earlier. We enjoyed the traditional turkey, with the usual fixings, but as always, Mama supplemented it with some of our favorite Shanghainese dishes. Mama Bao had also cooked and brought two of her best-loved Cantonese specialties. What a groaning board of food! Old habits die hard, I thought. It was a lovely, festive day, and I put my troubles out of my mind for a bit.

When we got home, Ana put the children to sleep in the room they shared, and then went to her bedroom. Wu had left right after dinner and gone to the restaurant to relieve the manager and close up. Matt and Xiao had taken the kids and me home. Wu came back at a decent hour and walked into the living room. I got up from the couch and shut the TV, deciding I would read in our bedroom, and avoid any conversation with Wu. He came in, changed into pajamas, and went into the living room. I heard the TV go on. I noticed he had forgotten to hang up his slacks. As I picked them up off the edge of the bed, a small gold earring fell from one of the pockets. I bent to find it. It wound up under the bed. I picked it up, knowing I had my answer to Wu's late evenings. In my heart of hearts, I had suspected, but now I knew. Wu was seeing another woman. The earring was a small gold hoop with pavé diamonds all around. It was beautiful and much more expensive than anything Wu had ever bought me. I wondered why he had only one. Walking into the living room, I stood before him and held up the earring. Wu put his head down. He didn't say a word for a minute, and the silence was deafening.

"All right, Yuming, now you know," he said at last.

"Who is she, Wu?" I asked.

"She's a customer of the restaurant. It wasn't planned; it just happened. She came in often with her friends, and it just evolved. One evening her girlfriends left and she lingered on, taking her time paying the check. One thing led to another. I'm in love with her, Yuming."

"Why do you have only one earring?" I asked.

"I'll be truthful with you. She lives with her parents, and so we meet at a hotel. She always leaves first, and tonight, when I showered, I found her earring on the bathroom floor. I put it in my pocket, intending to return it to her." He walked over to me and tried to put his arms around me, saying, "I'm so sorry, Yuming." I pushed him away, sick and disgusted. There was more I wanted to ask, like how long it had been going on, but I didn't. I just turned and went into the bedroom.

Wu slept on the couch that night. We had only been married for six years, and my marriage was falling apart. No, actually, it was over. This was no random affair. He had said he loved her. I thought about how embarrassing it would be when Ana awoke and found Wu sleeping on the couch. I didn't sleep at all that night. Again and again, I heard his words: "I'm in love with her, Yuming," as the tears rolled down my face. It was then I realized I didn't love Wu anymore. I hadn't for quite some time.

The next day Wu told Ana we had something we had to take care of, and we would be leaving early. We left the house to go to the restaurant to talk in private. No one would be there for several hours. Rain, yet unshed, made the atmosphere into a heavy gray curtain. It reminded me of the one in my school's auditorium. There was going to be a storm and not only the one from the heavens. He opened the gates and turned on the lights.

"I'll make tea," he said.

"No, thanks, don't bother," I said.

So we just sat down at one of the booths. Despite myself, I started to cry, and outside the skies opened up as well. I heard the sound of thunder, and I looked out through the tank with the fish swimming happily behind the window, watching the heavy downpour. The storm fueled my emotions, sparking my anger like the lightning from the heavy deluge. I ranted and raved, yelling loudly, accusing him of being selfish and weak. It was far from my nature to act this way, but he just sat there staring at me from across the booth. I knew that having our children hadn't been easy on either of us. My depression after my miscarriage had taken its toll on us, and Je's colic had been difficult, and had lasted a very long time. A stronger man would have been more supportive and never allow himself to become involved with women when he was desperately needed at home. Life is life, and a marriage is a commitment. I wondered who this girl was who had no qualms about taking a married man with two babies away from his wife.

When I finally finished my tirade, I sat there spent, quietly looking down at the wedding band on my finger. He said it had been innocent enough in the beginning. He had just killed time at the restaurant after it closed, hoping everyone would be asleep by the time he walked in. Later, he said, he started taking an occasional woman out, but never more than once or twice each. Then he met her. Wu said he never meant to hurt me. What stupid, empty, trite words. Unable to look me in the eye, he folded and unfolded the napkin on the table and said he wanted a divorce. He promised he would never abandon his children, saying he would support us, and always be in their lives. And so I was to be a divorcée with two small children. Outside, the storm was over, and I saw the sun coming out. That's how it was with thunderstorms. Fast and furious and over quickly, like our marriage.

A few weeks later, Wu moved out, and within ten months, we were divorced. I continued living in the house with the children, and I thanked God for our wonderful Ana. Wu married his girlfriend not long after the divorce papers were final.

Chapter Seven

Daly City, 1966

The years passed by, and Wu was true to his word. He saw the children often and provided well for us. Min was now ten years old, and our son Je was almost six. I decided to look for a teaching job closer to home and was fortunate enough to find a position teaching second-grade at a local school, not too far from home. I said goodbye to my wonderful principal and the many members of the staff I had become good friends with. Hopefully, I would be able to get together with several of the teachers with whom I had developed a close relationship. Min was now in the fourth grade, in a class taught by a lovely colleague of mine. Je started first grade. I was thirty-three years old.

Ana still lived with us but was planning to marry a very nice man she had been dating for over a year. She would be relocating because of a job offered to her future husband. Though both children now attended the same school I worked in, it would still be difficult for me to manage without her. I started to teach in the after-school program to make extra money, as well as to have a place for the children to be occupied and well cared for during that time. Mama and Baba were getting older, as was Mama Dai, but they were still active and were enjoying the time they spent at a local Chinese Community Center. I visited them often, and they vied for the chance to babysit if I had plans.

I started dating a little bit, but nothing serious, just a movie here, a dinner there. At the end of the school year, a party was always held at a local restaurant. I had become friendly with many of the teachers on staff, and we had put together a fun table of men and women. There was a buffet and a DJ. The group was lively and everyone was looking forward to the summer off as they shared their plans with one another. Sitting next to me was Edward Wong, a friendly man who taught fifth grade. He asked me if I wanted to dance. We found a spot for ourselves on the crowded dance floor, and after dancing to "96 Tears" and "Reach Out, I'll Be There," the music switched to something slower. Many of the dancers made their way off the floor as "Cherish" began to play. As I started to walk off, he grabbed my hand and pulled me back onto the tiny dance area, and I found myself in his arms.

Edward was tall for a Chinese, and I would imagine about thirty-four or thirty-five years old. I knew he had never married, and I also heard he had been engaged but wasn't any longer. The gossip circulated, as things do when people work together. He was an attractive man, and at lunch, several teachers passed comments along to me attesting to that fact after he left the room to go back to his class. Another slow dance came on and he pulled me close to him. I didn't pull away, and I rather enjoyed being in his arms.

The following week, I ran into him in the teacher's lunchroom while on a break. He asked me if I would have dinner with him that coming Saturday night. I said yes. Quietly, so as not to arouse comments, I asked one of my new colleagues if she knew anything more about Edward other than he had once been engaged. She said she didn't know much more, just that he was an American-born Chinese whose parents came from Beijing. This would mean that Edward's family spoke Mandarin Chinese.

I spent that Saturday afternoon going through my closet trying on dresses and shoes as I searched for the perfect outfit. I wanted to look classy, maybe even a little sexy, but not too sexy. I selected a knee-length, sleeveless red dress, and because Edward was tall, I accessorized it with black patent leather high-heeled pumps. My hair hung past my shoulders in soft waves. Small, dangling, gold earrings and a gold bangle bracelet completed the look.

When Edward came to pick me up at seven-thirty, I saw his eyes sweep over me as I answered the door. He took me to a lovely Italian restaurant that he said had good food. The ambiance was intimate, and he asked me if I liked Chianti. I answered yes. The waiter brought the bottle, and I watched Edward taste the small amount the waiter poured into his glass. He nodded to the waiter who filled my glass and topped off Edward's. We looked at the menus and decided we would share a Caesar salad and order individual entrees. We sipped our wine while we waited for the salad, and chatted about our respective classes, and how he was looking forward to the end of the term. I agreed.

He ordered lasagna, and I requested chicken Marsala. We chatted as we ate, and even tasted each other's dishes, agreeing the food was excellent. Over espresso and a shared slice of cheesecake, I told him I was divorced and gave some details about the children. He had already known this; the school's gossip mill worked in both directions. We finished the whole bottle of wine. In the car, I felt a tiny bit tipsy, but I didn't mind the feeling. We reached my front door, and once again, he pulled me close to him, as he had on the dance floor. This time, however, he planted a light kiss on my lips. He told me he had had a wonderful time, and asked if he might see me again. I told him I would enjoy that very much.

The months passed by, and we became a couple. He came to know the children well, and I finally introduced him to Mama and Baba, who liked him immensely. It was hard not to like him. He was handsome, stable, and sweet-natured. One evening, after we had been together close to a year, he asked me to marry him, producing a beautiful diamond ring. I said yes, and he slipped it onto my finger. I later found out that he had actually spoken to Baba beforehand. I thought back to how Wu had proposed, and how in love I had been. I loved Edward, too, very much, but not with the hot passion of youth, but rather the slow-burning desire of a mature woman who knew what she wanted. I was very happy.

We married in May. It was a small ceremony with a small reception. I wore a simple ivory dress with a small ivory hat and a veil that just covered my eyes. I carried a delicate bouquet of flowers in my hand. Edward wore a handsome three-piece black suit. Min, our flower girl, was feeling quite grown up in her peach-colored dress as she scattered rose petals down the aisle of the church. Je looked adorable in his little black suit, carrying our rings on a small pillow. Once again, Xiao was there, this time as my matron of honor. We had a small reception afterwards. Edward and I danced our first dance to "Cherish," and my life as Mrs. Wong began.

We agreed we would sell my house as it held the memories of another marriage. Edward lived in a small apartment he could sublet until his lease was up. We decided to stay in the same city, and after several weeks of searching, we found a house that we both loved. Edward had saved a nice amount of money as a bachelor, and fortunately, my house sold after two months. I split the money with Wu and donated the rest to purchasing the new house. We were able to move into our new place quickly and give our marriage a fresh start. Edward had grown to love Min and Je, and they grew to love him as well. Wu, true to his word, continued to spend a great deal of time with his children. I was very happy.

Chapter Eight

Daly City, 1970

Things were changing again in America as political awareness came to the fore. The hippie culture had waned and almost faded by the mid-seventies. A famine in Bangladesh was said to have claimed as many as one million people. In China, Mao Zedong died. In the Middle East, Egypt and Syria declared war on Israel. An Islamic republic, Iran was established under the leadership of the Ayatollah Khomeini. Economically, the 1970s were marked by the energy crisis. After the first shock, which peaked in 1973, gasoline was rationed in many countries. Europe in particular depended on the Middle East for oil; the United States was also affected, although it had its own oil reserves.

Gender roles changed during this time, and more women entered the workforce. However, the gender role of men remained as that of breadwinner. Stephen Hawking developed his theory of black holes. In 1963, President Kennedy had been assassinated after having accomplished his goal of landing on the moon, but now there was a growing sentiment that the billions of dollars being spent on the current space program should be put to other uses. The moon landings continued through 1972, but the near loss of the Apollo 13 astronauts in April, 1970, served to further the anti-NASA feelings.

The Sony Walkman and computer floppy disks were invented, and later the Apple II became the first personal computer. HBO entered the scene with pay-per-view television. Microwave ovens and VCRs began to be commonly seen in homes. Jimi Hendrix, Janis Joplin, and Jim Morrison all died at age 27. "The Godfather," "The Sting," "Rocky," "Annie Hall," "Jaws," and "Saturday Night Fever" drew crowds to movie theaters. Television was transformed. A new style of programming termed "social consciousness" ensued. Shows such as "All in the Family" and "Soap" broke down TV barriers. Strong independent females became central characters. Most notable was "The Mary Tyler Moore Show." Men and women both wore bell bottoms and platform shoes. Men wore turtlenecks and sported longer sideburns, while women wore their hair long and straight until Farah Fawcett unveiled her feathery cut. It was truly the times written about in Thomas Wolfe's "The Me Decade," and "The Third Great Awakening."

The years passed quietly, my marriage stable and happy. Late one afternoon, as I was preparing dinner, Min came bouncing into the house. She had been at her friend Sharon's house working on a science fair project. She was almost fourteen years old, and a typical teenager. She wore her dark wavy hair in a long ponytail, and wearing bell bottom jeans and platform shoes, she looked like a hundred other girls in our city.

"Mom, listen to this," she said, as she pilfered a slice of cucumber I was slicing for a salad. "I've decided to change my name. From now on, I want to be called Mina, like M-e-e-n-a," she said, drawing the sound out. "I hate Min; it's old fashioned. I'm an American girl, and I want an American name."

I was taken aback for a moment, but not completely surprised. She had subtly been rebelling against her Chinese background for a while now.

"Are you ashamed of your Chinese heritage, of me, your father, and your grandparents?" I asked.

"No, of course not, I just want to be more American," she replied.

"I'll have to discuss this with both your father and Edward," I told her. "I won't let you change it officially in court, but perhaps we can work something out for now. I will also want to talk to your grandparents."

She left the kitchen, and I stood there thinking. It didn't seem like such a strange request to me. I thought that perhaps I would agree, but as I had told her, I would have to discuss it further. By the following week, all had agreed, albeit grudgingly, to accept Mina's new name. Mama and Baba weren't happy at first, wanting to stay true to the family's roots, but eventually came around. She was perhaps the happiest kid in California. Our house was always noisy with her friends coming over after school to study, and on weekends just to hang out. The Beatles music played over and over on the eight-track stereo. The Jackson Five, Sly and the Family Stone, B.J. Thomas, and Three Dog Night were big favorites as well. Our home was lively and fun. Edward and I had always been open to Min's (I must remember to say Mina) friends at our house.

Je, not to be outdone, had his own group of friends, most of whom he saw out of doors since they loved to play ball.

There wasn't a sport Je didn't like. At ten, he was quite the young athlete, with soccer being his favorite. His coach had started calling him Joey, and somehow it stuck. My two Chinese children had American names!

Chapter Nine

Daly City, 1972

Our Mina was growing up. She would be sixteen in a few weeks, and it was time for me to spend some special time with her alone, just mother and daughter. One evening, when Edward was out grabbing a couple of beers with some of his buddies from the school, and Joey was watching TV in the living room, I decided the time was right. I called Mina into my bedroom, and remembering the day like it was yesterday, went to my dresser and retrieved from the bottom drawer, buried under my lingerie, a leather journal and a manila envelope, both of which had been placed in a large plastic bag to keep safe.

She was sitting on the bed, and I walked over and sat down beside her. "When I was your age, Mina, my mama sat me down, as we are sitting now, and handed me this book."

I retrieved the brown leather journal from the bag and handed it to her. Taking the large envelope out as well, I began to explain. "Of course you have heard me talk of *Nai Nai's* difficult life many times. Sweetie, you are almost sixteen, and I am passing on to you this journal, your grandmother's diary, which she gave to me after I turned sixteen. The envelope holds the translation from the Wu dialect in which she wrote her diary. There are also letters from Jun, her first husband, and from her family in Shanghai as well, which have also been translated into English. There are a few pictures from there, too. This is a very precious part of our family's history. Hopefully, you will marry, and if you have a daughter, I would like you to pass it on to her."

Mina took the book from my hands and opened the cover. Inside, the pages of the book were brittle, and the leather was starting to dry out. It was all in handwritten Chinese. This precious book was the heritage that my mother, Zhang Ling, had passed to me, and now was being passed down to her granddaughter. Mina opened the envelope and found a neatly typed English translation. As she began to read, fascinated, I stopped her and told her to save it for a time when she could really sit down and concentrate.

A week later, Mina came to tell me she had finished the diary. She had read it twice. We sat down together, and I made us both cups of coffee. Mina had just started drinking it. I think she just drank it because she thought it was cool, since she added so much milk and sugar it was almost not coffee. I was anxious to hear what she had to say.

"Wow, Mom, I can't believe what I read," she began. Your mother had some life. I can't imagine how she felt when Jun died, and then what Liwei Chen did to her… it's all unreal."

"Yes, I know," I answered. "She was fortunate to have escaped her life with him and so lucky to have met your grandfather, Bao. Then she had a good man to grow old with. Life has its terrible ups and downs, and all we can do is our very best to survive and look for our piece of happiness. This is something your grandmother Zhang Ling learned to do. Put the journal and the translation in a safe place, or would you like me to hold it for you? I have not told *Nai Nai* that you now have the journal, but she will know because you are turning sixteen, and that is what she wanted. It is best if you don't say anything to her about it, though."

"I think I want to hang on to it, Mom, if it's okay with you," she said. "I want to re-read it over the summer to absorb more about her life."

"That's fine, sweetheart. I'm glad you're that interested." I smiled encouragingly at her. "Perhaps after you're done again, we should put it somewhere safe."

"I agree, Mama," she said.

I liked that she still called me Mama, though she often called me Mom. I started dinner, thinking about how lucky I had been. My marriage to Wu had ended badly, but the children and I had a wonderful life with Edward. I couldn't ask for more.

A few months later, we gave Mina a lovely Sweet 16 party at a local catering hall. She wore a lavender dress accented with sequins on the bodice. With silver platform sandals on her feet and her long hair caught up on one side by a rhinestone clip, I thought she was beautiful, even if I was prejudiced. I caught Wu, who of course had been invited with his wife, watching Mina from off to the side. I was taking it all in. It was cute to see the girls whispering to each other as they checked out the boys they thought were cute. Like it or not, my little girl was growing up. Edward walked over to me, and taking my hand, led me onto the dance floor as he had done so many years before.

Four years ago, Edward had gone back to school to complete the necessary classes that allowed him to apply for a position as an assistant principal. Not long after he received his additional degree, he began submitting his resume and received an offer to interview for a position in an elementary school in Pacifica. Xiao and Matt had moved to Pacifica three years ago, deciding that Burlingame had become too quiet (which Wu and I had originally thought). It was a short drive for her to her job at the Mills-Peninsula Medical Center, while Matt had a longer commute to his Palo Alto office at Westinghouse.

Linda was two years younger than Mina and they got along very well. Matt and Edward were very good friends, and Xiao was like a sister to me. The men especially loved a day of golf, getting up at the crack of dawn so they could get out onto the links without a long wait. Edward hadn't gotten that first job, but several months later, another school, also in Pacifica, called him to set up an interview. After additional interviews, they offered him the position. We were very excited, and the raise in salary certainly wouldn't hurt. The principal wished Edward well when he told him he wouldn't be returning in the fall.

The next year flew by, and suddenly it was time for Mina to think about applying to colleges. It seemed that I had just done that. Where had those years gone? She already knew she wanted to major in Journalism and Mass Communications and hoped to go away to school. She wanted to apply to New York University (NYU) in New York, Northwestern University in Evanston, Illinois, and the University of Southern California (USC) in Los Angeles. We hoped she would be accepted at USC, as we would love it if she stayed close to home, but for now, as a high school junior, it was imperative she keep her grades as high as they were, and also do well on her PSATs. Next year's SATs would be of massive importance to the admission boards of every college and university. Mina was not only an excellent student, she was also head of her school's cheerleading team and editor of the school newspaper. I often wondered how she found time for it all, but she did.

At the end of that year, Mama became ill. The doctors found a tumor in her breast. The breast was removed surgically, and then radiotherapy was used, to no avail. Chemotherapy had been in use for many years, but the efficacy of this treatment was uncertain. The side effects were very difficult, according to Mama's doctor. Baba wanted her to try, but she refused. Just as Mina started her senior year of high school, and Joey his freshman year, Mama succumbed to her illness. She was sixty-seven years old. We asked Baba to move in with us, but like Wu's mother, he insisted on taking care of himself.

Mama's funeral was held in mostly traditional Chinese style. Both she and Baba had made it known to us that that was their wish. Mama and Baba were Presbyterians, but neither had completely given up the practice of Buddhism, and I guess, in death, she felt most comfortable returning to her original roots. When a Chinese person is gravely ill, a coffin is ordered beforehand, and we had done so. Mama Dai had explained what had to be done. We contacted a local Chinese funeral home to arrange for the wake and burial. Mama, according to tradition, was buried in her best dress. The deceased could wear any color other than red, as that could cause the deceased to become a ghost.

A Chinese wake could last for several days, but as Americans, we decided we would only keep one overnight vigil. During this night, Mama's picture, along with flowers and candles, were placed around the body while the family sat together. Additionally, she had asked us to use a Chinese coffin, the traditional style with three "humps." The few deities in the house were covered with paper. At the wake, held in the funeral parlor, there were no mirrors, as it is believed that anyone who saw the reflection of a coffin in a mirror would shortly have a death in his or her own family. We hung a white cloth over the doorway to Mama and Baba's home, and a small gong was placed to the right because a female had died. An auspicious date had to be chosen so as to avoid bad luck, and beforehand, invitations to the funeral were sent to friends and family. Those attending brought flowers, traditionally white irises, which would be in elaborate wreaths that included banners with couplets written on them. White envelopes with cash were also brought by the guests. The burial was held at a local Chinese cemetery. A traditional Chinese funeral ceremony lasts forty-nine days, with the first seven being most important. We decided we would only be able to observe that first week. Also, prayers that I had to learn had to be said once a week. And, while the funeral rites ended, mourning continued for the family for one hundred more days.

The next few months were quiet ones of mourning and reflection. I missed Mama terribly, as did the children. Baba seemed like a lost soul to me, but he insisted he was fine, and strangely, I realized he was.

Chapter Ten

Daly City, 1973

Edward's parents, Joyce and Roy Wong, lived in Seattle. Both had Americanized their names, finding it better for their careers. Edward was an only child. His father was an engineer for a company involved in Seattle's infrastructure, and Joyce worked as an administrative assistant for a large food distributing company in Seattle. They came down to attend Mina's high school graduation and were staying at a local hotel. It rained that morning, and the grass in front of our house was wet and shiny with reflected sunlight. Mina stood outside on the paved walk in her white cap and gown, smiling as we all took pictures of her. There would be plenty of time later to take more, during and after the ceremony.

A week earlier, Mina attended her Senior Prom, an exciting night for her. I looked at my little girl, once again all dressed up, and so grown up in her light blue dress, silver heels on her feet, and two pretty rhinestone combs holding back her beautiful black hair. Michael, an American boy, was her date and had come to pick her up in his dad's car. I answered the door, and as he stood there in his rented tuxedo, hair neatly combed, corsage box in hand, I watched his face as Mina walked down the stairs. She was lovely. Her eyes were dark, reflecting her Asian heritage, and they sparkled with excitement. Tall and slender, like her father and his father, she was a beauty. Perhaps I was a bit prejudiced, but surely every mother is when it comes to her daughter. Michael was clearly uncomfortable as Edward, who had come up behind me, welcomed him into the house.

"Can we get a couple of snapshots?" Edward asked, holding his camera aloft.

Michael, with an easy smile, handed the box with the wristlet to Mina, and she opened it and smelled the sweetness of the white gardenias. I watched him slip the corsage onto my daughter's wrist as they stood side by side while Edward snapped three or four pictures. After they had gone, Edward put his arm around my waist and asked if I'd like a glass of wine. A moment later, Joey came barreling down the stairs, barely stopping long enough to yell out to us that he was off to the movies.

"Don't be home past eleven, Joey," I called after him. I think he yelled back, "Okay." I walked to the window and saw he was already getting into a car in front of the house. I noticed his friend Bobby's dad was driving. All the parents took turns driving the kids around.

Now, a week later, we all piled into our Chrysler Town and Country van, and picking up Baba on the way, off we went to a local theater that had been rented for the graduation ceremony. Mama Dai was with us, too. Because Wu and his wife would be there, it would be very uncomfortable for me. While I often saw Wu when he came to pick up the children, I avoided any opportunity to be around his wife, Janet. She had been cold and standoffish from day one. I never understood that, since it was she who took MY husband away, not the other way around.

As we took our seats in the theater, Xiao, Matt, and Linda

arrived. I had saved seats for them so we could all sit together. I noticed out of the corner of my eye that Wu and his wife were sitting a few aisles up on the other side. Wu had come over to kiss his Mama, who in all fairness to him, he saw often. When Mina's name was called as Min Dai (first name, then last name, although we Chinese always put the last name first), she took her turn walking up to the podium to receive her diploma and shake hands with Principal Stanger.

Afterward, as we stood outside, Mina socialized with all her friends. Joey looked nice in a button-down shirt and a pair of slacks I had insisted he wear; this was a change of pace from his usual jeans and sweats. We stood chatting with Joyce and Roy, and finally spotted Mina's best friend and her parents. We waved, and they walked over to us. We had made a reservation for us all to have lunch at a lovely restaurant. Wu and Janet would not be joining us. Mina's father would take her out the following day, along with Mama Dai. The conversation at the restaurant was lively as the girls chattered about how they were looking forward to the summer, and their fears and excitement involved in their upcoming college careers.

The summer passed quickly, and I took Mina shopping for the many things she needed to head off to college. She was going to USC in Los Angeles. I was glad she would be just a short plane ride away. It would make it much easier, and certainly less expensive, for her to come home for the holidays and breaks. August arrived and we filled the van with bedding, a desk lamp, a small TV/VCR, some pretty curtains, and a lot of clothes and shoes. She would share a room with a girl named Sandra Gardini who lived in Cleveland, Ohio. They had written each other numerous times, and had spoken on the phone twice. Sandra wanted to major in Biology.

The drive to Los Angeles was long and we decided to stay over at a motel. We drove for about three and a half hours, stopped for lunch, and drove another hour to the motel. Mina was unusually quiet all day. Joey sat up front with Edward.

Mina finally admitted to us how nervous she was about leaving home. It was the first time she had said anything, although as the time to leave for school approached, we had been acutely aware that she was filled with apprehension. In the morning, we had breakfast at the motel and then continued on to the school. When we got there, we were directed to the parking area for the freshman quad. Upper classmen were there to answer questions for the new students. Mina inquired and was told which dorm she was in and where to go to obtain the key to the front door and her room while we began unloading the van. Her roommate had not yet arrived. Mina chose the bed closest to the window. The room overlooked a ball field. It was small and compact; it held two beds, two dressers, and two desks, one small, open closet they would share, and a sink and medicine cabinet.

We began to unpack, Mina filling her dresser with her belongings, while I made up the bed with the pretty new spread of pink and green, and tossed two little throw pillows on top. The girls had decided on the color scheme, and Edward hung the bright curtains that matched the girls" bedspreads. Her little TV/VCR sat atop the dresser, and she set up her school supplies in the drawers provided.

Joey was clearly bored. We left the room and set off to explore the campus. We had already explored the school, as we had all the others Mina considered. This would be Mina's home for the next four years. We found the cafeteria, the chapel, library, and various other quads. The campus was huge, and we only got to see a small amount of it. We headed back to the room. Sandra and her folks had arrived and were doing the same thing we had done earlier. Mina and Sandra shyly said hello to each other, while Edward and I shook hands with Sandra's parents. She told us she preferred to be called Sandy. Her parents had purchased the matching bedspread, as well as some posters for the walls, and the room looked cute and cozy, though cramped. Somehow college kids made the adjustment quite well.

Finally, it was time to say goodbye. I thought I'd be fine, but as I put my arms around my daughter, I felt my eyes growing wet. I didn't want her to see that I was about to cry, and I quickly gained control. Edward hugged and kissed Mina, and Joey shyly kissed his sister. Once we were in the van, I cried my eyes out. We arrived home late that night, as we had decided to drive straight through, although we had stopped for some dinner along the way. Joey ran up the stairs to his room, calling out a good night on the way. We were all exhausted, and as Edward and I got ready for bed, I felt overwhelmed by emotion again. I missed Mina already. My little girl was all grown up and gone away.

Chapter Eleven

Daly City, 1974

Mina was getting a ride home from college with a new friend's parents. We thought it was incredibly kind of them to offer. It seemed like we had just driven her up to start school. She had flown home to celebrate both Christmas and Easter and now her freshman year was over! She had taken Driver's Education in high school and was driving long enough that we now felt comfortable with our plan to buy her a used car over the summer so she could drive the long trip back for her sophomore year.

Edward and I talked about taking the kids on a vacation in the Los Angeles area. We thought a week at a beach resort would be nice, and I said I would call our travel agent that week. Mina would need some down time to see her friends and her father and just enjoy being home. It wouldn't be long before they wouldn't be caught dead going on vacation with their parents. Joey was worse than Mina, having reached that age where kids kept as far away from their embarrassing parents as possible. We had spoken with Mina earlier and knew they were already on the road. It was Saturday, and everyone was home. Mina arrived late in the evening, excited and bubbly, talking a mile a minute, and clearly happy to see us. I watched brother and sister hug each other, and then pull apart. Joey had really grown up a lot and even had a girlfriend, a sweet girl named Ellie. They were in several classes together, and she often came over, supposedly to study.

In the morning Edward went to pick up Baba to bring him to our house for a few days. He was still sturdy and self-sufficient, and I was so happy to see him. I went off to make sandwiches for lunch. I knew Baba would appreciate a home-cooked meal, and I had planned a simple dinner of fish and various side dishes. Monkfish was a favorite of Baba's, and I cooked it in Shanghainese style. Later, I made a huge pot of noodles with vegetables, and I enjoyed watching my father eat with gusto.

That evening, when everyone was preparing for bed, Mina came to talk to me in the bedroom. Edward was in the den watching TV, clearly to allow us some mother-daughter time. She sat on the bed, watching me take off my pearl earrings, and just looked at me.

"So, sweetheart, all in all, how was your first year of school?" I asked her.

We had talked many times over the school year, but I thought I'd engage her in some further conversation. She said it was wonderful. I knew she liked most of her classes, but that she had really struggled with a statistics class that was a requirement and had decided to get it out of the way. Despite the one difficult class, she finished her freshman year with a strong 3.7 GPA, and I told her I was very proud of her.

She had plans to see her father the next day, and she kissed me goodnight and left my room. I wandered into the den where Edward was watching TV, his stockinged feet up on the coffee table. I sat next to him, and put my head on his shoulder. Joey had gone over to his girlfriend's house for an hour or two and would be home soon. Papa had long since gone to sleep in the extra bedroom.

"It's nice to have her home, huh?" I asked.

"Yup, it sure is," he said. "I'm looking forward to going on vacation."

"Me, too, honey. I'll give the agent a call tomorrow, and get some suggestions from her." We watched a movie together until I felt my eyes closing.

"I'm going to bed. Are you coming, or do you want to watch a little more TV?" I asked.

He yawned and smiled sheepishly. "I guess that's your answer," he laughed.

We got into bed and in no time I could hear Edward's gentle snore, signaling that he had fallen asleep. I lay there, thinking that I loved him very much and that he was a wonderful husband who treated my children as though they were his own. I was truly blessed.

The following morning, I called Irene, our travel agent, and discussed some places that would be great for a family vacation. She recommended Venice Beach, as there were loads of interesting things to do other than just going to the beach. She told me about the famous "board" walk where people went to explore the waterfront scene and skateboard. She told me it was known for its street performers, skaters, artists, and myriads of vendors. She spoke of the famous muscle beach, which I knew Joey would love.

"Then there are the canals," she told me, "which are north of the Venice Pier, and beautiful to see." She also suggested we not miss the Venice Beach Graffiti Walls, where artists with permits paint exhibitions with high-quality flair.

She checked to make sure we would be traveling during a week the show would be available to see. She recommended several places for us to stay that would comfortably accommodate the family without breaking the bank. She particularly liked the Venice Beach Suites, with two bedrooms, as well as a small kitchen, which would allow us to be together. This way we could keep breakfast items, cold drinks, and snacks, which would help offset the costs.

I told her I wanted to discuss it with Edward and that I'd get back to her. In the morning, Edward and I talked about it, and then we ran it by the kids as well. Mina would use the second bedroom, and Joey would sleep on the pullout in the small living room. Everyone seemed to be excited, and I called Irene asking her to book us for the first week in July, as she suggested. Joey had accepted a job as a stock boy at a local pharmacy and was able to negotiate his starting date around our trip. Mina wanted to work at a local summer camp, but had put in her application too late, so she was unable to obtain a counselor's job. We weren't unhappy about that. She had her whole life to work. We thought taking the summer off after her first year of college was a good idea. Besides, she had worked at "Get It Done," the dry cleaning/mail/and other services store throughout the school year.

We had booked an early flight out of San Francisco Airport, and we arrived in Los Angeles after an uneventful flight of just over an hour. We retrieved our luggage and found our way to the Hertz Car Rental kiosk. Irene had reserved a car for us. It was a simple procedure, and not long after, we were on our way, following the TripTik that AAA had provided for us.

Venice is relatively close to LAX, and we were told it would take us anywhere from fifteen to forty-five minutes, depending on traffic, to get to Venice. We were happy vacationers and arrived at the Suites in a little over half an hour. Edward went to check in while the bellman got our luggage and took it up to our room. The suite was lovely, with two bedrooms, a small living area, two bathrooms, and a well-supplied small kitchen. After we unpacked, we went out to find a place to have something to eat, and to pick up some groceries. We ate at a local diner, and then found a supermarket close by where we were able to pick up some staples. We bought milk, cereal, cookies, popcorn, pretzels, peanut butter, and jelly, as well as butter, a loaf of bread, eggs, soda pop, paper towels, napkins, and various other items. The kitchen had everything else we needed. We planned, of course, to eat our dinners and most of our lunches out. We dropped the groceries off and changed into bathing suits. The kids were anxious to get to the beach for a bit. Earlier, Edward had asked at the desk for a recommendation for dinner and the clerk suggested a good seafood restaurant close by and offered to make a reservation for us. At dinner, we'd plan our week's itinerary with the suggestions from the lovely front desk clerk and the many brochures she gave us.

I saw Mina come out of the bathroom wearing a red, two-piece bathing suit that made me stare. I remembered her buying it, but when had she filled out so? When had she become a woman? With her long hair and large dark eyes, my daughter was a head-turner! Well, maybe this was just from a mom's perspective, but I thought she looked stunning.

Joey wore board shorts, a tee shirt, and sandals… ready to "hang ten," as he said, but first he'd need a couple of surfing lessons. Mina said she was happy to work on her tan, so we grabbed our small insulated beach bag, and filling it was some cans of soda pop and a load of snacks, we grabbed the towels and sun tan lotion I had packed. Tossing them into my beach bag, off we went.

At the beach, the blueness of the sky was offset by some cumulus and striated stratus clouds. The cloud formation resembled large balls of cotton candy, with long wisps trailing behind as if someone had been pulling pieces off. The sun was strong, and I told the kids to be careful of getting burned. I had recently seen a story on the news, and I made sure they applied plenty of sun tan lotion, the kind with an SPF marked on the bottle. SPF was a new innovation, meaning sun protection factor, and lotions and creams were starting to be called sunscreens. They were designed to block ultraviolet-A and B radiation. Who knew that sunlight could cause cancer? There were more and more discoveries every day.

Back in the fifties and sixties, there had been increased public concern about the impact human activity could have on the environment. In 1970, President Richard Nixon proposed an executive reorganization that consolidated many of the federal government's environmental responsibilities under one agency, a new Environmental Protection Agency. The EPA began regulating under the Clean Air Act what were known as greenhouse gasses, caused by mobile and stationary sources of air pollution.

The Public Broadcasting System (PBS) began operation, succeeding National Educational Television (NET). Watergate, a political scandal, occurred as a result of the June 17, 1972 break-in at the Democratic National Committee headquarters at the Watergate office complex in Washington, D.C., and the Nixon administration's attempted cover-up of its involvement. Those caught had been attempting to wiretap phones and steal secret documents connected to President Nixon's re-election campaign. Eventually, the scandal led to the resignation of President Nixon on August 9, 1974—this was the first presidential resignation in the history of the United States. As part of a plea bargain during the Watergate trials of 1973, Vice President Spiro T. Agnew also resigned. In 1974, the president was impeached. Gerald Ford became the first president of the United States who wasn't elected. Additionally, he pardoned Nixon.

Apollo 17 was the final mission of the United States' Apollo lunar landing program; it was the sixth of its kind. It was launched on December 7, 1972. A year lat-

er, Skylab, the USA's first space station, was launched. Hank Aaron of the Atlanta Braves broke Babe Ruth's home run record by hitting his 715th career home run. In 1975, Saigon in South Vietnam fell, captured by The People's Army of Vietnam. Bill Gates founded Microsoft and the future would never be the same again. President Ford survived two assassination attempts in a 17-day time span. The television series "Wheel of Fortune", and "Saturday Night Live" premiered on NBC. Also in 1975, Sony's Betamax became the first commercially successful home video recording unit. Automobiles were huge, but downsizing was beginning.

The role of women in society was changing, both at home and abroad. A significant number of women became heads of state outside of monarchies, and heads of government in a number of countries across the world. Isabel Martinez de Peron was the first woman president of Argentina. Indira Gandhi was prime minister of India, and Golda Meir held the same position in Israel. Later, in 1979, Margaret Thatcher became England's first female prime minister.

The Feminism movement of the sixties carried over to the seventies. Gloria Steinem, Betty Friedan, Betty Ford, Shirley Chisholm, and Bella Abzug were some who continued, among others, to lead the movement for women's equality. While Coretta Scott King called for an end to all discrimination, the election of political figures such as Harvey Milk to public office, as well as the many celebrities, including Freddie Mercury and Andy Warhol, who "came out" during the decade, brought gay culture further into the limelight.

In music, it was the start of the popularity of folk music. James Taylor, The Carpenters, and Carol

King came to the fore. Rhythm and Blues (R & B), by way of Motown artists such as Stevie Wonder, The Temptations, and The Jackson 5, became extremely popular. The mid-seventies brought about the rise of disco, which dominated the last half of the decade with bands like the Bee Gees, ABBA, the Village People, Donna Summer, and KC and the Sunshine Band. In response, rock music became increasingly hard-edged with artists like Led Zeppelin, and Black Sabbath. Pink Floyd's "The Dark Side of the Moon" (1973) became the highest-selling album of the year. It remained on the Billboard chart for 741 weeks!

In movies, "Patton," "The French Connection," "The Sting," "Annie Hall," "One Flew Over the Cuckoo's Nest," "The Godfather Parts I and II," "Rocky," "Jaws," "Star Wars," "The Exorcist," "Grease," "Close Encounters of the Third Kind," and "Saturday Night Fever," many of which were Oscar winners, dominated the box office.

Television changed by virtue of minority-centered programming such as "Sanford and Sons" and "Good Times," while shows such as "Soul Train" premiered as an alternative to "American Bandstand." Bawdy humor, such as "Charlie's Angels" and "Three's Company," and game shows and soap operas were all popular. Cable TV became more affordable, and HBO, in the race to bring the silver screen to the small screen, commenced with the launch of pay television with a continuously deliverable signal via satellite. It offered the "Thrilla in Manila" boxing match between Muhammad Ali and Joe Frazier.

Our trip was just what everyone needed. We all had a fantastic time, and there was still a lot of the summer left for the kids to enjoy before Mina had to go back to college and Joey to high school. When I missed my period in July, I was stunned, and finally called Xiao, my "go-to" person.

"Can you do lunch on Saturday, Xiao? I have something I want to discuss with you," I said.

"Sure," she replied, "I'll call you on Friday, and we can decide where to meet."

I hadn't said a word to anyone else, but I was over ten days late and had bought a home pregnancy test. This was a new innovation, just on the market a year or so. After urinating on the "stick," the change in color told me I was pregnant. It was then that I had decided to talk to Xiao and ask her if she would go with me to my gynecologist. I was so excited I could barely contain myself, though I knew I had to calm down. It was probably not true. Edward and I had been trying for so long that we had stopped talking about it, assuming that for one reason or another, I wasn't going to conceive a child with him. Suddenly, at the age of forty-two, it seemed that I was pregnant. Of course, I didn't know how accurate those new home tests were, so I would say nothing to Edward until I had seen the doctor. No sense building false hope.

Xiao and I met for lunch at a small Italian restaurant we both loved to go to for their personal pan pizzas. She had no sooner settled into the booth when I blurted out, "I think I'm pregnant, Xiao."

"What? How do you know? Have you seen the doctor, Yuming?" She was astonished at my announcement.

"Not yet," I said, leaning across the table to touch her hand. "I wanted to talk to you first. I bought one of those new home pregnancy tests; have you heard about them? I know that it's probably ridiculous, but it says I'm pregnant. Will you go with me to see Dr. Frank? I'm going to call for an appointment. He has late afternoon hours on Thursdays; can you make that?"

"Of course I can," Xiao agreed. "Have you said anything to Edward?"

I took a sip of water, my throat dry. "Not a word, I'm too scared that it's not true."

We didn't discuss it further during the meal. It seemed better to just leave it alone until I saw my doctor. When I got home I knew I was very on edge, and I tried to calm myself down as I picked out something to change into for our dinner plans with friends later. I just had to wait until it was confirmed, one way or the other.

That Thursday, late in the afternoon, Xiao picked me up at home, and we drove to my gynecologist's office. The room was filled with women with swollen bellies of varying sizes. I hoped that I would soon be one of them. Soon I was ushered into the examination room where I talked with Dr. Frank and was tested. When I walked back into the waiting room after seeing the doctor, Xiao took one look at my smile and knew. I was pregnant. My baby was due to be born the beginning of April. After Xiao dropped me off at home, I went inside and started dinner, my mind racing. My doctor told me that, because of my age, it was considered a high-risk pregnancy, and he recommended that I undergo an often-used procedure called amniocentesis. He carefully explained the actual procedure and why it was important. Using ultrasound, which had only recently been introduced in the procedure, a needle would be inserted to draw out a small amount of amniotic fluid. This would be cultured, and after approximately three weeks, we would have the results. The test would determine whether the baby had certain genetic disorders, such as Down syndrome or others. It could also tell the gender of the fetus.

Edward got home, and finding me in the kitchen, came up to me as I was seasoning steaks, and planted a kiss on the back of my neck. Opening the refrigerator, he poured himself a glass of white wine, and asked if there was anything he could do to help, and did I want a glass of wine, too. I said no thanks, as drinking liquor during pregnancy had recently been linked to something called Fetal Alcohol Syndrome.

I told him there was something I wanted to discuss with him. Neither of the kids had gotten home yet. I sat down at the dinette table, and as he stood beside me, a puzzled look on his face, I took one of his hands and placed it on my belly. "Edward, I've just come from the doctor. We're having a baby." I blurted it out, just like that.

He stared at me as if I had told him an alien ship had landed outside. Clearly, he was stunned. Then he took me in his arms, and I began to cry from happiness.

The summer waned, and soon Mina was back at school. My pregnancy was progressing nicely, and though I hadn't started to show yet, there were numerous mornings I spent in and out of the bathroom. I had switched grades and I loved working with fifth graders after years of having taught the younger students. I notified my principal that I would hopefully be applying for maternity leave in March. Edward and I decided we would hire a nanny so I could return to teaching when the leave ended. While it would have been wonderful to stay home and raise the baby, with Mina in college and Joey starting his junior year of high school and his time for college just around the corner, we knew that the second income was needed to make ends meet.

Xiao and Matt's daughter, Linda, though a little younger than Joey, was also in her junior year. Soon both families would begin the college process for them. Of course, we were already seasoned college parents, having been through the process with Mina. Everything was so surreal, with children in high school and college, and a baby on the way. It was a crazy, wonderful time for us.

Initially, when Mina and Joey heard the news about the baby there had been mixed reviews. Mina was ecstatic about having a baby sister or brother. Joey, on the other hand, being a teenage boy, was embarrassed by the whole thing, and found it difficult to deal with it. His friends all had siblings around their own ages. No one's parents were having babies in their forties.

We hoped that when the baby was born he would come around. In the third week of August, Mina packed and got ready to go back to school. She and Sandy had pledged a sorority last year, and would now be living in the sorority house. She would be sharing with a girl in her junior year named Jennifer Stark. The day she left I thought to myself that, when Mina came home for Thanksgiving, I would be more than halfway along with the pregnancy. That afternoon, Joey came in with an attitude, something we had been seeing a lot of lately. Edward and I had already discussed this situation, and we had decided that he would be the one to sit Joey down and have a talk with him later in the week before school started.

The pregnancy was still normal and uneventful, and the morning sickness finally abated. All my friends worked, and many of them were colleagues from my school. I started knitting during my breaks and missed Mama more than ever. How elated she would have been over this happy news. Baba was thrilled, and we knew that he, too, was thinking about Mama. I cranked out lots of adorable green, yellow, or white sweaters, booties, hats, and blankets. One afternoon in early December, having just gotten home from work, I watched a touching movie and found myself feeling vulnerable and blue. I got up to get myself a cup of chamomile tea, and suddenly the baby kicked. It was not a strong kick, but not being a first-time mother, I recognized the sign of life immediately. I couldn't wait for Edward to get home later so I could tell him.

When I was sixteen weeks pregnant, I had the amnio, as it was called, and three weeks later, we knew we were having a healthy baby boy! It was so exciting to know the sex of the baby. Christmas was just around the corner and we had been shopping for gifts for weeks. When Edward brought the tree and trimmings down from the attic, it suddenly hit me that I was having a baby in less than four months. The holidays were always a wonderful time for our family but this year we were truly blessed.

Joey calmed down, finally resigning himself to the fact that soon he would be a big brother. Mina came home from college and helped me shop for our Christmas Eve meal. We invited Xiao, Matt, and Linda, as always, and Edward would pick up Baba who would stay for a few days. To honor Mama, I always cooked some traditional Chinese food and had made little eggrolls and other small specialties that were passed around before we sat down for our dinner. I served turkey and ham with a lot of side dishes, and Xiao, who was a fantastic baker, outdid herself with an apple pie and cookies. There was the usual overabundance of food. Platters were served family style, and I was so stuffed that I told Xiao, Linda, and Mina that I had to sit for a while before even attempting to clean up.

"Just sit and relax," Xiao said. "We will handle it."

Baba went into the living room to spend some time with his grandson, Je, as he still called him. Joey didn't seem to mind, but only his grandfather could get away with it. We had trimmed the tree the day after Mina had gotten home, and now, as darkness fell, Edward turned the lights on. Next year at this time, a new little person would be with us to witness the beauty of our tree. The presents were stacked underneath, and our home was filled with love. Xiao loaded the dishwasher while Mina and Linda wrapped up the leftovers, making sure to put together a "doggy bag" for the Danners family to take home.

The following day was Christmas. In the morning, we exchanged our gifts. Mina got a lot of the clothing she had asked for, particularly the brown fringed boots she had pointed out to me in Macy's just after she got home. Joey, as always, had requested sports equipment and was extremely happy with his new soccer ball and tennis racquet, as well as several eight-track tapes. He was very into current music and had recently asked if he could take guitar lessons. We thought it was a great idea. I had gotten Edward a beautiful cashmere sweater in the softest gray, as well as two button-down shirts he could wear to work. The children got me (subsidized a bit from Edward), an elegant black leather handbag I had admired with Mina a week earlier. Edward's gift for me was lovely. He bought me a gold bracelet studded with pave diamonds. As he closed it around my wrist, he leaned over, kissed me, and whispered he had never been so happy. I was happy, too. Baba sat quietly on the side, watching. Edward and I had bought him two shirts, several pouches of his favorite pipe tobacco, and a handsome teapot, similar in pattern to Mama's original one. While nothing could replace Mama's pot for its memories, it was badly chipped from years of use while having tea leaves steep in it. We decided it would be safest in a place of honor on Baba's kitchen shelf. He still boiled water in a kettle on the stove and poured it into the new pot, making tea the way it had always been done by the Chinese. The kids had gotten him a robe and slippers to replace the old ones he kept at our house.

It had become a Christmas Day tradition for Edward and me to drive to the San Francisco Presbyterian Mission Home where Mama had lived so many years ago, and without which, Mama and Baba would never have met. My parents had always gone with us, but now, with Mama gone, Baba refused to go. The Home's mission had changed down through the years. Now, rather than physically rescuing women, they helped, via various programs, to empower women to participate in and contribute to society. They offered counseling, education, group support, and other forms of community involvement. Mama had loved to visit there, though the memories were sometimes painful. We always brought with us a basket filled with home-baked goodies and a generous check. When we returned home, we all ate a delicious meal of leftovers from the night before. There was so much food, there would still be enough for sandwiches throughout the week.

The winter vacation ended with the temperatures dropping to unusual lows. It was in the mid-forties for several days. I actually didn't mind it, though. Mina had gone back to college after picking up one of her friends who lived close by, and Joey would be going back to his school in a few weeks. Edward, Joey, and I settled into the usual routine of work, school, and knitting. The baby was due March 27, the due date having been changed from the original in April, and I had a nice round belly to prove it. I felt healthy and strong, though there was many a night I was awakened by a strong kick, as my little boy moved around in my ever-expanding womb.

The months flew by. I had stopped working a few weeks earlier. It was almost Easter, and eleven days past the time for our baby to make his welcome appearance. The doctor said if I didn't go into labor right after Easter, he would induce. Mina had come home the day before and was a big help to me around the house. I was miserably huge and had swollen feet. I hated getting into shoes and spent most of the day in house slippers. We went to Xiao and Matt's for Easter every year, and we planned to pick up Baba on the way. The night before Easter, I couldn't sleep. The baby's kicking kept me up, and I felt nauseous. Around four in the morning, I got out of bed, which was no mean feat. I heard Edward snoring peacefully as I padded over to the bathroom to get a drink of water. Halfway across the room, my water broke. I woke Edward; he was excited but tried to appear calm. He called Dr. Frank, who told him to wait to take me to take me to the hospital until my contractions were twenty minutes apart, then call him again and leave for the hospital.

I was going to deliver at St. Luke's, which was less than five miles away. Edward helped me get dressed, and in my slippers, we grabbed my bag and got ready to go. Eventually, the contractions were about twenty minutes apart. Earlier, Edward had gone into Joey's room and awakened him with the news. He was scared for me and asked Edward if he could go to the hospital with us. Edward said no, but he could stay home from school and wait for a phone call with the happy news. Mina was also told to stay home and wait along with her brother until Edward called. Then we left for the hospital.

At 5:25 that afternoon, I gave birth to a beautiful boy. We named him Lawrence in memory of Mama Ling. Ling meant spirit or soul, and we thought it fitting that Mama's amazing spirit be honored by her grandson. He weighed seven pounds, eight ounces, and was twenty inches long. That evening, Xiao, Matt, and Linda came to the hospital. It was a room filled with joy and the wonderful sound of a crying baby. We brought him home three days later and settled him into a bassinet in our bedroom. Edward's parents were on their way. Our house was now too small for our family, and we would begin searching for a larger house as soon as I was up to it. The house rang with Lawrence's lusty voice as he signaled that he was hungry.

Chapter Twelve

Daly City, 1975

We began our search for a larger home. We knew we wanted to stay in the Daly City area. We spent our weekends toting the kids around to open houses as we hunted for what would hopefully be our last house. We knew just what we wanted, and when we saw it, we looked at each other, nodded, and decided to make a bid.

Prior to the day we were going to make our bid, we sat down with pencil and paper and carefully figured out our finances. We knew approximately what we would get for our house, and after two days of discussion, we made our decision. After we looked at the house again, we knew this was our dream home. We brought in an engineer to make sure all was as it should be, and a few weeks later, we bought the house. We put ours on the market immediately and were fortunate enough to sell to a young family of three, with the stipulation that we needed two months to move out.

Our new house was still in Daly City. The area was very upscale, and this beautiful one-family house had four bedrooms, two-and-a-half bathrooms, a two-car garage, and a nice-sized back yard. There was a finished basement where Baba could stay when he visited.

We moved on a cloudy day. At one point the sky was dark, and rain threatened to fall any moment, which would make it difficult for the movers. It drizzled a few times, but fortunately, it held out until later that evening. Joey would be going to a new high school in the fall. With his likable personality, he was sure to make new friends and adjust. He was driving, as were his long-time friends, so he was able to get together with them. We bought him a used car, a blue, four-year-old Dodge Dart, and he was thrilled.

Mina had her car and drove home, along with two girlfriends who lived not too far from our new home and who shared the gas and tolls with her. It was the end of May and Mina finally got to meet Lawrence. She hugged and kissed us all, and then picked up the baby, who struggled in her arms. He was a chubby little boy, hungry and smiling all the time. She handed him back to me, and ran upstairs to her room, which we had decorated together via telephone consultations. It reflected the taste of a young woman, not a girl. Furnished in shades of turquoise and brown, the oak furniture was beautiful, and she would now add her own finishing touches. Her old, favorite stuffed toys sat on a shelf, while a large photo album sat on one side of the desk. She loved that she now had a double bed, covered with a turquoise, white and brown comforter, with lots of throw pillows to match. On the windows, blinds and matching café curtains made the room warm and cozy-looking, and the brown shag carpet completed the look.

Later, Joey came through the door, and running up the stairs, waved hello to his sister, being at the uncomfortable age where he would prefer not giving her a kiss in greeting. He was a typical teenage boy. Mina was planning to visit her father and his family in the next few days. They had a decent relationship, and she saw them whenever she came home. Joey, however, had never been that close. They were big kids and had to make their own choices, so I never got involved.

The years were measured by our Thanksgivings, Christmases, New Year's Eves, and the myriad birthdays. They seemed to fly by. Thanksgiving was a lovely day. Lawrence was close to eight months old. It was sunny and mild as I popped the turkey into the oven, and began to put together the dough to make biscuits. Edward would pick up Baba later. For the past six months, Baba had been living at Atria Daly City, a lovely assisted living facility for seniors. His health had deteriorated over the last two years. He had never been the same after Mama passed away, though he had given it a great try. He refused to move in with us. He had developed diabetes several years earlier, and while it was controlled, this year he suddenly refused to eat properly and forgot to take his medication. When he fell getting into the car on Lawrence's birthday, he broke his hip. After surgery, he was sent to a nursing home for rehabilitation, and we knew he would never be able to return home. He accepted it gracefully. We were pretty certain he had known the inevitability even before the accident.

Over dinner the night before, Mina mentioned her boyfriend John several times. He and Mina had been a couple since they met earlier in the year while both were working for the Journalism Department's newspaper. She talked about her long-term plans as we ate. There was little doubt that she would pursue a career in journalism. We had started looking at schools with appropriate Master's degree programs over the summer. She was extremely interested in the University of Florida's J-School. It was very well-respected in the field. She told us only about two hundred students were accepted into the program at the College of Journalism and Communications each year. She would apply elsewhere as well, but really had her heart set on Florida. As we ate, she talked about John a great deal, and Edward and I noticed that. John was also planning on a journalism major and was interested in writing for television newscasting. He had also applied to UFL. John Harvey was a tall, slender, Caucasian man whose family lived in Los Angeles. USC had been local for him, and he had lived at home throughout his college career. His father was an accountant, and his mother a teacher. He had two older sisters, both of whom were married. His oldest sister, Barbara, was married to a doctor, and they had a two-year-old son. His sister Jane was a teacher and had only recently married a man who did some kind of work for the city.

On Thanksgiving morning, Mina slept in, having gotten home late the night before from visiting Wu and his family. She came into the kitchen and kissed me on the cheek. "What can I do to help, Mom?"

"Plenty," I answered, handing her an apron. "Would you mind peeling the sweet potatoes?"

She was always a great help in the kitchen, and I knew that, when she married, her husband would be the recipient of all she had learned from me. Sadly, though, there were very few Chinese dishes that she knew how to cook. I taught her some basic dishes, but she wasn't terribly interested, though she liked to cook in general. I was sad to see our wonderful heritage dying in the kitchen. The language was already gone to us. I guess something was better than nothing. We worked side by side for a while, chatting about everyday things. Joey wandered down looking for something to nibble on. It seemed he was hungry all the time. I told him to have a small bowl of cereal as we would be having a large meal later. That wouldn't stop Joey, who could eat all the time. What a typical teenage boy. Edward was in the dining room setting the table. I could always count on Edward for help around the house. As we were preparing dinner, Lawrence, who had been asleep, woke up. Mina went to pick him up while I finished what I was doing so I could nurse him. My sweet baby nursed for a while and then fell asleep at the breast. I nudged him awake. I wanted him to have a full nursing so he would be full and comfortable and allow us all to enjoy our holiday meal. Now, happily content, he was throwing his toys all around his playpen.

When things were in order, I went upstairs to shower and change my clothes. Xiao and her family were expected soon. Just as I started putting on some makeup in the bathroom, I suddenly felt dizzy, and began sweating; my face looked gray in the mirror. My stomach hurt, and I felt nauseous, and it was difficult to catch my breath. I knew I was having a heart attack.

BOOK THREE
Dai Min (Mina)

Chapter One

Daly City, 1975

We lost my amazing mother Yuming that Thanksgiving afternoon. She had called down to us from her bathroom, and when we saw her, we called for an ambulance immediately. Ironically, they took her to St. Luke's, the same place where she had given birth to Lawrence less than a year ago. The doctors said she had a congenital birth defect. Apparently, her heart had never been totally healthy, but symptoms had never manifested themselves, and somehow it had never been diagnosed. She had never gone to a cardiologist.

How could her other doctors have missed this? How did this happen? They explained that pregnancy stresses the heart and circulatory system. My mother had delivered a baby quite late in her childbearing years, never knowing the complications that had been going on during those nine months. The doctors further explained that during pregnancy there is a very large increase in blood volume. This, of course, is to help nourish the growing baby. The heart rate also increases, causing the heart to work harder. My mother's labor, which wasn't easy, caused changes in the blood flow and pressure.

During labor, all the pushing caused stress to the heart. Because the delivery put a terrible strain on her heart, the heart attack occurred three weeks later.

After my mother's death, my family's life was in shambles. Lawrence suddenly had no mother. To say my stepfather was a mess was an understatement. He was unable to accept it. No one knew what to do. After the funeral, which was an ordeal no one should have had to live through, my mother's amazing friend Xiao took over. In her quiet, strong way, she quickly placed an ad in two local newspapers, interviewed several women, and found a nanny who could live-in full time. Rosa was a single woman of thirty-six who had come to America from Mexico to make a better life for herself. She told Xiao she had just lost a position with a wonderful family with two children who had moved to Chicago, and she had been anxious to find another job. Our lives were in an upheaval that words couldn't describe. Lawrence had to be weaned, and he had a hard time accepting formula from a bottle. Eventually, he adjusted, though not without a lot of tears. Joey and I were another story. Edward had taken an immediate family leave from his school. The principal was kind and understanding. How could he have been anything else?

Linda had been my rock, as Xiao and Matt had been my mother's. She spent as much time with me as she could. My brother Joey withdrew into himself. Two weeks after the funeral, he returned to school. My boyfriend John had been accepted to UFL to do his graduate work. He wanted to change his plans, but I insisted that he go, and at the end of August, John had moved there, sharing an apartment that he had taken with a young man whom he had never met. It had all been arranged through the school's message boards. I, too, had been accepted, but not wanting to go far from home under these circumstances, I applied late and was accepted at San Francisco State College to study for my M.A. degree in Journalism. I needed John more than ever, but understood that he had to go to school as planned. Just before leaving for Florida, John asked me to be his wife and placed a small engagement ring on my finger. He would be home for Thanksgiving. This was the one truly bright spot in my life. We loved each other, and everything would somehow be all right, I told myself.

Joey graduated from high school, and continued his studies at a local community college, not really having much of a head for school, and truly no real direction toward his future at that time. Edward had eventually gone back to work, trying to pick up the pieces of his broken life. Rosa turned out to be a terrific choice, and Lawrence thrived under her care. In the short time during the Thanksgiving break, John and I got married. We had a small religious ceremony at my family's Presbyterian Church. Afterward, we had gone for a lovely lunch with the family. I remember how difficult it had been to say goodbye when the holiday was over, but we both had to return to our respective schools. We never even had a honeymoon. It would have to wait until the time presented itself. It seemed much of my family's lives revolved around major holidays.

Two years later, we both graduated from school. We went on a short, wonderful honeymoon in Napa Valley. We moved into a lovely one-bedroom apartment not far from my family and began the difficult search for work in our chosen respective fields, he in radio and me in television. John hoped to work in radio programming. After a series of interviews, he found an entry-level position with a small, unknown radio station. He more or less "cut his teeth" there. He spent some time making photocopies, pulling and filing away albums, and doing whatever odds and ends the station manager found for him; he found it boring, but he learned a great deal. A friend from grad school, whom he had kept in touch with, called him and said he had heard of an opening as an assistant program manager at a popular rock radio station that was local to us. John interviewed for and got the position. He worked for KZAP radio for almost two years when, in 1980, the station was bought by KROY, which changed its format from rock to country music. While this was far from John's field of expertise, he was promoted to programming manager by the new owners based on his experience. He had to quickly learn about country music, which was very popular both locally and countrywide. Unfortunately, the new station's style was not a hit with the listeners. After updating his resume, John sent it out to several local stations and interviewed with KFRC. He felt it wouldn't look good that he had moved around so much in so short a period of time, but he wanted to like what he was doing. They offered him the programming manager's position and he accepted. They had recently changed to a nostalgia format by playing the rock hits of the sixties and seventies. This station's new format was well-received, fortunately for us. It was nice to hear rock music again. Truthfully, I had never loved country music.

I was working at a local TV station which became an affiliate of CBS News. I was unhappy, finding that there was very little opportunity since I was basically nothing more than a "gofer." Like John, I sent out my resume, and after several misses, I finally hit a new job. This position, which was in local cable news, offered much more room for growth. I liked the people very much, and felt as though this place could become "home.'

We still lived in our small apartment, working, spending time with our friends, and of course with Edward, Joey, and Lawrence. We settled into a happy pattern, decided to try for a baby, and I became pregnant within two months. My pregnancy was easy, and I never even had morning sickness. I was able to work until the beginning of my ninth month, and in May, after a reasonably easy labor, I gave birth to a beautiful baby girl. We named her Susan. When Susan was born we knew that, as a child of mixed race, she might struggle with identity issues. But we were convinced that we could bring her up in a home of love and support so that she could be happy and feel confident about who she was.

In the 1920s, a union between races was punishable by law. The Chinese Exclusion Act of 1882 was the beginning of restrictions to create a closed society. Later, in the 1940s in Nazi Germany, people were forced to walk through the streets identified as defilers of the race for marrying or having intimate relationships with those they called non-Aryans. In Africa, during the Apartheid era, 1948-1994, interracial relationships were punishable by law. The Ku Klux Klan called for the purification of American society with movements both in the 1860s and the 1920s. Klansmen in the South wore white hooded robes and masks to conceal their identities. African Americans had their houses burned down and entire families were lynched.

We planned for me to take off three months, which was what the station would allow me for maternity leave. After that, Susan would go into daycare. We had asked friends for recommendations and found a lovely place that made us feel comfortable about leaving our baby. It was so popular that we had to sign up when Susan was a month old to secure her a place. Daycare was expensive, but instead of hiring a nanny (equally expensive), we thought the interaction with other children as she grew would be invaluable. The next four years went by in a wink. Our lives were settled and calm, both of us happy with our careers, and the family at peace. Susan grew in leaps and bounds and time passed happily.

One afternoon, after a long day at the studio, I came home smiling. John kissed me hello, and said, “You seemed cool and collected.”

I had finally made it to stand-in anchor, which I been offered after my time writing stories called “readers” and "sacks" that involved the anchorperson explaining a news story as footage was shown. I also wrote "voice-overs," (similar to sacks), and handled other assignments leading up to my opportunity to actually appear on camera. After being a stand-in for some time, I was asked to replace the current anchor who was leaving to have a baby and become a stay-at-home mom. It seemed strange that she would give up her opportunity for a great career, but the truth was her ratings were poor, she wasn't well-liked, and everyone felt she left to save face. So this was my magic moment. It was a very small station, but I jumped at the offer.

Today was my very first broadcast working as a full-time newscaster. I told John how I tried to remain calm as I waited for the light on the camera signifying that I was "on the air." I told him I'd thought about the experience I had gained when I covered myriad times for the woman who left, and how I'd tried to be calm and steady as I reported a shooting, stock market changes, and other breaking stories. Although I had a great deal of experience by now, when I received my cue and saw the camera on me, I was terribly on edge, aware that this was my first telecast as a permanent anchorperson.

"Oh, John, I was a nervous wreck," I told him. "Not so much about my ability to deliver a good report, but I kept thinking that this time people were going to see me with different eyes because it had been announced beforehand that I was taking over the anchor spot. I knew I was being judged by both my bosses and the viewers."

John wrapped his arms around me and swung me in a circle. "You were fantastic, Mina, and you looked beautiful, as always. The blue dress was just the thing to make the viewers take notice of you."

"I hope so, John. The ratings will be in soon enough."

Chapter Two

Daly City, 1985

The eighties were a very different decade than the seventies. Ronald Reagan was president. The term "yuppie" became popular, denoting upwardly mobile young people. Popular TV shows like "Thirtysomething," as well as movies like "The Big Chill" and "Bright Lights, Big City" depicted this generation of young men and women who were plagued with anxiety and self-doubt. While they were successful, they were not necessarily happy. The expression "More was more in eighties fashion" was the truth. Loud colors, blue mascara, yellow eye shadow, and huge shoulder pads were the norm for women. Women wore "big hair" styles teased and sprayed to the hilt. Parachute pants and Wayfarer jeans were all part of the unisex styles of the time. Guys wore Member's Only jackets and heavy gold chains, while the girls wore tons of plastic jewelry.

In March of 1981, an assassination attempt was made

on President Ronald Reagan. He was struck by a bullet fired at him by a deranged twenty-five-year-old man, John Hinckley, Jr. It punctured his lung, but fortunately, he survived. In July of that year, Sandra Day O'Connor became the first woman appointed to the Supreme Court. That same year, as millions watched, Prince Charles of England married Lady Diana Spencer. The AIDS virus was identified, personal computers (PCs) were introduced by IBM, Beatle John Lennon was assassinated by a so-called fan, Mark David Chapman, and Egyptian President Anwar Sadat was assassinated, as well.

During the years 1982-1984, the movie "E. T.: The Extra-Terrestrial" was a box office sensation, while "Return of the Jedi," "Raiders of the Lost Ark," and "Beverly Hills Cop" made hundreds of millions of dollars at the box office. This was also the heyday of teen movies, with films like "The Breakfast Club" and "Pretty in Pink." Throughout this decade, family sitcoms became a new type of TV programming. "The Cosby Show," "Family Ties," "Roseanne," and "Married...With Children" were great favorites. VCRs were all the rage and people were able to rent videos of movies to watch on their TVs through these machines.

Next came cable television, a way of delivering TV to paying subscribers via radio frequency delivered through coaxial cables, or light pulses sent through fiber-optic cables. Cable TV had been around for some time, but by the end of the 1980s, sixty percent of American TV owners had cable service, the most revolutionary of all stations being MTV in 1981. This station played music videos that made stars out of the bands whose videos were shown. Michael Jackson's elaborate "Thriller" video helped sell 600,000 albums in the five days after its first broadcast. Additionally, MTV also influenced people worldwide, as many tried to copy fashions and hairstyles they saw in these videos. Artists like Madonna and others became fashion icons. Other popular hits were "Start Me Up," by the Rolling Stones, "I Just Called to Say I Love You," by Stevie Wonder, "Careless Whispers," by George Michael, and "Like a Virgin," by Madonna. "We are the World," created by Michael Jackson, was a video with many mega-stars of the time. It was recorded with a cause: to provide aid to Africa. "Do They Know It's Christmas?" recorded by Band Aid, was written in 1984 in reaction to television reports of the 1983-85 famine in Ethiopia.

The president announced a new defense program called Star Wars, Sally Ride became the first American woman in space, and Cabbage Patch kids—silly looking dolls, each totally different, that came with names on birth certificates—became all the rage. In 1983, the first artificial heart transplant surgery was performed on Barney Clark, a 61-year-old man who was too old to be eligible for a human heart. After the transplant, he lived for 112 days. In 1986, the space shuttle Challenger exploded, while the Russians launched the Mir space station. Elsewhere, in Chernobyl, Ukraine, a nuclear disaster occurred as a reactor exploded, releasing more than a hundred times the radiation of the bombs dropped on Hiroshima and Nagasaki during World War II. Thirty-one people died from the devastating blast, but there was no knowing the number of people who would eventually die from the long-term effects of radiation. The explosion dramatically changed the world's opinion about using nuclear energy for power.

October 19, 1987 was referred to as "Black Monday." Stock markets around the world crashed, shedding a huge value in a very short time. A London to New York Pan Am flight exploded over Lockerbie, Scotland on December 21, 1988. A total of 270 people were killed. Two Libyan terrorists were blamed for the bombing. One was found guilty of murder, but the other was acquitted. On November 9, 1989, the East German government announced that travel through the border to the West was open. This was referred to as "The Fall of the Berlin Wall." People were shocked and went to the border to see if it was true. Confused border guards let them through, and there was huge a celebration.

Our daughter Susan was sitting at the kitchen table having milk and cookies. She wore her brown hair in two short pigtails that always made me think of little horns. With her Chinese/Caucasian heritage, she was a very attractive child, as so many half-Asian children are. Her eyes were large, and one had to look twice to notice she was half-Asian. A bright and outgoing child, she was full of mischief. One way or the other, both in nursery school and now in Pre-K, if there was a melee, Susan was sure to be at the bottom of it. Several times we received notes and even phone calls from the teacher telling us about an incident in class. It was never anything serious. Susan wanted a toy another child was playing with so she grabbed it. Susan didn't raise her hand and instead called out, cutting off another child who was speaking. Susan didn't want to lie down on a mat for her nap as the other children happily did. Our pediatrician said she would outgrow the aggressiveness but would be bright, and probably a leader.

John was home and said, "By the way, Susan had another tiff with Julie today. It was nothing serious, just a doll Julie was playing with that Susan wanted. She actually pushed her and made her cry. I expect there will be a phone call later from Julie's mother again, and possibly Mrs. Rayburn, as well. I told Susan she couldn't watch television today, and she wasn't happy."

"I hope she starts to outgrow this stage soon," I answered, shaking my head.

After John left for the station, I ran upstairs to change out of my blue dress. Susan was playing in her room, banging her toys around. After her cookies and milk, she had stomped upstairs from the kitchen, clearly angry about her punishment of no TV that day. Checking on Susan, who was working on a puzzle and said she wasn't talking to me, I thought about how she had her Great-Grandmother Ling's feisty spirit. I hoped she would inherit her kindness, too.

All week I had been thinking about re-reading my grandmother's journal, which I did every so often. I retrieved the journal from the top shelf of my closet and began to read it. I had read it many times since my mother Yuming had given it to me. When Susan turned sixteen, she too would be given the gift of the diary. She would be the third generation female to own Ling's diary, I thought, opening the sturdy plastic box I kept it in. I read for forty-five minutes or so. Each time I read the translated journal, I felt I had more insight into the matriarch who had so bravely written this journal through all her adversity.

I peeked in on Susan often, and I looked at the clock and saw it was almost two-thirty. Her half-day of school brought her home at noon. The children were fed lunch a little before eleven, and she had her little snack when she got home with John and his news about her little tiff in school. I thought I would spend some time with her now that she had calmed down. In her room, she was playing with her two Cabbage Patch kids. She had a boy and a girl. They were so popular that last year when they came out, they were virtually impossible to buy. I remembered the news items from that past Christmas. The manufacturer claimed each doll was different. Head shapes, eye shapes, hair styles and colors varied, along with clothing options, too. Inside each box, there was a "birth certificate," with that particular "kid's" first and middle name on it. This made them as singular as the kids who adopted them. We had been fortunate to obtain them through a friend of Linda's who worked for the company. Susan's girl "kid" was named Viola Carmela, and the boy Garrison Rudolph. Such fancy names for the silly-looking dolls that the children were so crazy about, I thought.

I went into her pretty peach-and-mint green room. Her daybed was made up in a dainty floral print, with café curtains on the windows to match. "Are you tired, sweetie?" I asked.

"No, Mommy, I'm fine," she answered. "I wanna play."

"Please say I want to instead of I wanna," I said, thinking, good she's talking to me again.

She was seated at her little table. It was a small, square wooden table, painted mint green, and had four matching chairs.

I leaned down to her. "May I play, too?"

She nodded at me and I sat down on one of the tiny, low chairs. I saw that her plastic tea set was spread out on the table. "Should I pour tea for the children?" I asked.

"Garrison Rudolph hates tea, Mommy, don't you remember?" She gave me a questioning look.

I didn't, but making a quick recovery, I gestured to the little pitcher and said that perhaps Garrison Rudolph would like some apple juice.

"Yeah, he likes apple juice. Viola Carmela has a cold, and wants tea," she said matter-of-factly.

I didn't correct her for saying yeah. She had a wonderful imagination. "Maybe they would like to lie down for a little nap after their tea and apple juice," I inquired hopefully.

Susan rubbed her eyes, and I could see that she thought it

sounded like a good idea for the "kids" to have a nap, along with her. I tucked the three of them into her bed, making note of the time. I didn't want her to sleep too long or she'd never get to sleep later after her dinner and bath. Often, these little naps made the difference between a pleasant dinner for the two of us, or a confrontation with her complaining about the broccoli, or another healthy vegetable I placed on her plate. The variation in our schedules didn't give John and I a lot of time together, but there had been buzzing about changes at the radio station. John was hoping for a promotion to station manager this year, and with that, the possibility of different hours, and of course, more money. We might have to find an alternative means of taking Susan to and from school, but we would cross that bridge if we came to it.

While Susan napped, I went back into my bedroom and read a little more of Zhang Ling's journal. I was at the part when she and Liwei Chen, her second husband, had arrived at Angel Island in San Francisco. What a horrible man Liwei had been! I looked at the clock, and though it was always hard to put the journal down, I wanted to get a start on dinner while my little one napped. I planned to wake her as soon as I had put things together for our meal. I had defrosted chopped meat and was going to make a meatloaf, which Susan loved. Hopefully, she'd eat the mashed potatoes and carrots, two of the few vegetables she liked other than corn and string beans. I hoped dinner would be an easy affair for us tonight. As I prepared the meatloaf, John called.

"Just checking in," he said when I picked up the phone.

"All's quiet on the home front," I replied. "She's napping with the Cabbage Patch Kids and I just started putting dinner together."

Laughing, he said, "That's great. I just wanted to say hello, babe. I'll see you later."

John usually walked in around ten, ten-thirty. I reported to work at four-thirty A.M., and after Susan had eaten and been bathed, I put her to sleep. Shortly thereafter, I headed to bed myself. John would hang out in front of the living room TV for a while, and nuzzle me with a goodnight kiss when he finally came into bed. Half the time I slept through it. No sooner did I hang up with John when the phone rang again. It was Julie's mother. I listened to her tirade for a moment or two, and then I apologized, telling Mrs. Kleiner how sorry we were about the incident, and that Susan had been punished. I said hopefully she would get past this stage quickly. Mrs. Kleiner seemed appeased (until the next time, I thought), and hung up. I put an egg, breadcrumbs, and some salt, pepper, garlic powder, and onion powder into the ground beef and just as I immersed my hands in the gooey mixture, the phone rang again. I'd never get done at this rate, though it was still early. I quickly ran my hands under the water, the greasiness not really coming off under the tap. I grabbed the phone with a dish towel.

"Hello," I answered.

"Hey, what's doing?" It was Linda.

She and I had been best friends all our lives. Everyone thought she would marry her boyfriend from college, but it had ended quickly and quietly, and the following year, she met and eventually married her wonderful husband, Paul Russell. They had had a lovely wedding, and I had been her matron of honor. Two best friends had married two guys who had become best friends. Paul worked in customer relations. He had recently changed positions and now worked locally for a new, unique office supplies company called Staples, based in Framingham, Massachusetts. With branches blossoming all over the country, the company threatened to be a force to contend with. Linda and Paul also lived in Daly City, and we got together as often as we could, considering our crazy schedule. After getting her B.A., Linda changed career plans and wound up going to nursing school. Initially unable to find work in a local hospital, she had worked for an obstetrician in private practice for a while, but now was in the neo-natal unit of U.S.C.F. Benioff Children's Hospital. It was a small local hospital with an excellent reputation.

Paul and Linda had twin sons, Joseph and Ricky, whose name was actually Richard. They were three years old; sweet and well-behaved little boys. They were the exact opposite of Susan. Somehow, though, when they were together, they got along well. They had a wonderful nanny to take care of the boys, not unlike Rosa, who still lived with my father and had cared for my brother Lawrence when my mother died. We chatted for a while, catching up on everyday things. I told her it was my father Wu's birthday next week, and that I would see him for dinner, but I would feel uncomfortable, as usual. Although I had always had a reasonably decent relationship with my father and his family, I truly felt that Edward was my real father. Hanging up the phone, I made a mental note to call my father tomorrow. I would shower and get into bed myself after Susan was down for the night. I loved and worried about Edward, and basically I knew I just saw my real dad to assuage my guilt. It had taken quite a while for things to adjust after my mother's death. Edward seemed like he'd never recover, and though he worked and functioned, he wasn't the same. Lawrence was the great joy in his life.

Joey lived in San Francisco, and was happily ensconced in his job as a computer programmer. He had finally found himself, and had made a wonderful career choice. He was single, and liked being the free agent he was, dating first this girl, and then that one. Thank heavens Rosa had stayed on, no longer a nanny, but actually a wonderful housekeeper. My father was so grateful for her. My brother Lawrence was a sweet young man who had infinite patience with Susan's tantrums. Fortunately, she didn't have them too often with him. She seemed to have a better rapport with boys than girls. Lawrence had straight, dark hair, flashing black, slightly lidded eyes, unusual for a Chinese, and a somewhat broad-bridged nose. Lawrence and Joey were the last unmarried children of all Asian stock in the family. My grandfather, Song Bao, had passed away two years ago, as had Mrs. Dai, Wu's mother. There was no one left from that generation to pass on the traditions of our Chinese heritage. Sadly, neither Mandarin, Cantonese, nor Shanghainese would be heard in any of our homes any longer. I was married to an American, who of course spoke no Chinese, and Joey preferred to date American girls.

Chapter Three

Daly City, 1988

This year Edward met a lovely Chinese woman who had recently started teaching at his school. They were friends first, but eventually, he invited her out to a movie. He hadn't had a very active social life since my mother passed away, and we were very happy to see him trying to get out of his rut. He was still an attractive man, hardworking, and devoted to all of us. Helen Chu was also widowed, having lost her husband several years earlier. She had two grown daughters, both of whom were married with families of their own, and they no longer lived in California.

We got together for the first time on a Sunday afternoon after she and Edward had been dating for about six months. We chose a local restaurant with a quiet atmosphere where we knew we wouldn't be rushed and we could spend some time getting to know her a little over a light meal. In the car on the way home, John and I exchanged thoughts.

"I actually liked her a great deal," I remarked to John after the dinner.

"I did, too," he said thoughtfully. "She seems bright, and

she's certainly attractive enough. I think Edward has grown to care for her."

Helen was a tall woman, almost Edward's height and a couple of years his senior. She had thick, short brown hair that framed her pretty face. While she wasn't beautiful, she had wonderfully expressive eyes, and always seemed to be smiling. We both found her warm and charming. Four months later, Edward asked Helen to marry him, and she accepted. We thought it was wonderful. What a terrific woman she must be to be willing to share in the raising of Edward's thirteen-year-old son, Lawrence. We were so pleased that finally he wouldn't be alone. They seemed to have so much in common. They were both teachers, extensive readers, and had the time to travel because of their summers off when Lawrence was away at camp.

They planned and quickly executed a lovely wedding. We were thrilled to watch the simple ceremony. They got married in church with our family, as well as Helen's, present. Her two married children and their spouses attended, along with her three grandchildren. Helen wore a simple pale gray dress and a small hat with a veil. One of Helen's little granddaughters was the flower girl. Lawrence was Edward's best man. Friends of both the bride and groom's side joined in wishing them happiness for their future together. They held a small reception in a private room in a local restaurant.

It was wonderful to celebrate the usual yearly holidays with Helen at our table. She was a second generation American. Her grandparents had come from a small town in China, where Mandarin was spoken. An only child, she had been born in Indianapolis. Both her American-born parents had been teachers, and it seemed a natural progression that she too would teach. Her mother was a college professor who had been given an opportunity to teach at a small college near San Francisco, so they made the decision to relocate. Her husband had taught high school Biology in Indianapolis, and fortunately, he was able to secure a position, too. Helen was eleven when her family moved. Unfortunately, neither of her parents were still living, one having succumbed to cancer, the other to a horrible car accident. All the more reason she was so happy to have been welcomed into our family. They bought a lovely townhouse in the Daly City area because Edward was thoughtful enough to realize it was unfair to expect Helen to live in the home that he and his family had shared.

Susan had settled down a great deal. No longer as pushy and difficult, she was very well-liked by both her teachers and friends. She had a lovely circle of girlfriends that she spent time with. Several of them attended the same dancing school she went to. She had been taking ballet and tap for several years now, and while she would never be a ballerina, she was learning a great deal about grace and poise. Her recital was only a few weeks away, and we were looking forward to it immensely.

Along with her dance classes, she had begun learning to play the violin. She seemed to have a musical ear and didn't balk too much when she had to practice every day. We had an established routine of dance class after school on Tuesdays and her violin lesson on Thursdays, both of which John was able to take her to since he had become station manager and his hours had changed. Still, it was difficult for him as he often needed to stay at the station after his usual time to leave. Because of our now-overlapping schedules, we decided to hire a live-in nanny. Ana, our previous nanny, had recommended a friend of hers who had recently become divorced and needed the money. Donna Rodriguez was the perfect match for us. We all liked her immediately, and she was wonderful with Susan. She drove her to both her dancing school classes and her violin lessons.

The day of the dance recital was a beautiful day in mid-June. Susan was dancing in two numbers. I particularly loved the tap dance "Don't Worry, Be Happy," by Bobby McFerrin.

The other song was more of a jazz number called "Hippy, Hippy Shake," sung by a fun group called the Georgia Satellites. The costume for the hippy number was baggy black and neon print pants that were tight at the ankle; they were covered with multi-colored peace signs. This was paired with a neon pink crop top. We were told to tease their hair and apply a lot of makeup. The jazz costume was only a little less outrageous. It consisted of acid wash shorts and a blue tee shirt with a large smiley face superimposed on it. With this outfit, their hair was to be in high ponytails. Two of the mothers had volunteered to help them change between numbers and re-do their hair.

The whole family came to see the show, including Joey, and of course, Donna. It was held in the auditorium of a local high school. We cheered and whistled for each of her numbers and when it was over, Susan came running out to find us in the lobby. It had been her fourth recital, and she was a real trooper. I handed her a wrist corsage of pink carnations and told her how fantastic she had been. Helen had bought her a box of chocolates, and Donna an adorable little handbag that made her feel like she was very grown up. All her dance friends came over to say good-bye. We went to a lovely Cantonese restaurant where we had made a reservation. It was a truly wonderful day, and John and I were so proud of our little girl.

Chapter Four

Daly City, 1991

The nineties were the last decade of the 20th century. It felt like a big deal, as if everything would be different in the last decade of this second millennium. Culturally, it was a time of multiculturalism, as well as alternate media. Movements such as "grunge," the "rave scene," and "hip hop" spread around the world to young people via cable TV and the Internet.

The Gulf War saw Iraq left in severe debt after the 1980 war with Iran. President Saddam Hussein accused Kuwait of flooding the market with oil, thus driving down prices. As a result, on August 2, 1990, Iraqi forces invaded and conquered Kuwait. The United Nations immediately condemned the action and a coalition force, led by the United States, was sent to the Persian Gulf. United Nations forces drove the Iraqi army from Kuwait in just four days. The Kurds and Shiites then rose up in revolt, and Saddam Hussein barely retained power. In November 1990, England's Prime Minister

Margaret Thatcher resigned, having been in office since 1979. Hurricane Andrew struck Florida, leaving great destruction in its wake. In the Persian Gulf, a massive oil spill caused considerable damage to the wildlife, especially in areas surrounding Kuwait and Iraq. The Belfast Agreement was signed, declaring a joint commitment to a peaceful resolution of the territorial dispute between Ireland and the U.K. over Northern Ireland. The decade was seen as a time of great prosperity in the United States under the Presidency of Bill Clinton.

A major happening was the dissolution of the Soviet Union, which led to a realignment and reconsolidation of economic and political power across the world. The Union of Soviet Socialist Republics (USSR) ceased to exist on December 26, 1991. Soviet President Mikhail Gorbachev resigned, and new Russian President Boris Yeltsin took control. It was an unprecedented time of peace and prosperity. Israeli Prime Minister Yitzhak Rabin and Palestinian Prime Minister Yasser Arafat agreed to the peace process at the culmination of the Oslo Accords. This was negotiated by United States President Bill Clinton on September 13, 1993. The Palestinian Liberation Organization (PLO) would now recognize Israel's right to exist, while Israel permitted the creation of an autonomous Palestinian Nation Authority.

While things had quieted down in the Middle East, in Rwanda and Bosnia, ethnic conflicts arose leading to genocide. In Rwanda, there was a genocidal mass slaughter of the Tutsi and moderate Hutu that was perpetrated by the members of the Hutu majority. During an approximate one-hundred-day period from April 1994 to mid-July, an estimated 500,000 to 1,000,000 Rwandans were killed. In Bosnia, an ethnic cleansing campaign took place. The term Bosnian genocide refers to the genocide committed by Bosnian Serb forces in 1995. Additionally, the term refers to the ethnic cleansing campaign throughout areas controlled by the Christian Orthodox of the Army of the Republika Srpska that took place during the 1992-1995 Bosnian War.

Major league baseball went on strike on August 12, 1994, thus ending the season, canceling the World Series for the first time in ninety years. American NBA basketball player Michael Jordan became a major sports and pop culture icon idolized by millions worldwide. U.S. President Bill Clinton was caught in a media-frenzied scandal involving inappropriate relations with White House intern Monica Lewinsky. This was first announced on January 21, 1998. After the U.S. House of Representatives impeached Clinton on December 19, 1998 for perjury under oath following an investigation by federal prosecutor Kenneth Starr, the Senate acquitted Clinton of the charges on February 12, 1999 and he finished his second term.

The 1990s were an incredibly revolutionary decade for digital technology. Cell phones were large and expensive. Only a few million people used online services in 1990, as the World Wide Web had only just been invented. Computers, the Internet, and the World Wide Web had been a groundbreaking idea. Now, their time had come. They began to appear in the home, not just the workplace. Computers operated by being connected to a telephone line. The screeching sound of the modem, as it was called, was loud, and the connection didn't al-

ways happen. It often took several tries to connect. By now, the Internet and the World Wide Web had caught on in schools, too. Individuals began to create what was known as web pages. Schools allowed students to use the Internet as a source for papers and projects. Basically, it was an "online" library. There were ways for schools to install web servers and provide faculty with a way to these instructional web pages. The first web browser went online in 1993. Search engines, a way of accessing information, sprang up. Yahoo! and Google were two of the popular ones. No one could have predicted at the time what a huge impact they would have on the entire world!

"Y2K" spread fear throughout the U.S., and eventually the world, toward the end of the decade, particularly 1999. All feared possible massive computer malfunctions on January 1, 2000. Many people stocked up on supplies for fear of a worldwide disaster. Ultimately, there were no globally significant computer failures when the clocks rolled over into 2000. The Intel Pentium processor was developed, and people started using email. Instant messaging and Buddy Lists were popular with people using AIM, AOL (America Online), and Yahoo! to communicate. The MP3 player, iMac, CD-Rom drive, CD burner drives, Microsoft Windows on PCs, Netscape Navigator, and Internet Explorer came to the fore.

Cars became rounder in shape, and Lexus and Infiniti became new upscale coveted brands. The Human Genome project began. The Hubble Space Telescope, which revolutionized astronomy, was launched in 1990. Comet Shoemaker-Levy 9 broke apart and collided with Jupiter in July 1994. On October 3, 1995, in a hugely followed trial, O.J. Simpson was found not guilty of double-murder of ex-wife Nicole Brown Simpson and her friend, Ronald Goldman. The Hale-Bopp comet swung past the sun for the first time in 4,200 years in April 1997. Global warming as an aspect of climate change became a major concern.

Baby Boomers, born post-WWII (1946-1964), Generation X, and Generation Y (the Millennial Generation, early 1980s through early 2000s) brought tattoos and body piercing to great popularity. "Retro" styles of the sixties and seventies were also prevalent. Mother Theresa died, John F. Kennedy, Jr. and his wife died in a plane crash. Best Picture Academy Award winners were: "Dances With Wolves" 1990, "The Silence of the Lambs" 1991, "Unforgiven" 1992, "Schindler's List" 1993, "Forrest Gump" 1994, "Braveheart" 1995, "The English Patient" 1996, "Titanic" 1997, (which became the highest grossing film of all time at 1.8 billion dollars worldwide), "Shakespeare in Love" 1998, and "American Beauty" 1999. On television, sitcoms were popular. "Seinfeld," "Cheers," "Friends," "The Fresh Prince of Bel Aire," and "Everybody Loves Raymond" were favorites. People were watching medical dramas like "ER" and "Grey's Anatomy." The teen soap genre, such as "Beverly Hills 90210" became popular throughout the decade. "The Simpsons," an animated sitcom, which had debuted earlier in December 1989, became a domestic and international success. It would eventually be considered an institution of pop culture. It spawned others such as "Beavis and Butt-Head," "South Park," and "Family Guy."

In music, the nineties were a decade of change. MTV shifted away from the video format and radio splin-

tered into separate niches. U2 was the most popular band of the time. "Grunge," "gangsta rap," "R&B," (rhythm and blues), "teen pop," "Eurodance," "electronic" dance music, "punk rock" (mainly because of the band Green Day, which would also help create a new genre, "pop punk"), were popular. This would be the decade that alternative rock became mainstream. Nirvana, Pearl Jam, Soundgarden, Blink-182, Weezer, The Offspring, Red Hot Chili Peppers, Gin Blossoms, Third Eye Blind, Soul Asylum, Stone Temple Pilots, Three Doors Down, Smashing Pumpkins, Everclear, Bush, and Alice in Chains were some of the popular alternative bands.

Across the pond, in the U.K., other alternative bands like Oasis, Radiohead, and The Verve were big sellers. Female pop icons The Spice Girls became the most commercially selling group since The Beatles. Contemporary R&B, popular among adults, included Kenny G, Michael Bolton, Celine Dion, Mariah Carey, Whitney Houston, Sade, En Vogue, Destiny's Child, and Boyz II Men. In country music, Billy Ray Cyrus, Shania Twain, and Garth Brooks took over the charts. Throughout the decade, videogaming on TVs was constantly offering newer and better ways to play. Sony's PlayStation became the top-selling game console and changed the standard media storage type from cartridges to compact discs. My Little Pony produced by Hasbro was popular in the early part of the nineties. Skip It, Transformers, Care Bears, Jenga, Furby, Pokemon, roller blades, and Razor scooters were a hit with youngsters and teens alike. Harry Potter books were all the rage, as was the Goosebumps series. Young women rushed to have their hair styled in the "Rachel," after Jennifer Aniston's character on

"Friends." Doc Maarten's shoes and flannel shirts in the grunge vein were popular with guys and girls. Light-up sneakers and jelly shoes were also well-liked among the younger set.

John and I had thriving careers. Between us, we had a comfortable income that afforded us the opportunity to give a good life to our daughter. John and I had been trying for a long time to have another child, but that joy had evaded us for now, so Susan was our one and only, and at times we over-indulged her. She was almost eleven and was going through a shy stage, feeling uncomfortable with her pending puberty. She looked a great deal like the few pictures of her Great-Grandmother Ling in the back of the journal. They had been taken long ago, with the few other family pictures that had been mailed from Shanghai many years earlier. Slender, and not very tall, Susan was a fifth-grader and would go to middle school in the fall. I had no idea where the time had flown. For a number of years now, John and I had been lucky enough to be on fairly overlapping schedules. With me a prime-time news anchor and John a station manager, it gave us a greater amount of time to spend together as a family. Donna was no longer with us. We had given her plenty of notice so she could find another position. She had been wonderful, and we kept in touch with her. The schools had closed for the Christmas break and my brother Lawrence was coming to stay for a few days. He was in high school, and was a very good student.

After John and I got married, I had taken over the special joy of creating Christmas for my family in the tradition of my mother, Yuming. Edward, Helen, Joey and his girlfriend and Lawrence were joining us, and Linda, Paul, and their twins Joe and Ricky were coming, too. Christmas Eve was Monday night and I wanted to finish my food shopping for the holiday meal. This year we wouldn't be going to The Donaldina Cameron House, as it had been known for some time. Donaldina

Cameron, my grandmother's savior, known as the "Angry Angel of Chinatown" had passed away in 1968. It had changed so much that we decided to just mail our yearly contribution, along with a letter expressing our heartfelt thanks for what its existence has meant to our family. There was no one there who might have remembered Zhang Ling.

Susan and I planned to go food shopping on Saturday. She had grown up so much and loved to help in the kitchen, the way I used to with my mother. At times like these, I missed her a great deal. We were planning to bake on Sunday, as well as prep for the actual meals. I had bought an attractive new cloth tablecloth with matching napkins. The ever-thoughtful Linda always brought a beautiful flower arrangement for the table and it would look lovely on my new tablecloth. I washed all the larger serving pieces that hadn't fit in the dishwasher the night before, and Susan helped dry them. Both Xiao and her husband were in a nursing home and it was too much for them to join us. It was heartbreaking to see the last generation leaving us little by little.

Later, in the supermarket, Susan ran into her close friend Lisa Taub, also shopping with her mom. Not only did they spend a ton of time at one another's houses, but they had gone to dancing school together since they were five. I had a brief conversation with Lisa's mother while the girls made tentative plans to get together during the school break. A woman walking with her daughter and son came down the aisle we were in, and after they had passed the two girls covered their mouths, whispering and pointing to the boy whom they obviously thought was cute, or whatever almost-eleven-year-olds thought about boys. We parted, wheeling our carts in opposite directions, calling out Christmas and Hanukkah greetings to one another. Later, just after we unpacked the groceries, Lawrence, Edward and Helen arrived. It was wonderful to see my little brother, as always.

"Wow, Lawrence," I exclaimed, as he came through the

door, “you must have grown another two inches since Thanksgiving!”

He smiled, shyly, as he did when someone complimented him. He was really growing up. His face, still broad, was changing. He looked so much more mature. I noticed he was breaking out a bit and wondered if I should mention skin care to him or just mind my own business. I decided to say nothing. He was a typical teenager, thinking he knew everything, and probably would not want my opinion on anything. Helen could handle it. I had a hard enough time dealing with Susan’s pre-teen moods. Lawrence went upstairs to put his bag in the guest room as he would be staying over. He usually shared the room with Joey, but his brother was bringing his current girlfriend this time, and wouldn’t be coming until tomorrow. We planned to order pizza for dinner tonight as I had too much cooking and preparing to do. By seven o’clock, everyone had arrived. Edward, John, Paul and Lawrence all sat down to talk and watch a football game on TV. The men were drinking Heineken beers and eating chips and dip. I had put out cans of Coke for Lawrence. I knew he would have preferred a brew like the rest of the men, but I didn’t think it was appropriate. He could do what he wanted outside. I looked back into the living room and thought for once all was well with the world. Helen was a great help in the kitchen. She was so lively and warm, and I enjoyed her company very much.

The following morning I took a fast shower and threw on a pair of jeans and a hot pink tee shirt. It was early, and a lot of the house was still sleeping, including Helen. I was surprised but figured she’d be up soon enough and offer her talents in the kitchen. I wanted to get started on the chocolate cake and apple pies. I would make the pies first, since Susan didn’t mind helping to peel apples, and I could use the help when she got up. I always made two pies, since they were the “best sellers” every year. I made sure there was plenty so anyone who wanted to could take some home. There were always takers. Susan came to help, and not long after, Helen showed up. I handed them both aprons.

Christmas Eve dinner was lovely. My cooking was well appreciated. We started with a crisp salad of baby greens with cranberries, pears, and pecans with a fig and balsamic vinegar dressing. Everyone oohed and aahed over the prime ribs and gravy. I had made a traditional Christmas ham as well. Mashed potatoes and a medley of roasted root vegetables completed the meal. There was a lot of food, and everyone dug in until they were quite full. Despite that, dessert was well received. We sat over coffee and tea, eating way too much of the fattening, but deliciously decadent desserts I had baked. Xiao had baked a huge fruit cake as well, and Helen, who didn't bake had brought a platter of fresh fruit. We all had a wonderful time reminiscing, as we always did on this night, remembering lost loved ones and some of the wonderful times we had all shared. I thought about how the meal was so entirely American and felt a moment's regret that I hadn't served anything from our Chinese heritage. Later, the women all helped me clean up. Joey's girlfriend Amanda seemed lovely, and thanked me profusely for the invite, telling me how much she had enjoyed the meal, and how kind it was of us to invite her. Her parents lived in Boston and she had decided to relocate to California. I wondered why she hadn't gone home for Christmas but kept it to myself. Everyone finally headed home with their "doggy bags," exchanging hugs and kisses with all of us, as well as New Year's greetings.

"I'll talk to you before the holiday," Linda said, as she headed home with Paul and the boys.

"Yes, Lin," I said, and then, "see you all next year!"

In the morning, we opened all our gifts, and I made bacon and eggs for everyone. Later, after more football, we would eat the ton of leftovers from last night's dinner.

This year, New Year's Eve was a quiet night. We went to an early dinner at a lovely Italian restaurant with some good friends of ours from John's station, and after, the small group stopped back at one of the couple's homes to ring in the New Year with champagne and toasts for all good wishes in the coming year. Susan had gone to a sleepover. Five other girls had been invited, and Mrs. Connors, her friend Allison's mom, planned to order pizza and had bought loads of snacks that would be a hit with the girls. One day they were on diets, the next they ate all the junk food they could find. It was very sweet of Mrs. Connors and her husband to host this little get-together for the girls. John drove her over before we went out, and on New Year's Day, he picked her up and she came home all bubbly and excited, asking if she could get some more posters for the walls in her room. It was already hard to find the walls, but it took so little to make her happy these days. A poster and a couple of bottles of bright nail polish, and she was thrilled.

I decided that I wanted to celebrate Chinese New Year this year as we had occasionally in the past. Sometimes I just felt so nostalgic, as I had at Christmas dinner. My mother, Yuming, had loved the holiday. It fell on February 15th this year and I thought it would be a fun thing to do. I wouldn't be cooking, but rather I wanted us to go to lunch at one of the local restaurants, Dim Sum King. We all really enjoyed the traditional food and decor associated with Chinese New Year. Outside, there was a dragon parade, and myriads of Chinese people, as well as Caucasians, filled the streets. We had done this several times in Susan's lifetime, and I was always happy to enhance what little she knew of her Chinese culture.

The winter passed uneventfully, and the school year came to a close. Susan and her friends had been going to Camp Loma Mar for the past two summers. They had gone away for two weeks each time. This year, she had begged us to let her stay longer. We agreed to allow her to go for the whole month of July. The camp was located about an hour's drive from us in the city of the same name and was a YMCA camp. I had begun shopping for new clothes for her in early June, and she would be packed and ready to leave right after the 4th of July. Aside from Lisa, only one other friend, Allison, was going this year, but would also be staying for the month. Their friend Ellen's parents were in the middle of a divorce, and she and her younger brother would be spending the summer with their grandparents who lived in the Poconos in Pennsylvania. Susan and Lisa told me what was going on several weeks earlier. They were very upset about the whole situation.

We spent a fun 4th of July at a barbecue at Linda and Paul's house, and that Sunday we loaded Susan's trunk into the car and headed off to Loma Mar. Susan was bubbly and excited, having been in touch with several of her friends from past seasons who were also returning to camp. We got there around noon and helped her settle into her bunkhouse of nine girls. We had lunch there and said hello to many familiar faces. Lisa and Allison were already there, and shortly thereafter, Aileen, a girl they knew, arrived with her parents and her older sister Jackie, who also attended the camp. Jackie was almost fourteen, and while she considered Susan and her sister and friends to be babies, we were happy she was there and knew she would keep an eye on the girls. Finally, it was time to leave. We kissed Susan goodbye and got into the car.

"Bye, Mom and Dad," she called, running alongside as we drove away.

"Have a good time, sweetheart," I told her. "Please remember to write."

"I will, Mommy," she agreed, "I will. Bye, Daddy."

She looked very young as we drove away. We had decided to go on vacation ourselves and would be leaving for Vancouver Island in Canada the following Monday. We were staying at a small resort for a week, and we were both looking forward to it very much.

We had a fantastic time on our vacation which seemed to be over before it even started. That's the way good times are. Susan kept her promise and wrote us every week. She was having a great summer until suddenly there started to be incidents of her being bullied by three girls in her bunkhouse. Although of similar age, Susan was not as grown-up as these girls, having turned out to be a late bloomer. She was a little babyish regarding her style of dressing, no desire to wear lip gloss, and was shy around boys. I didn't push her; she was still a little girl in my eyes. These other girls were much more socially advanced, wore clothing that was just a little too grown-up for their age, (what were their mothers thinking, these kids were ten-eleven years old?), and had picked Susan to be their victim. They made fun of her and teased her about her clothes. When Ethan, one of the boys at camp, asked her to dance at one of their little parties, Susan was extremely flustered and barely able to respond to him. Later, in the bathroom, three girls had approached her and made fun of her.

"Uh, uh, um, uh, no thank you, Ethan," one of the girls said, parroting Susan's uncomfortable response to the boy.

"Duh, duh, dumb, duh," another said, laughing. "Chinee girl no like boys," another said.

Later, back in the bunkhouse, they whispered about her to the other girls, all of whom looked at her and laughed. This was just the start of the harassment and bullying that Susan would be subjected to. Aileen stuck up for her, but it was a waste of time. Lisa and Allison were in a different bunkhouse, so they weren't aware of how bad the bullying had become. After two weeks of teasing, whispering about her to the other girls, hiding all of her underwear, and general abuse, she finally said something to me during a phone call.

John and I were terribly upset and decided to drive to the camp and discuss the situation with the managers. Unfortunately, it wasn't the first time they had seen this behavior, and they were quite upfront with the ringleaders regarding the repercussions involved if it didn't stop immediately. There would be no further warnings. The next step would be involvement of their parents, possibly leading to prorating of the money paid, and asking the girls to leave. The girls must have felt the threat to be serious and left Susan alone after that. Still, she was wary and on edge, and clearly was happy when the month was over and she could come home. It was a shame since she had greatly looked forward to her time at camp.

Chapter Five

Daly City, 1996

Middle school started and ended with barely a blink of the eye. Susan was pretty and petite. She was still close friends with Lisa and Allison and even started to socialize with the opposite sex a bit, though she was still shy. She got good grades and loved all her English classes. By the time she started high school, she blended in well with the potpourri of kids coming in from various other middle schools in the area. From middle school on, the students had more independence as they moved to different classrooms and teachers for different subjects. In high school, every grade counted toward their official transcripts, which would be used in their college applications.

Susan's self-assurance had finally grown, and she was now a teenaged version of the smart, personable little girl she had been. Now, at almost sixteen, and in her sophomore year of high school, she excelled in English and French, and did well in history and science, although she was never a good math student, and algebra gave her a run for her money. She landed a coveted job as one of the writers for the school newspaper. Additionally, she had tried out for, and been accepted as a cheerleader, and she had a huge circle of friends, many of whom were boys. There were still sleepovers, but now the girls spent their time setting and styling each other's hair, giving each other manicures and pedicures, and pouring over magazines like Teen, YM, Cosmopolitan, Glamour, and Seventeen. These teen magazines functioned on the assumption that a dumbed-down version of grown-up information was the way to go. Many of the articles included their peers' false embarrassing moments. They offered perspectives on timely information, many silly and quite able to misinform these easily-persuaded, gullible girls. Susan had been out on a few dates with local boys, with either John or the boy's parent driving them to the movies. Occasionally, the boys had their own cars. John was nervous about this, but Susan was growing up and had a good head on her shoulders. She, too, would be driving soon. We knew all the kids well, and put our trust in Susan to execute good judgment. It was a happy time for our family.

My brother Joey was also happy. He was now married to a lovely woman named Joanie, and they still lived in Daly City with their two girls, Jeanine and Cheryl. He was doing quite well for himself in the computer industry, having gotten in at just the right time. Joanie worked in marketing. My grandfather had passed away peacefully several years earlier. He had lived a long life, but had never been the same after my grandmother died. He was found by a nurse who went into his room at the nursing home one evening while he was sleeping. I saw my father Wu and his family occasionally but our relationship had become very strained over the years.

Later that year, Susan complained about a cold that was lingering longer than seemed usual. She was tired, pale, losing weight, and very run down, and her glands were swollen. I took her to our doctor who decided to run some basic tests. He suspected mononucleosis, also known as the "kissing disease." Infectious mononucleosis, "mono", was usually transmitted through kissing, but can be transmitted through a cough or sneeze, or even sharing a glass or food utensils, he explained. The tests didn't confirm his suspicions completely, even though her symptoms fit the norm. She had a bad sore throat, and occasionally fever, which got worse over two weeks, and she was constantly fatigued. The glands in her neck, as well as other places in her body, were swollen, and she had a lot of headaches.

Because of the swollen glands, the extreme fatigue, fever, and night sweats, he began to suspect a more serious problem and referred us to an oncologist. Multiple symptoms pointed to a much more serious disease; he wanted us to see a specialist about possible Hodgkin's lymphoma, a cancer of the lymphatic system. He suggested we make an appointment to see Dr. David Saperstein at Davis Medical Center, part of the University of California. He said it was a top-ranked facility with a specific department called the Section of Pediatric Hematology/Oncology. Dr. Saperstein was the right person to see. Our doctor offered to get in contact with the office to speed our ability to get an appointment. No one slept much that night, and the following morning we obtained an appointment to meet with Dr. Saperstein two days later. Susan was strangely calm. I can't say the same for John and me.

Dr. Saperstein turned out to be a man in his mid-fifties, with a pleasant smile, and kindly manner. He told us a bit about the specialized center he was affiliated with. There were teams of specialists who specifically dealt with children and teenagers with cancer. He explained he couldn't make a diagnosis without many tests. He started by giving Susan a complete physical examination, and made a detailed record of her medical history. Blood and urine were taken. We left and headed home, anxious for the results of the tests, yet scared of what we might be about to face.

The next day we went back, and Susan had a chest X-ray and a CAT scan. The scan was done using contrast material that made abnormal areas easier to see. After receiving those results, which took agonizingly long, the doctor asked us to come back as he had ordered a lymph node biopsy where a sample of tissue would be removed from the right lymph node in Susan's neck. After several more days, Susan had the biopsy done, and we once again went home to wait for results. Finally, we sat in the doctor's office while he confirmed that Susan did indeed have Hodgkin's leukemia. He explained that it is cancer of the lymphatic system, whose job it is to fight disease and infections. He told us that cells in this system abnormally reproduce, which eventually cause tumors to grow. It can spread to other organs and tissues in the body. The next step, he said, was for Susan to have a PET scan to further determine which three possible types of the disease were active, and if it had spread to other parts of the body. His office scheduled that test for the following day. Fortunately, John and I had no problems getting coverage from our jobs.

The results of the PET scan were received by the doctor a day later. He told us that it was doubly certain that she had Hodgkin's lymphoma. He explained that most often at Susan's age the disease progressed quickly because of the sudden onset of symptoms, and because these lymphomas grow quite fast. This disease is very common in children and teenagers. I started to cry, but composed myself as John put his arm around my shoulder. Susan just sat in the chair across from Dr. Saperstein. Her face was unreadable, but I couldn't help but think how stoic she was. The doctor was calm and gentle as he explained to us what treatment he recommended. He described to us the many members of the Section's team. He himself was a pediatric oncologist. There were surgeons, radiation oncologists, pathologists, and pediatric oncology nurses. He explained that the center also had psychologists, social workers, nutritionists, rehabilitation and physical therapists, and others, all of whom could support and educate the patient and the entire family. There would be chemotherapy.

He suggested that we consider harvesting some of Susan's eggs to be frozen prior to the chemotherapy. He went on to tell us that the first chemo that would be used would most likely not make Susan sterile; however, if that didn't give the results we hoped for, the egg harvest would be a back-up as the next type of chemo would most likely cause sterility.

"How is that done?" Susan asked, her face even paler than before.

"Well, Susan, you'll be working with a fertility specialist. You'll be taking daily injections of hormonal drugs, which you will be able to administer at home, to stimulate your ovaries. You and your parents will be taught how to do this. After this treatment, your eggs will be harvested during a surgical procedure. Then your eggs will be frozen. You'll be asleep during the procedure, and you won't have to stay overnight in the hospital. When this has been accomplished, we'll begin the chemotherapy." He went on, "In many cases, with children or teenagers, the lymphoma may not cause symptoms until it has grown or spread. Your disease is at stage IIB, Susan. This is a common scenario because of the sudden onset of the symptoms," he explained, "as well as the fact that these lymphomas tend to grow very quickly. What's happening in your body is the cells in the lymphatic system are reproducing abnormally. This is causing the tumors that we found in your lungs to grow. These cells are abnormally large, and are called Reed-Sternberg cells. We have found these cells in one side of your diaphragm, but not in your lymph nodes, which is favorable. Certain factors help us make this determination. As with any type of cancer, the prognosis varies greatly from patient to patient. Your treatment, Susan, will be structured specifically around you. The treatment will be aggressive in order for us to achieve the best prognosis. I will tell you that it is the most treatable type of Hodgkin's lymphoma."

I sat there listening, but not believing. How could this be real? Susan was only going on sixteen. My mind wandered as

I tried to accept the reality of the situation.

"I'd like to begin the fertility injections immediately," Dr. Saperstein was saying.

"Is my hair going to fall out?" Susan asked.

"Yes, Susan," he said gently, "more than likely."

We drove home in silence. Everyone's fear was palpable. When we got to the house, Susan went up to her room, wanting to be alone with her thoughts. I sat down at my computer and did a lot of reading. I learned some specifics about the disease. I read that it was a cancer of the lymphatic system, part of the immune system that fights disease and infections. I remembered about swollen glands, which sometimes accompanied a cold. I had them many times myself. Who could imagine that these cells would grow into tumors? The doctor told us that Susan had three in her chest area. This cancer is the third most common childhood cancer in the United States. I read and read.

The next day my heart was heavy, and I was unable to concentrate. I went to the studio and did my job by rote, knowing that I hadn't been my usual charming self when I presented the news report. I hadn't been my charming self for a while. Later that day, when I got home, I knocked gently on Susan's bedroom door. She had stayed home from school again.

"Come in, Mom," she said, shutting off her TV.

I sat down on the side of her bed, pulling her into my arms. She began to sob, and I just held her until she finally stopped.

"We're going to beat this baby, we are," I told her, my heart breaking.

"Why did this happen to me, Mom?"

"I can't answer that, sweetheart, but we'll follow the instructions the doctors give us, and we'll get through this together. I know it's easy for me to say."

Susan just nodded, lay down, and turned her back to me. I left her to her thoughts, knowing that nothing was going to calm her tonight, or for many nights to come. John had come home, and was in the living room trying to watch TV.

"Want some coffee, honey?" I asked.

He glanced up at me and smiled. "Yes, as a matter of fact, I'd like some"

"Are you hungry? I'll make us all some sandwiches."

Susan came down when I called her, and forced herself to eat some of the tuna fish sandwich.

Chapter Six

Daly City, 1996

Time seemed to be suspended. Susan took a health leave from school, and we were able to arrange home schooling for her. Surprisingly, after the initial shock, she became very strong and stoic, with an attitude of self-control and hopefulness. John was a basket case, trying hard to keep a positive attitude around her. As for me, I was so out of my mind that I didn't know how I was functioning, but somehow I did because I had to. At night, in bed, John held me, and I cried myself to sleep many nights. Susan's friends were amazing, coming over after school to cheer her up with the latest school gossip. It was sad that Susan had to work from home, but it clearly couldn't be helped. The tutor, Mrs. McElroy, was a lovely woman, a retired teacher who treated Susan as she would any other student. Hopefully, Susan would be able to return to her school after the chemo was finished.

The team at Davis was wonderful. The egg retrieval process began. I injected Susan daily with the hormonal drugs that would cause her ovaries to produce several mature eggs during one menstrual cycle. Then, as Doctor Saperstein and his team explained, the eggs would be removed by aspiration during a small surgical procedure. In the meantime, while this was ongoing, we tried to maintain a reasonably normal life, but it was next to impossible for me. I often caught John staring out into space, clearly deep in thought. I continued to show an upbeat attitude in front of Susan. The rest of the family was wonderfully supportive, but nothing really worked. The only one with a true positive outlook was Susan, and for that I was grateful. The rest of us just muddled through with words of encouragement and hopefulness.

We were given the name of two wigmakers in our area. We made an appointment with one and went to the store one morning. The woman who worked with us was kind and supportive. Susan tried on several wigs. We were able to match her beautiful, long wavy hair with a shade that was almost exact. Her wig could be worn with or without a headband. It took two weeks for the wig to be ready, but they did a fabulous job. You would never know Susan was wearing a wig. It was made of human hair and was very expensive, but worth every penny. At least Susan could look like herself when the time came. Somehow, the weeks passed, albeit slowly. Susan underwent the surgery to harvest the eggs, and then we were told the awful news that none of them were viable. It was all for nothing. There was no explanation. Sometimes the procedure worked, and sometimes it didn't. It was that cut and dried. We had no choice but to proceed with the chemotherapy. We hoped that this particular drug wouldn't cause infertility. Dr. Saperstein and his team prepared us for the first treatment, explaining again the possible side effects. They were more than likely to happen, he said. There would probably be nausea, extreme exhaustion, and of course, the dreaded hair loss.

On a chilly Tuesday morning in February, we arrived at the Davis Medical Center and checked in at the Chemotherapy Suite of the Oncology Department. Susan was surprisingly calm, as she had been throughout all of this. The nurses were kind as they hooked her up to the machine that would take hours to deliver a terrible poison to her body that would hopefully kill the cancer cells, even as it destroyed healthy ones, and wreaked havoc in other ways. The hours passed slowly as the first treatment slowly dripped its insidious way into Susan's body. The chemo would be given in cycles. There would be a rest period to allow her body to recover. The treatments would last for several months.

After what seemed like an interminable amount of time, we finally went home. Susan went right to her room. I heard her on the phone, probably talking to her best friend Lisa who had been her rock since the diagnosis had been given to her. A few days later nausea hit her like a ton of bricks. She vomited several times during the day and was extremely tired. She had been prescribed an anti-nausea drug, and by late afternoon, the medicine kicked in somewhat. She was able to eat a scrambled egg and a slice of toast. I was grateful that she kept it down.

And so began the routine. One week on, one week off. After a few weeks, Susan's hair began to fall out. Eventually, the single hairs became clumps that would fall to the floor. We went to the salon and had her hair cut very short. At least she had the wig. Susan's attitude was still amazing. She had good days and bad but was always exhausted. She lost weight, but never lost hope. The kids kept her as busy as she was able to handle. They came over to visit, even dragged her to the movies when she was up to it, and called often. Finally, the chemo was done. There was a short period of relief that the treatments were over, but now the waiting began. Doctor Saperstein wanted to see Susan regularly. He had her come in for a careful physical exam.

"I'll be paying attention to the size and firmness of the lymph nodes," he explained.

His office arranged for a CAT scan the following day. Blood tests would be done as well, to check her blood count for possible additional problems. The blood work would be done frequently. When the results of the scan were in, a mass was seen. Dr. Saperstein wasn't certain if it was an active lymphoma or scar tissue, so he ordered a PET scan, which would give him more information. Susan had the PET scan the next morning, and in the afternoon Doctor Saperstein called us and asked us to come into the office. I knew from the urgency in his voice that he must have received bad news from the scan. I was right. The chemo hadn't worked. The three masses that had originally been found were still there. There would be a new round of chemotherapy started immediately. This time, the drugs would almost definitely cause infertility. Susan would not only have to deal with having cancer, but also have to come to grips with not being able to have children. That night I sat down to talk with Susan in her room.

"Mom, I never thought about having kids," she said. "I mean, I'm not even sixteen. What kid thinks about that?"

I didn't know how to respond, just hugged her close to me. "We knew this was something we might have to deal with. The most important thing is for you to get well," I said, knowing I sounded like a fool. "This is unfair, and something you'll have to adjust to. I know you're incredibly upset and that's normal. Losing your fertility is a big deal, Susan." There was nothing else I could say. What was there to say to your child who has just been told she'll never have children?

Two days later, my daughter donned her wig and went back to the medical center to begin the chemotherapy that would take her fertility away. John and I tried to be calm, but we were both aching inside. It was a repeat of the last round of chemo, but this time there were new drugs. The nausea was just awful. It was cumulative, the virulent chemicals circulating throughout her body, and she vomited constantly as every other week the drugs were pumped into her body. Since she was so ill this time, she would be unable to continue her home-schooling until the chemo was over.

The months passed, and warmer weather arrived. Susan had just finished her chemo, and it was time for her next PET scan. We headed off to Davis, but I saw the look on her face as she changed into the gown and walked out of the small dressing room to enter the scanning room. I had no more words left to comfort her with. All I could do was whisper, "Good luck, baby."

Doctor Saperstein called us in the morning, asking when we could come in. I went to work, and afterwards, Susan and I went to the hospital late in the afternoon. John would meet us there. The station had been amazing in altering his schedule as needed.

The look on the doctor's face was different from last time. "I won't beat around the bush, guys," he said. "Two of the three tumors are gone, but there is still one left. I am going to suggest some very intensive chemotherapy. I would like you to begin stem cell transplantation. Let me explain, and then you can go home and do your own research. This is the only viable way to proceed. "First, you will have injections of various growth factors before and possibly after the transplant," he continued. "These growth factors are proteins that make bone marrow produce blood cells. Next, we'll collect some stem cells through IVs set up in both of your arms. One will remove the blood; the other will replace it. Then you will be given high doses of chemotherapy, and possibly more growth factors, both of which can give us a better chance of curing the lymphoma, or at least controlling it for a long time. Bone marrow is a spongy substance inside your bones that makes stem cells. These cells develop into blood cells. When we use high doses of chemotherapy it kills off your bone marrow cells, as well as any remaining lymphoma cells. This means you cannot make any new blood cells. After the harvesting and the chemo are completed, you will be given your stored stem cells back through this transfusion. Then you can make the blood cells you need again."

We went home, digesting the latest news. It was unusually hot that day. John drove, Susan sat next to him, and I sat in the back seat with a pounding headache, feeling the air conditioning blowing strongly on my face. I was chilly but I didn't say anything, I just moved over a bit, avoiding the stream of cold air coming from the vent. Susan was quiet, as usual, her head down. At home, I offered to make dinner.

"No, thanks, Mom," she said, "I can't eat.

John didn't want anything either. He was running back to the station to do some pressing work and said he'd pick something up on his way. He hugged Susan and left. There was nothing more for him to say to her. I made myself a cup of coffee. I didn't know whether to be elated or really upset. Two of the tumors were gone, yet one remained, an interloper growing quickly and sending its tentacles into other parts of Susan's body if we didn't stop it. I chugged down my coffee, and walked over to the window, staring out into the backyard. A stray cat ran by. It was twilight, but it had suddenly gotten dark, and it began to rain. It was an early-evening storm on an overly warm spring day. Soon, it was coming down pretty heavily. I looked at the black clouds moving quickly overhead. They certainly matched my dark mood. There was a sudden flash of lightning, and shortly after I heard a rumble of thunder off in the distance. I remember learning something about counting the seconds between the lightning and the crack of thunder and dividing the number by five. That would tell you how far away the lightning was. Suddenly, the cat ran behind the shed and under some bushes in our backyard. Street cats must really know how to fend for themselves, I thought. I guess it was just looking for a dry place to hide out until the rain abated. I wondered where it foraged for food. It made me sad to see the poor animal. Life could be very sad. I thought about eating something but I just walked down the hallway to the room John and I shared as a home office and sat down at my computer. I read article after article online until I didn't know which hurt more, my eyes, or my head. I went into the bathroom and took some Tylenol. Looking at myself in the mirror over the sink, I saw that I had aged over these months. New lines had appeared around my mouth, and my usually lively eyes were dark and lifeless. I had dark circles under them, too, and a perpetual frown on my face. The studio had their work cut out for them before I went on camera each time.

Our baby was terribly ill and John and I were helpless. Susan would need us more than ever. We had prayed that this last round of chemo would take care of the tumors. Now, all we could do was hope that the stem cell therapy would be the answer. I wondered if Susan was hungry, but she would tell me if she felt she could eat something. I started to knock on her door and then thought, why am I always offering food? I guess it was somehow a way I could feel useful and nurturing, in some small way. It was painful to see how thin she was. As I went into my bedroom, a scary flash of lightning lit up the dark room. A moment later, a huge clap of thunder exploded overhead. I could hear that it was really pouring now. I thought about the gray tabby I had seen, wondering if it had found a dry spot to ride out the storm.

I stood at the window watching the violence outside, then I walked across the hall and knocked on Susan's door. "It's me; can I come in?"

"Come in, Mommy." I noticed she called me Mommy, something she hadn't called me in a number of years, Mom having always been her usual way of addressing me.

"Do you want to go over some of the research I've done on how the procedure is performed, time frame, and prognosis for teenagers undergoing this treatment? I've printed it out. I thought we could talk about it, and if you like, you can read what I printed." I paused so she could think about her answer.

"Okay, Mommy, I might as well get it over with," she said, resignation in her voice. She had her own computer but hadn't wanted to research it on her own.

We were waiting for a call from the medical center to tell us what time to come in tomorrow. I began explaining to Susan, that this procedure had extremely high success rates as far as eradicating cancer completely. We talked for an hour, Susan being her usual strong self. I don't know how she did it; I was on the verge of breaking into tears several times as we spoke. I left her the detailed information and went back to my room. The hospital finally called telling us to come in at noon. Susan would be staying there for a few days. I helped her pack a bag, and packed one for myself as well since I planned to be sleeping there. I called the station, asking them to arrange for another anchor to cover for me so I could have the next two days off. I had taken a lot of time off, and I was glad that my producer was so caring about the serious situation. Everyone was rallying around us. John, too, had been fortunate in how understanding his people were at work. He was the station manager, but he had to report to a woman higher up at the station. I would be at the hospital for the first two days, John the third. We were told it would be three days, at least. We also knew there would be more miserable side effects.

The next day we drove to the medical center and Susan was admitted for what we prayed would be the final ordeal in her battle. Engraftment is the term used after the transplanted cells enter the bloodstream. This time between the therapy and engraftment would make Susan feel generally unwell. The bone marrow must start to recover. The blood count is at its lowest two to three weeks after the transplant, and fever, infection, bleeding and anemia, including vital organ damage could occur. Susan would be kept in isolation to reduce the chance of infection. Her healthcare team would be monitoring her very closely. As her blood count reached better levels she would be checked in other vital areas before releasing her. She would be weak and tired for six to twelve months, as her immune system needed this time to recover.

Chapter Seven

Daly City, 1997

A year after Susan was diagnosed with cancer, the last PET scan, X-rays and blood tests showed no more tumors, and she could return to school. Doctor Saperstein told us about a follow-up treatment he was considering but decided to hold off for now based on her recovery. She had missed a lot of the second term of her sophomore year, but home schooling and summer school kept her current with the curriculum. I didn't know where she found the strength. She had the strongest will of anyone I had ever known. She made me think of her Great-Grandmother Zhang Ling yet again. That woman had survived every adversity thrown her way. Susan had inherited her genes. Now, cancer free, with a good prognosis, she would try to get some semblance of normalcy back into her life. She would be returning to school the following week, and she was terribly excited to see all the kids. Her immediate friends, Lisa especially, had been there for her through it all. What great young people they were, I thought time and time again. I hoped their parents realized what amazing children they had. As always, the family was wonderful.

That Monday morning, Susan's first day back to school, it was raining again. Huge drops of rain pounded the sidewalk in front of our house. I stood staring out the living room window, watching the trees in the yard shaking from the wind and remembering how I had watched that street cat seek shelter in our back yard a while back. Newly grown leaves were snatched from their bough-beds and blew all around. It was a dark and dreary day, yet it was filled with the sunshine in our hearts. Susan came down the stairs, looking adorable in a simple navy blue jacket over dark jeans. She wore trendy sneakers and looked every bit the stylish teenager she was. She was wearing the wig. I knew she was extremely tired and she looked too thin. She and John left and I stood with the front door still open, lost in thought. We all knew it was a tremendous challenge for her to go back to regular classes. But she had dealt with summer school, and she would handle this, too. She knew there would be whispers about the girl with cancer, and the wig would add to it but Susan had weathered a lot more than gossip. Her guidance counselor had worked hard at setting things up, and had been a wonderful liaison between the high school, her home-schooling program, and summer school. We had no doubt that Susan could easily take her junior year in stride. I closed the door and went upstairs to shower.

Several months later, she took the PSATs, and considering she hadn't taken a review course, she did extremely well with a score of 1245. Later that year, she would take a course for her first try at the actual SATs. Then, early in her senior year, she would take them again. These would be the final scores colleges would receive. The term passed quickly, another Christmas came and went, and suddenly it was time for finals. She had gotten some of her strength back. It was amazing, and frankly, I don't know how she did it. But, she was determined to beat this thing and go on with her school career and her life. What a trooper!

She would be taking two Advanced Placement classes in her senior year, AP American English, and AP French. Her grades were excellent. She landed a job in a local day camp as a junior counselor. Lisa also found work in the camp. We were concerned that it might be too much for her but she had spent enough time at home. The following week, it was time for Susan's PET scan and X-rays. She had them every three months, and each time we went to the medical center with fear in our hearts. As always, waiting for the results was awful. But, once again, the test results showed she was still in remission. When we got home, John went to do some work-related research on his computer in our office. Standing in the doorway I said, "Honey, I need to ask you something. Is this a bad time?"

"No, Mina, I'm just doing some research on a couple of new groups. What's up?"

"I think it's time to pass my grandmother's journal on to Susan. According to my family's tradition, it should have been given around her sixteenth birthday. Clearly, it wasn't the right time then. Do you think she's ready to read it now?"

"She already knows the story," John replied. "It will be interesting for her to draw comparisons between them, as we have done."

"Okay, tonight's the night," I said. "I'll do it right after dinner."

Dinner was a pleasant affair. John cooked some delicious ribs on the grill, along with corn on the cob. I made a salad, and we sat outside eating and enjoying the nice weather. Susan told us it was great to be back at school and that the kids had all been nice to her, though she said some didn't know what to say to her. I looked around our backyard, watching a squirrel wave his bushy tail as he scurried along and quickly climbed a tree, an acorn in his mouth. My tomato plants were growing nicely. I had planted them as I did every spring. I smiled, feeling for the first time in a long time that maybe things would be all right with the world. After we finished eating, Susan and John helped bring in the things from the table, and Susan and I loaded the dishwasher and wrapped leftovers. There was a companionable silence, and I could feel Susan's happiness that I hadn't been aware of for a very long time.

"Susan, sweetie, I've had a thought," I said, popping a slice of tomato from the leftover salad that I'd been putting into a container into my mouth. "You know it's been a tradition for the first daughters from each generation to be presented with Great-Grandmother Zhang Ling's diary. I was given it by your grandmother, Yuming, when I was sixteen, and she was the first to read it, also at sixteen. Under the circumstances, it clearly wasn't the right time for you to read it when you were turning sixteen. Now I think you're ready. I want you to see the hardships Zhang Ling endured. You've already heard the stories verbally, but only by reading her journal will you understand her. Honey, you are a great deal like her, as was my mother, Yuming. You have inherited her strength and incredibly strong ability to face life's challenges. I hope you enjoy reading her journal. When we finish here, I'll get it for you."

"Thanks, Mom," she said happily. "I look forward to reading it."

For the next few days, the weather turned unusually gray and cool. In our house, no one cared. Susan continued to feel great as she studied for and then finished her finals. She did well, as always, and her junior year of high school came to an end. Her friend Ellen, whose parents had gotten divorced, invited Susan to spend a week with her and her brother at her grandparents' home in the Poconos. We thought it was a great thing to do before her camp job started, and we made arrangements through Ellen's mom for the kids to fly to Pennsylvania. It was just what she needed. Once again, her amazing friends came through!

We had hoped to go on vacation while she was away. John's and my studios came through once again and I had spoken with Linda and we agreed that our favorite vacation, a week at a beach, would be great. Their boys were going to sleep-away camp for the summer. She was waiting to see if she and Paul could get the week off. Our travel agent suggested Stinson Beach, which was only a two-hour drive from us. Linda called saying they had been able to get the time. Our travel agent booked rooms for both of us at a hotel she recommended, and the following week we drove down and met our friends there.

The place was lovely, and it was wonderful to just lie on the beach, swim, and have some quality time to catch up. We spent our days lazing under big umbrellas on chairs we had rented, grabbing fast lunches, and enjoying delicious dinners every evening. It was very relaxing, and we were happy to be spending time with Linda and Paul. Linda had been wonderful in keeping me grounded during Susan's ordeal. The weather was perfect. We called Susan a couple of times and she told us what a great time she was having with Ellen's grandparents. A week later she flew home by herself and we picked her up at the airport. She was feeling happy and relaxed. Ellen hadn't been interested in the camp job and had stayed on with her family. Susan and Lisa were starting their jobs as junior counselors the day after July 4th.

Susan came home after the first day of camp and told me that she had been given the seven and eight-year-old girls and how cute they were. They were old enough to understand what they were supposed to do and weren't too difficult to handle. One little girl stood out from the rest. Jillian was the youngest in the group, having just made it into the group by a month or so, and she was a quiet, solemn child. Susan told me that as she got to know the little girl they began to bond. Jillian's older brother was attending the day camp, too. Lisa had been given the five and six-year-old girls. Late one afternoon, about ten days after camp started, Susan got dropped off home by the camp bus, and wiping the sweat off her face, threw her cap onto the hall table, yelling that she was going to take a fast shower. John wasn't going to be home for dinner. I had leftover chicken and some angel hair pasta from two nights ago and figured it would be perfect for just the two of us. Perhaps it was the pasta that made Susan talk about Jillian.

As she set the table she said "Mom, let me tell you about this little girl in my group. The kids were making macaroni picture frames. You know, they paint the elbow macaroni silver or gold, and when they're dry they're supposed to glue them onto the frames that the arts and crafts counselor gave them. So, the girls were laughing and talking as they worked on their projects. The boys were playing baseball with their counselors, and I noticed that Jillian had moved to the empty table alongside ours and was sitting by herself. I went over to help her and we worked on her frame together, but she barely uttered a word.

"Later, when I had my break, I asked my counselor if she knew if something was wrong or was upsetting Jillian. I told her how Jillian had sat alone. She said she had noticed too and was glad I had given her some special attention. She told me the little girl's mother had died from cancer about six months ago."

"Oh, poor child," I said.

I watched Susan's face as she related the day's event to me and I knew she was thinking about herself.

"I know where your head is right now," I said, walking away from the microwave where I was warming the food, "and you of all people will be kind and understanding with this child."

In our case, I thought, it was the parents who had to watch the child suffer. This little girl had to watch her mother suffer and then die. "You're in a different situation, sweetheart. You're going to be fine. Your whole life is ahead of you. Help Jillian, is that her name? Find a way to see if she will play with the others, and try to take her mind off things, even for the few hours a day she's in camp. You have such a giving nature, I'm sure you can help this little girl."

"I know, Mom, but it's just so sad." Susan was clearly involved with this child's story.

"Come," I said, motioning to a chair, "sit down, dinner is ready."

Later that evening I thought about Susan and how it would be that everywhere she turned she would hear about cancer. She would have to deal with that, even as she would have to live with the constant fear of its return. I wondered how she felt about working with children, knowing her own situation. My heart was heavy as I turned on the television and sat down to watch. Susan was upstairs in her room, and I could hear her talking on the phone.

Chapter Eight

Daly City, 1998

The summer passed uneventfully. Susan was a senior in high school. In another month it would be time for her latest PET scan and X-rays again, and John and I knew this was always uppermost on her mind. She told us that so far she liked her teachers, and while some of her classes seemed like a challenge, she knew how to apply herself. Her weekends were busy, and she was rarely home. She talked a lot about a boy in her Global History class named Robert Jacobs. He had an interest in the law and was participating in Moot Court in the hopes of getting a real feel for the subject. They had plans to go out on the coming Saturday night. Lisa, too, had been hanging out with a boy that she seemed to like, and the two couples were going to see a movie. At this point, she started spending a lot of time with Robert, and I guess I could say he was her boyfriend. We liked him a lot. Robert Jacobs was tall, probably about 6'2", and had wavy dark hair that he wore slightly long. He lived close by, and though he had a car, he lived close enough to walk over to our house, and vice versa. Susan liked his folks a lot and got along well with his sister,

Bonnie, who was a freshman at their high school.

Susan began attending a course to prepare for the SATs, which she would be taking soon. We scheduled an appointment for her tests for the following week. That day I had to go to work early to take care of some things, so John took her. She was used to the procedure, but it wasn't the tests that were so unnerving, it was always the awful wait for the results. Hours later, I finally got home and I went up to her room and knocked. I remembered how many times I had stood outside her door after these tests.

"Mom?" she responded. "I'm on the phone."

Well, that's a surprise, I laughed to myself. I was glad. Everything seemed as it should be. John was still at work and tomorrow, Friday, he was leaving in the morning to attend a taping of a show featuring one of the new, hot bands. He'd be home on Saturday. I opened the door and asked if she wanted to go out for pizza.

"Yeah, sure, that would be great. Give me ten minutes, okay?"

"Okay, honey," I agreed.

She was on the phone a lot longer than ten minutes but I had nothing but patience with her. We went to a local restaurant that had delicious personal pan pizzas. We shared an antipasto salad, and I had a plain pizza, while Susan opted for her usual pepperoni and mushroom pie. I watched her devour hers. We enjoyed our meal, skirting the obvious. There was no reason to discuss it. There would be more scans in her future, hopefully with good results.

She had never said a word to me about her great-grandmother's journal, which I had given her a while back. I decided to ask her about it.

"Susan, I didn't want to bother you, but tell me," I said, "did you ever find time to read Zhang Ling's journal?"

"Oh, yes, Mom, I just never got to talk to you about it." She leaned toward me, her elbows resting on the table. "I was overwhelmed by the horrible things she lived through. It seemed like I was reading a novel, not someone's real life story. It was fascinating to learn about my culture, too. We're so American. I'm so glad she found such happiness with my Great-Grandfather Bao."

"So you can see why I say you have a great deal of her personality. You have inherited her strong nature and her ability to see your way through the things that come your way. Hopefully your life's happiness is just around the corner."

I asked her how the test prep was going, and she told me it was grueling but she was confident she was going to score at least a hundred points higher than her PSATs. We had just begun the college process, and what a process it was. Last year we had talked about schools and had even gone to look at one over the summer, but now it was really upon us. If she intended to apply early decision anywhere, we had to really get moving and visit some colleges. Susan had always wanted to go away to school, but under the circumstances, we thought it would be better for her to attend a local school she could commute to. Still, we would consider allowing her to dorm if the school wasn't within a decent driving range of home.

Two schools she was interested in were very highly rated, and we planned to visit them once we got her latest test results. We were all thinking positively. Sacramento State, we learned, is part of California State University. The school is known for its beautiful campus of 3,500 trees on three hundred acres. Sacramento is known as the City of Trees, and the campus had received many awards and great recognition for its famous University Arboretum. It was about a two-hour drive from home. We also wanted to visit the University of the Pacific, which we found out is the oldest chartered university in California. It was highly rated and one campus was located in San Francisco, which was a half hour from us by car.

Finally, after what was always an interminable amount of time, the results of the PET came in. We sat in the doctor's office waiting for him. My heart was pounding as the door swung open, and Dr. Saperstein walked in holding a folder.

"The results look good," he said. "There are no changes."

We had developed a lovely relationship with him, and he smiled warmly at us, standing up from his desk and putting his arm around Susan. I looked over at John, who was looking at our daughter. The relief showing on their faces was incredible. Another day for celebration! At this point, our story had actually become minor, local news. Because I was an anchor with a station that reported local news, as well as national, they had asked for our permission to feature the story if Susan agreed. She actually thought it was wonderful to share her journey so that other young people could see her as a role model for positivity. The outpouring of love everywhere was amazing. In a world torn with strife, the sheer kindness of strangers was incredible. John's bosses were wonderful as always, and we knew we were fortunate to be employed by people with such open hearts. After shaking the doctor's hand, we happily headed home.

We made plans to attend an open house for parents and students who were interested in touring Sacramento State. The following weekend we made the two-hour trip to the campus. It was overwhelmingly beautiful because of the multitude of trees. We toured the school, looking at the buildings housing the many subjects being taught. We saw a gym, a large, bright dining hall where we grabbed a bite to eat, a couple of standard freshmen dorm rooms, and the state-of-the-art library with many small, private, separate areas, each with a desk, chair and computer. The student guides were hand-picked for their knowledge and outgoing personalities. They walked us around the campus, chatting with the potential students and their parents. Susan ran into several kids she knew from her high school that were also visiting with their parents. Later, we attended a presentation in the auditorium, where an a cappella chorus provided terrific entertainment after various people discussed the many opportunities the university offered. We left there impressed and excited.

Two weeks later, we attended a similar program at the University of the Pacific's campus in San Francisco. We noticed that Susan paid careful attention to the dormitory rooms, most of which housed two students. Old and elegant, it had a totally different flavor from the other school. Both had so many things we liked. At each, we had attended financial aid presentations that had encouraged visitors to ask many questions about a topic that was of the utmost importance to the parents of graduating high school seniors. We had a lot to think about and ultimately this choice would be Susan's. Her friend Lisa was traveling away to school, being interested in a career in graphic arts. She had applied to several schools across the country. Her first choice had been the School of Visual Arts in New York City. She had also applied to the School of the Art Institute of Chicago, as well as UCLA in Los Angeles, which had an acclaimed Bachelor of Fine Arts program. Her parents were hoping she would choose to stay close as finances were an issue, and while they were more than prepared to take loans and there would be some financial aid, the airfare to New York or Chicago would be prohibitive several times a year. The program at UCLA in Los Angeles was critically acclaimed, with a ranking in the top ten of art schools in the U.S. The girls were sad about the separation that was imminent, but each had to strike out and follow life's path. We were at an important time in Susan's life. Her health was good, her social life was good as well, and for once everything was falling into place. Susan chose Sacramento State, and so my little girl was almost a college student.

BOOK FOUR
Susan Harvey

Chapter One

Sacramento, 1999

I graduated from high school, and now summer is waning. I attended an orientation at my college two weeks ago where I spoke with an advisor and picked my first semester subjects, shopped with mom for bedding, accessories, and some basic school supplies. When I got to my new room at Sacramento State, my new roommate Melissa George and her parents were already there. We'd never met, but we'd chatted on AOL, and made several phone calls to each other over the summer, planning our room décor, and in general, discussing our excitement as well as trepidations about college. Melissa and her parents lived in Tacoma, Washington, along with an older sister, a younger sister, and a brother.

Melissa was really pretty. She was very slim, with long, dark auburn hair. Both her mom and younger sister had similar coloring. Her other siblings had not come, so I assumed I'd meet them another time. I was very nervous as we all introduced ourselves, and while everyone was smiling and friendly, clearly Melissa was as nervous and shy as I was. Melissa's dad, a balding, nice-looking man, and my dad stood off to one side chatting as Mom began unpacking. Melissa had chosen the side of the room by the window, and her bed was already made up. Mom and I unwrapped one of my new sheet sets, two pillows, a big "husband" pillow that all the college kids use, and the brightly colored matching comforter and sham. We began to make up my bed. Most college beds are longer than usual twin beds, and we had purchased the special bedding needed. Melissa and I already decided on a color scheme of purple and green and bought the same bedding from a home store that had locations in both our areas. Mom had picked up short curtains and rods, which our fathers proceeded to hang, and Melissa's dad gave my dad his share of the cost. A lot had to be done, including making sure the cable connection to the Ethernet was set up and getting the phone plugged in. There were helpful people all over to answer our questions, so we easily got it all taken care of by visiting one of the local offices.

I had brought a small refrigerator, and Melissa brought a microwave. We each had a TV/VCR player. We would be sharing a lot of items, and I hoped we would hit it off. Finally, my parents and I trotted off to find the dining hall so we could get some lunch before we said our goodbyes. Melissa's family had said their goodbyes and left a little earlier as they had a flight to catch back to Tacoma. Melissa had tears in her eyes as she hugged her parents. After we ate, we headed back to my building where it was my turn to kiss my parents goodbye and walk them to their car. Mom cried a bit, and I did, too. I guess most moms do. I don't know how I felt. I was excited, yet my heart was beating fast as I saw them drive away. I turned, and using my new key, I entered the dorm building and went up a flight of steps to my room to continue unpacking. Two days later, my classes began and I threw myself into college life with real gusto.

Later that week, Lisa and I had an opportunity to have a heart-to-heart chat. It was reassuring to be able to pick up the phone and share my feelings with her. We talked about our classes, professors, new roommates, the cute guys on our co-ed floors, and how weird it was to have co-ed bathrooms and showers. I missed her a lot, but the possibility of new friends abounded, though she would always be my best friend. I began settling down into a routine, thinking that Melissa was a very nice girl, though we didn't seem to have too much in common. She was majoring in history. I decided I wouldn't be quick to judge until I had gotten to know her. I was at a brand new beginning. I had been given an amazing second chance, and I aimed to grab the brass ring of the merry-go-round.

Robert had chosen the University of the Pacific, commonly known as Pacific. He was studying at the Stockton campus. He planned to major in economics, and then go on to law school, but everything changed for him early on in the summer. His father suddenly passed away from a massive heart attack, leaving the family in major upheaval. His dad hadn't had a history of heart problems, and it came with no warning, as these things sometimes do. No one had found that out faster than my family when my grandmother Yuming died, and when I had gotten cancer. Robert wanted to delay his first year of college so he could help his mom get their family's life in order, but she wouldn't hear of it. So he stayed local. It was a terrible time for them, and I could do nothing more than find time for phone conversations where he was able to unburden himself to me about how hard it all was. He was grief-stricken; heartsick for his mom and sister Bonnie, and overwhelmed. He still felt that he should have taken at least the first semester off, but his mom had prevailed. I wondered over and over again why life has to be so hard for some. I knew it was irrational, but I often looked at others, thinking that they seemed to lead such charmed lives. Of course, I also know that one truly never knows what goes on behind closed doors.

My days were filled with routine but were never boring. I

liked most of my professors. I hoped to major in Journalism. I had lots of basic course work to complete for that major. My favorite class was History of News Writing, Media, and Reporting. The professor was a small, intense man with a strange way of walking back and forth across the classroom over and over again as he spoke. I found it unnerving, but I was there to learn, not judge. Sociology 101 was a basic class intended to introduce us to the study of "Humankind's most important creation, the social group." It was very interesting. I also needed a basic science course, and since I had studied both biology and chemistry in high school, I thought geology might be something new to study. There was a lab class necessary as part of the geology curriculum. When I gave it consideration, I realized it might be too much for my first semester so I decided to skip it. There would be plenty of time to take a science class. Then there was calculus. I had always been a so-so math student, having done decently in pre-cal last year, but I immediately found myself struggling with the calculus class. A math class was one of the requirements, but it was very early, and I knew that I could always go for peer tutoring if I didn't start to get a handle on it soon. Professor Ng was a bit odd, and she spoke very softly. We all had to be very quiet in class in order to hear everything she said, particularly when she had her back to us as she worked out problems on the whiteboard, a recent innovation in teaching and business workplaces. My last class was Corporate Communicating/Public Relations. Professor John Rollings was an extremely tall and stately black man, with a booming voice and quick smile. I liked him immensely. All in all, I thought my program was interesting, and aside from the math, which I hoped I would do well in, I was pleased with my classes. I had a short period of time within which I could drop the math if necessary, and fill it with something else.

I fell into the routine easily. Boys and girls from many different places filled the rooms next door, across the hall, and on other floors of my freshman building. Every room had the occupants' names on the door, and before we arrived, the college, and later the kids decorated them with paper cut-outs and pictures of things they were interested in. The hallways, too, were decorated with welcoming words for the new students. Melissa and I were getting to know each other. I was finding I liked her quiet demeanor and sweet nature very much. Next door to us were two girls, one of whom, Esther Goldman, had been very warm and friendly from the start. She and her family lived in Henderson, Nevada, which I learned was close to Las Vegas. She was a modern Orthodox Jew, and not knowing much about that I was intrigued to find out more about her. I wondered why she hadn't attended a more "Jewish" school like Brandeis in the east, or perhaps something even more religious like Yeshiva University. Her mother taught high school in what was probably one of the few Yeshivas in her area, while her dad was in some sort of business of his own. She had two sisters; one was older and married with three young daughters, the other sister was younger, having just started high school. She also had two older married brothers with families. Esther kept kosher, and observed the Sabbath, which I knew started on Friday night and was observed until sundown on Saturday. Chana Rabinowitz, her roommate, was also modern Orthodox.

Esther and I began spending some spare time together since she was also hoping to major in journalism. I began to learn some of her traditions. I was confused by the fact that she wore jeans. I had been under the impression that Orthodox Jewish women always wore skirts. She told me her mom didn't wear a *sheitel* except for at work. She explained that this is a wig that many devout, married Jewish women wear to cover their own hair. I told her I was familiar with the term. She said her mom also wore pants, but never to work either. This was the modern part of their orthodoxy. We ate together when we could, Esther choosing her meal from the many choices in the kosher section of the cafeteria. She was part of the Hillel organization on campus, a group that Jewish students could join to continue or expand their Jewish lives. Once again, I was surprised at her school choice because the school didn't have what she called a Chabad House on campus, which was a much more orthodox institution. Hillel afforded the Jewish students the opportunity to meet each other by attending Friday night and Saturday morning Shabbat services, as well as a place to celebrate the various holidays. I was totally amazed at the various sects of Judaism. I had only heard of Orthodox, Conservative, and Reform, yet I learned from Esther that there were subdivisions within each group, some more devout, others less so. Esther was basically Conservadox, though she attended Orthodox services at home. I was raised Presbyterian, and I knew that originally my family had been Buddhists. I was fascinated by her stories and explanations of her practices, holidays, and general attitude. What an interesting friendship ensued as I shared what I knew of my family's Asian heritage with her, and she shared hers with me. Robert and I spoke every couple of days, and because he was also Jewish, he enjoyed hearing about my friendship with Esther. Robert's family was Reform, but far from religious, so Esther's much more modern Orthodox lifestyle was a source of learning for him, too.

October came, and with it Parents' Weekend. It was wonderful to see the kids walking around campus with their families, occasionally seeing small children in strollers, and toddlers in tow. My parents arrived on Friday evening and checked into the motel where they were going to stay. I was so happy to see them, and even though there had already been a care package with Mom's home-baked goods (which I shared, though not with Esther because they weren't kosher), seeing them was fabulous. We went out to dinner at a local restaurant that was packed with other students and their families.

The next morning they came back and we walked around

campus as they exclaimed about the masses of trees that had started changing to the vibrant palate of autumn. Reds, rusts, purples, and yellows; what an amazing diversity! Walking about you could hear a cacophony of sounds. There were students calling across the quad to one another, the chirping of birds probably getting ready to fly south, and the underfoot crackling of the dry leaves that had already fallen from some of the trees. The time with my folks went too quickly, but we had participated in many of the activities the college had set up for the weekend, and it had been fantastic.

My workload was huge, and I had to learn time-management skills quickly to keep up, but who knew better than I did how to keep up with schoolwork? It surely was a lot harder than high school, but I was doing okay in the calculus class, and the other classes were fine. October was almost over, and it was suddenly Halloween. There were all kinds of goings on planned around campus, and the kids were looking forward to the parties and the fun of the holiday. Esther and Hannah (she preferred that to Chana since non-Jews have a hard time with the guttural *"ch"* sound) wouldn't be participating. I learned that because All Hallows' Eve was originally a Druidic celebration of the harvest, Halloween is a pagan celebration. Esther explained that the Torah, which is the first part of the Jewish Bible, prohibited Jews from adopting customs that have roots in idolatrous religions. I was intrigued by her faith more and more each day.

Melissa and I, as well as some of my other new-found girlfriends on our floor, were into the holiday full blast. We planned to go to one of the sorority parties we were invited to. It seemed appealing to me. I had chosen to dress as a geisha, nothing original, but a costume easily devised because of a full-sleeve, floral robe I had. Melissa was going as Princess Leia of Star Wars; her long hair was perfect to make the two buns that were such an important part of the look. We had a great time that night, dancing, drinking hard apple cider (welcome to college life), and getting to know a lot of new people. It was just what we needed to brighten up the season. At one point, I noticed Melissa deep in conversation with a cute guy with reddish-brown hair. I thought that with her auburn hair they looked like they could have been brother and sister. They seemed to be hitting it off, and the next day Melissa told me they had made plans to get together again.

I was doing well in all my subjects, but there was a lot of reading, and I was valiantly continuing to use my time-management skills. College was a big undertaking, and it was important for students to have just the right mix of schoolwork and social life. I felt healthy, and since I've always been a good student, I knew I would do fine. Melissa and Esther were in the same Spanish class and were lucky to have each other for feedback when there was a tough assignment. I had studied French and Latin in high school but decided to skip taking a language for now. I was thinking that perhaps it would be helpful for me to continue Latin next semester. The months raced by; I took tests, turned in papers, went home for Thanksgiving, and then it was December and almost the end of my first semester at college. Everyone was looking forward to going home for the holidays in two weeks. One evening, Alex, a friend from down the hall, was hanging out in my room.

"Hey, Susan," he said, looking at me sideways, "The "Green Mile" is opening this week, wanna go see it? It looks terrific."

I knew Alex liked me, and I wanted to see the movie, so I thought, why not go? Freshmen were permitted to keep cars on campus and he had his at school. I had taken Driver's Ed over the summer and my parents had bought me a used, white Nissan Sentra, but they weren't comfortable with me driving long distances alone just yet, and had asked me to wait until next semester before I drove back and forth on my own. They felt the school break would give me some time to practice.

Although Robert and I continued to talk all the time, we had no commitment to anything more than friendship. I had hung out with lots of new guy friends on campus, but never anything more than a friendly chat in one or the other's room, and rarely on a one-to-one basis.

"Sure, I really want to see it. When do you want to go?" I asked.

I had seen commercials for the movie on TV for the past two weeks, and who didn't love anything Tom Hanks was in, or for that matter, anything based on a Stephen King book? We decided to go Friday afternoon, and while it was opening that day, he had an early class and I had none, so we chose the first showing at noon, knowing it wouldn't be too busy at that time. The movie was edgy and a little scary, too, as it told the story of Paul Edgecomb and the supernatural events he witnessed on his job as a death row correction officer. I saw Alex watching me at one point.

"Scared?" he asked, taking my hand.

"It's freaky," I responded.

I began hanging out with Alex a bit more. He told me his family was from Russia, Ukraine to be exact. Many Russian Jews had immigrated to the States for the opportunities offered, and for religious freedom. His family had made their home in California. Alex's mom worked for a bank, having graduated from college in Russia. His dad had been a college professor there but was unable to teach since his degrees weren't recognized in America. He worked in sales for a mid-sized furniture manufacturer. While they were not religious Jews, he said his family observed the most significant holidays.

I was fascinated by all the Judaism around me. I liked Alex; he was a really nice guy. But Robert was still an important part of my life. I thought it was interesting that Robert was also Jewish. I laughed to myself one night thinking about what if a half-Chinese woman married a Jewish man? What would our kids look like, I wondered? Then I remembered that I probably couldn't have kids. That was sobering. Besides, it was all too silly. I barely knew Alex, and Robert was just a good friend. A few weeks later, I told my crazy thoughts to Esther because I was trying to understand what the draw was for me. She couldn't answer that, but she could, she said, make me better informed about Judaism in general. That appealed to me very much. Maybe I should study Hebrew rather than Latin next year, I laughed to myself.

Chapter Two

Daly City, 1999

I was home, on the phone in my room talking to Robert. My folks had picked me up yesterday, and it was so great to be home with all its familiar surroundings. I looked forward to a quiet day of unpacking my things and settling in to spend the Christmas and New Year's holidays with my family and friends. Robert and I made plans to get together in the next couple of days. Lisa was already home and coming by after dinner tonight for a real catch-up in person. We had scheduled my tests with Dr. Saperstein for two weeks later. I was very nervous about it. Mom and Dad were in their usual high spirits at holiday time. Other than the appointment for my scan and X-rays, we never talked about the Hodgkin's.

Lisa came over around seven o'clock, and we called Allison to make plans to get together. Allison said she had just spoken with Ellen. We had all gotten home within a day or two of each other. I couldn't wait to see them. We finalized the plans to hit the mall the next day to shop for holiday gifts for our families, and then Lisa and I sat down for our long-awaited face-to-face chat.

"Lisa, I want to ask you something," I told her. "You know that I went out with this guy Alex a few times, and he's really nice. But he's kind of pushing me to be his girlfriend. It's way too soon, and besides, I'm just not sure about him. I mean, he's a good kid, and all that, but…oh, I don't know."

Lisa grabbed an Oreo from the pack on the bed that I brought up after dinner. "What about Robert?"

"Robert and I are great friends, but I don't know if I like him, like him… you know, that way. I mean, we can talk about anything, and I feel very close to him, and I can't wait to see him, but…" I just stopped without finishing my thought because I didn't know what I was thinking.

"Well, I think he likes you," Lisa replied, pushing the pack of Oreos toward me.

I got up and put them on the dresser, saying, "No more cookies, I'll get fat, and then neither one of them will like me."

"I wish I had your problems," Lisa sighed. She was always on a diet, though she really didn't need to be. We hung out until ten o'clock and I was suddenly tired from the long day. She got up to leave and I walked her downstairs.

Putting on her jacket, she said, "I'll pick you up at noon, and then we'll go get the girls.

"Okay. Night, Lise," I said, closing the door.

In my room, I finished most of the unpacking and switched on the TV. I couldn't concentrate. I kept thinking about Robert. We were such terrific friends. I was sure he thought of me only as a friend… or did he?

In the morning I grabbed some cereal with half of a banana for breakfast and ran upstairs to shower and dress. Lisa came by at noon, and we picked up the other girls. At the mall, we split up into two groups of two, heading off into different stores with plans to meet up in an hour and a half at the food court. We all had lists of stuff we wanted to get for the holidays. Even though Hanukkah was over, I planned to get Robert some CDs. We talked about music all the time and I knew what bands he liked. We had exchanged gifts for the past couple of years.

Allison and I went to Macy's to buy gifts for our moms, and she for her sister, as well. I had saved up money from my job last summer, and I always made sure to save a little each time my parents deposited money into my bank account at school. I bought my mom a beautiful red, light weight cotton sweater, and a black-and-white checked scarf. Allison copied my idea and got her mother the same sweater in blue and a bright, multi-colored striped scarf. For her younger sister she had planned on some CDs, so we left Macy's and headed off towards the music store. Cassettes had pretty much died off by now, and almost everyone had a Walkman for their CDs. I bought Robert "Human Clay" by Creed, "The Fragile" by Nine Inch Nails, "Issues" by Korn, and "Significant Other" by Limp Bizkit. I wasn't a big fan of any of them, but I knew he loved them, especially Creed. If he had any of them, he could exchange or return them. Allison bought "Millennium" by Back Street Boys, "Baby, One More Time" by Britney Spears, Christina Aguilera's CD of the same name, and "Fan Mail" by TLC for her sister.

After meeting for lunch at the food court, we headed off to the stores again. We went to The Gap and I bought my dad a blue polo shirt and a gray striped button-down collar shirt. I had checked with Mom on his size just to be sure. Allison got her dad a hoodie and a tee shirt. Finished, we met back at the food court as planned, then headed home. It was quiet in the house when I got in, and I went up to my room and put on my TV. I watched the end of the news and a game show for about an hour when Robert called. We made plans to get together two days later. He suggested going for lunch to a local diner that we always went to, and then maybe grabbing a movie. I went back to my show and shortly after I heard my Dad come home.

"Hey, kiddo, what's up?" he asked standing in my open doorway.

"Not much," I said. "I spent the afternoon with the girls at the mall doing some holiday shopping."

He never seemed to have the same hours. Still, he had a fantastic job and was grateful for the decent living he made.

"Did you hear from your Mom?" he asked.

"Nope, she didn't call."

"Okay, I imagine she'll be home in about an hour and a half." He started out the door. "I have some work to do. See you in a bit when Mom gets in."

I watched for a while longer, and then went downstairs to set the table. Years ago, Mom had gotten into the habit of cooking in advance on Sundays so there would be food for dinner during the week. She never liked the idea of "ordering in" too often, saying that it was important for a family to enjoy home-cooked meals. Even though she was a well-known anchor person, she always made it a point for us to have dinner together at home if schedules allowed. I loved that, and our home felt warm and welcoming because of it. I appreciated that neither of my parents let their jobs, and my Mom's so-called "celebrity status" interfere. At home we were just a regular family. I saw that she had defrosted a meatloaf and I peeled some potatoes and put them on to boil. I'd make mashed potatoes. I found a fresh head of broccoli in the fridge, and after I rinsed it, I cut it up and put it in a saucepan with some water and salt. My mom had taught me well. She always told me that someday I'd make someone a wonderful wife. The phone rang and I grabbed it. It was my mother saying she had just left the station and was on her way. I told her I had started dinner and she told me I was amazing.

We discussed holiday plans over dinner. As always, Christmas Eve would be at our house. I promised Mom that I'd help as usual. It was ten days away, so there was plenty of time to shop and make arrangements. My tests were just before the holiday. We talked about grades and I would be carefully watching for my transcript to arrive. I was pretty sure I had done well, my only concern being the calculus, but I was feeling confident that I had done all right. After dinner, I went back upstairs to rearrange my closet and drawers. I had kind of thrown stuff in because I was anxious to get my unpacking done. Finishing that, I decided to give Esther a call. Hanukkah had just passed, and it had been her first time celebrating away from home, and while Hillel had wonderful plans for their Jewish students, it had still been hard for her. I grabbed my phone book and looked up her home number. Her mother answered.

"Hi, Mrs. Goldman, this is Susan Harvey."

"Oh, hello, dear, how are you?" she replied.

"I wanted to wish all of you a belated Happy Hanukkah," I told her.

She thanked me, wishing my family and me a wonderful Christmas, and said she'd call Esther to the phone. I had met Esther's parents at the school and I liked Mrs. Goldman very much. There was something very warm and kind about her, I thought, as I held on waiting for Esther.

"Hey, what's going on?" Esther said in her bright, cheerful manner.

"All's good, just wanted to say hi. I want to wish you and your family a belated Happy Hanukkah and see how things are going out there in the desert," I said.

"It's good to be home, but in some ways, it almost feels strange to be back in my old regimented lifestyle." She paused for a second, then asked, "What about you? Are you missing the freedom yet, or still too soon?"

"I think it's still too soon." I laughed. "I saw my old gang of girls two days ago. We went shopping for holiday gifts and grabbed some lunch at our mall. It was really nice to see them. I made plans with Robert to go to the local diner and see a movie on Wednesday. Let's see, what else? Oh yeah, I have my appointment for my tests next week, and I'm nervous about that."

"Yeah," she replied, "I certainly understand that. Good luck. Heard anything from Alex? Do you think he'll be in touch?"

"I don't really know, but if I had to guess, I'd say yes," I said.

"I think you're right," she agreed.

We spent the better part of an hour on the phone. We talked about our grades again. She thought she had done well but was anxious to see the transcript. I asked about the gifts she'd given and gotten for Hanukkah, and a million other things. It felt great to chat with her. I really liked this girl. She was just so sweet and genuine. I'm not saying that my lifetime friends weren't wonderful; they were my rocks who had been and would continue to be there for me through thick and thin. I couldn't put my finger on what made our friendship so close in such a short time, but I was happy Esther had come into my life. We ended our call with her again wishing me good luck with my scan, and asking me to call with whichever came first, my results or my transcript. She wished me a Merry Christmas but was sure we'd talk before then.

The next morning, I allowed myself the luxury of sleeping late and then continued to lie in bed reading for more than an hour. I was reading Harry Potter and the Prisoner of Azkaban, the third in the series of Harry Potter books, which were the biggest thing since sliced bread. It was nice to read about his studies at his school, Quidditch, and not have to worry about mine for a while. My stomach started growling, and I looked at the clock on my night table and thought, no wonder! It was a quarter past one already. I hopped out of bed, washed my face, brushed my teeth, and wandered downstairs in my pajamas to make myself some lunch. The morning paper was laying on the table. Mom usually ate something and scanned it before she left for work… there would be lots of news waiting for her when she got there. Dad always just flew out the door with a travel mug of coffee to accompany him on his drive to work. I looked through the fridge and found nothing particularly appealing. I put the teakettle on to boil, feeling like a cup of tea instead of coffee, and rummaging some more, I found a couple of bagels that seemed fresh. I grabbed one with sesame seeds, sliced it, and threw it into the toaster. I was lost in thought as the whistle of the kettle pulled me back to reality. I had been thinking about Robert and our plans for the next day. I grabbed cream cheese and a jar of grape jelly, and after making my tea, which I liked super-sweet, I sat down at the table to read the paper and eat. When I finished eating, I rinsed the dishes, put them in the dishwasher and headed for the living room couch, hoping to find a movie or some afternoon talk show to watch. Today I was just going to veg out. "Dirty Dancing" was on, and I settled down to watch Baby carry a watermelon for at least the fourth time. I must have dozed off because Mom called and woke me. I guess I was really tired. We spoke for a few minutes, and she said she'd see me later. The movie was over, and it was just a little before four. I continued my afternoon of indulgent hanging out, eating pretzels along with a diet Coke, as I channel surfed. Robert called around five to make plans to get together the next day.

"Hey, what's up?" he said when I answered.

"Nothing, nada," I replied, "I've been sitting on my butt all day, just reading, noshing and watching TV."

"Yeah, I'm kinda tired, too." I heard the smile in his voice. "It's nice to be home. Anyway, are we still on for lunch tomorrow? We can really catch up, and if you like, we can do a movie after. I'm dying to see "The Green Mile."

"Oh," I said, "I saw it when it first opened, but I'm sure we can find something else we'll both like."

"Sounds good. I'll come by around twelve. Is that okay for you?"

"That's perfect," I told him. "See you tomorrow."

We never got to a movie. We sat in the diner for an hour and a half. He had a cheeseburger with fries and a Coke, I had a chicken salad sandwich and a diet Coke, and I'm sure I ate more of his fries than he did. Our conversation started off on a light note—classes for next semester, new friends at school, just general stuff. I gave him his belated Hanukkah gift, and he seemed pleased by the choices I had made. He said he had something for me for Christmas. By the time we finished our lunches, we had gotten into some pretty heavy stuff about his family. We decided to skip the movies. I tried to grab the check, but Robert wouldn't let me even split it. I wondered if there were money problems at home, but I allowed him the dignity of paying the inexpensive lunch bill. Outside, we walked to his car and drove over to Gellert Park, passing the Chinese cemetery on our way. He was quiet during the short ride. After we parked, we started walking and the conversation turned heavy again. He told me that he knew his mom was having a hard time emotionally, but he hoped she was okay financially. I told him I was scared of my upcoming CT scan and X-rays. We passed the tennis courts and stopped for a while to watch a couple who seemed to be pretty decent players. We said maybe we'd play next week. The playground was filled with moms sitting on benches while their kids ran around, going on the slide and the swings. An ice cream truck came by and we both got pops, chocolate for me, vanilla for him. After we finished our ice cream, we sat on a bench and Robert took my hand. We both looked down at our hands locked together but neither of us said anything. We sat like that for a few minutes, holding hands, but not speaking. I felt something different at that moment, and clearly, Robert felt it, too. We leaned forward and kissed… our first kiss. Suddenly, we were both shy and not sure what to do.

I spoke first. "Do you want to walk some more?"

"No, I want to kiss you some more," he said.

We kissed once more, this time with an obvious passion. We had suddenly moved into a whole different realm of our friendship. It all seemed so clear to me now. As Lisa had said, Robert DID like me, and I realized I liked him that way, too.

I smiled at him and stood up. "Let's walk around some more, huh?"

I didn't want to wind up having a make-out session on a park bench for all the world to see, so we walked a bit and then headed back to the car. He dropped me home, but not without making plans to get together again the next day. I opened the door to get out and he pulled me to him for another kiss. So, just like that, I guess we were seeing each other.

My parents and my girlfriends approved. Lisa had given me an "I told you so" when I called her. My grades came in the mail the next day. I got an A in History of News Writing, an A in Soc, a B+ in Corporate Communicating, and a B- in Calculus. I was pleased with my grades, though the B- wasn't great. Still, a 3.7 wasn't bad. A day later, Robert got his transcript, and he had aced all his classes, starting off his college career with a 4.0 GPA! Boy, was he smart, I thought. Melissa called to tell me about her transcript and was mostly pleased. She had had a hard time with one of her science classes and was disappointed at getting a C+, but it was only the first semester, and hopefully, things would get better. Lisa, Ellen, and Allison were also happy with their first semester grades. I had gone for my tests, and once again, my results were good. I was still cancer-free. Esther and I spoke several times. She, too, had done very well. What a bright bunch of kids we were.

Christmas Eve finally arrived, and it was the amazingly wonderful get-together that it always was. Lawrence and Joey and his family arrived, as well as Linda, Paul, and their boys. Unfortunately, Matt had had a stroke in the nursing home, leaving him partially paralyzed on his left side. Xiao had passed away from natural causes earlier in the year. Mom and I had cooked and baked up a storm, and everyone had a wonderful time. We reminisced about Yuming, my grandmother, and Ling, my great-grandmother. The next day, we opened our gifts and ate our yummy leftovers. Robert dropped by late in the afternoon. The whole holiday season had been a very difficult time for him, his mom, and his sister. He had bought me a pink fleece hoodie, a small beige crossover bag, and a graphic tee shirt with an asymmetrical pink heart on it. The gifts were great, and I was sure his mom or sister had helped pick them out.

A week earlier, I had re-read my Great-Grandmother Zhang Ling's journal. How far my family had strayed from our heritage! Other than yummy pork buns called *cha siu bau*, and a few other traditional Chinese dishes Mom made, our home showed very little reflection of the fact that my mother was full Chinese, and I was half-Chinese. Robert and I had become a committed couple in the past month, and I decided to bring this up to him. We were hanging out at his house one evening when I spoke about what was on my mind.

"Robert, I have to ask you something," I said. "How does your family feel about you dating a Chinese girl?"

"Well, we've never actually dated until now, Susan. We've just been great friends forever," he replied.

"But we are a couple now, and I'm half-Chinese. My background is different than yours, and I look different." I peered at him, watching for his reaction.

"I don't see that, Susan. I just see you," he said. "I don't care what you are, Susan, I love you for who you are, just the way you are. This is about us, not my family." Suddenly, he must have realized what he had done. He had used the "L" word.

He took my hand, just holding it in his gently, and looked me in the eyes, and said, "Yes, Susan, I love you."

It was then I knew I loved him too… and I told him so.

Chapter Three

Sacramento, 2000

I was back at school. Lying in bed the Sunday night before my first class of the spring semester, I thought about how my life had changed on New Year's Eve. Robert and I had had sex for the first time. Robert hadn't been a virgin. I was sure he had had a sexual relationship with a girl he'd been dating during our senior year of high school, and maybe even one other girl, not to mention the possibility of anyone new at college, but I was still a virgin. It was strange in this day and age, and although several of my girlfriends were already sexually active, somehow no one had come along until now that made me want to have sex. Oh, sure, there had been some make-out sessions with Alex, but that was it. I let my mind wander back to New Year's Eve before I got out of bed to start my day.

Mrs. Jacobs and Bonnie went to visit her sister and brother-in-law in San Diego for the holiday. Robert didn't want to go so he stayed home. He and I had gone to a New Year's Eve party. There was the usual amount of drinking, pot smoking, and who knew what else? Dick Clark's New Year's Rockin' Eve was on, and people were clustered around the TV watching The Backstreet Boys perform "Everybody," their smash hit. At midnight, we sang "Auld Lang Syne," none of us quite sure what the words were or what they meant, and everyone kissed and hugged each other. Outside, people yelled and car horns tooted loudly. Robert and I kissed, and our kiss was passionate and lasted a long time. We pulled apart and looked at each other with meaning. We had known we would be drinking, and fortunately, while it was a bit of a hike, we had decided to walk to the party. I had done something that was a really big first. We said our goodbyes, wishing everyone a Happy New Year one more time, and leaving, we walked back to Robert's house. It was a beautiful night. My folks knew I was staying over at Robert's house, but I never told them Robert's mom and sister would be away for the holiday. Lying like this was a big deal, and I had to hope I didn't get found out. Back at Robert's house, he put his arms around me, and after several kisses standing in the hallway, we somehow wound up on his bed. We had sex for the first time.

How can I describe the experience? I had thought it would be painful; Lisa had said it was when she and her boyfriend had sex the first time, but it wasn't awful. There had been some pretty heavy make-out sessions, and then some, but we both knew this was the night to actually have sex. We kissed, and slowly undressed bit by bit until we were both naked on his bed. Robert had a condom. It was over very quickly. We just lay there in each other's arms, talking quietly, with Robert kissing me over and over. It was sweet and romantic, but not what I had expected. Robert got up, saying he was thirsty, and asked if I wanted something to drink. He threw on his jeans and tossed me his shirt to wear. He came up with two glasses of iced tea, and a box of chocolate chip cookies. We ate the cookies, getting crumbs all over the sheets, but we didn't care. Soon we had sex again. I was a little sore, but I quickly forgot about that as this time there was pleasure that sent shock waves through my body. I had no basis for comparison, but it was wonderful. Surely the fact that we loved each other contributed. We fell asleep in each other's arms, and in the morning, because we both knew it had been more than just a sexual encounter, we were shy with other.

"Let's have some breakfast. Eggs okay?" he inquired. "We have English muffins, too."

"That's great," I answered. "I can do it." I was wearing his shirt again and he had put on a pair of shorts. Downstairs, he went to the fridge and found the eggs and muffins.

"Scrambled okay?" I asked.

"Sure," he said as he split the muffins and put them into the toaster.

He asked if I wanted coffee or tea. I told him coffee and he started the Mr. Coffee. The simple domestic chores made our shyness fade. I finished making the eggs, and after we ate, we felt sated in more ways than one.

"Wanna just hang out, or go out and find something to do?" he asked. "We could go to a movie," he said unenthusiastically.

"Let's just chill and watch TV," I replied.

I had called home earlier, wishing my folks a Happy New Year, asking about their evening, telling them Robert would drive me home later in the afternoon. His mom called, saying they'd be home around 3:00 o'clock. We realized that it would be a good idea to get me home sooner rather than later.

A week and a half later, it was time for Robert to go back to school. Our schedules were really different as I didn't have to return until one week later. We crammed as much as we could into the time we had together, but it was really hard saying goodbye. The good news is that my folks allowed me to drive my car back this semester. Robert and I went to schools only about an hour's drive from each other, so we would be able to get together on weekends. My roommate Melissa showed up with dark gold highlights in her already beautiful, auburn hair. It was great to see her, and we picked up just where we had left off. Esther and Hannah were happily ensconced next door. Alex had been in touch over the break, but now it was incumbent upon me to tell him I was in a relationship. This semester I was taking Geology, Latin, Feature Writing, and Book and Magazine Publishing. Things settled down to the usual routine of classes, studying, and socializing. For the most part, my professors were okay. The Geology teacher was a bit strange in a "lost-in-the-clouds" scientist way. The lab work was interesting. Alex showed up at my door on the second day back and I casually mentioned to him that I was now in a relationship. He smiled and said he was happy for me. I thought I saw a look of disappointment cross his face when I mentioned it, but I couldn't be sure. I began to fall into my rhythm and two weekends later Robert came to my school on Saturday with plans to stay over. I enjoyed introducing him to my friends and it was wonderful to be together. Somehow, Melissa managed to sleep out that night, though I had made it clear that I didn't expect this of her when Robert came for a visit. We decided I would visit him at Pacific the next time, probably in two weeks. And so the semester passed happily with us getting to spend time together. I was doing extremely well in all my classes. I had always been good in Latin, and it was easy for me to continue. I really liked the Feature Writing class. Then it was time for the Mid-Winter Recess. It was short, and just came and went. I tried to pack as much into it as I could. I enjoyed the family, my friends, the holidays, and every second with Robert that I could. I went back to school and myriads of tests, papers, on-campus get-togethers, and visits with Robert.

Melissa and I had a wonderful friendship and I was closer with Esther than ever before. We all bemoaned the fact that we lived far from each other. When Spring Break finally arrived, once again I headed home to be with the family, the girls, and of course, Robert. A lot of a college student's year is measured by these wonderful breaks when we got to go home. My relationship with Robert had grown to the point that it seemed abundantly clear that this could be "it" for us. This was a long break, encompassing both the Easter and Passover holidays. Robert and I discussed our future together. I felt calm and settled, and very grown-up.

On September 11, 2001, known as 9/11, there were a series of four coordinated terrorist attacks on the United States by the Islamic terrorist group al-Qaeda. Four passenger planes were hijacked by terrorists. Two of the planes crashed into the North and South towers of the World Trade Center complex in New York City. Within an hour and forty-two minutes, both 110-story buildings collapsed. A third plane crashed into the Pentagon, the U.S. Department of Defense headquarters. The fourth plane, headed for Washington, D.C. crashed in Shanskville, Pennsylvania after its passengers tried to overcome the terrorists. The attacks claimed the lives of 2,996 people, including the terrorists, and caused at least ten billion dollars in property and infrastructure damage. That year, the war in Afghanistan began as the U.S., the U.K., Italy, Spain, Canada, and Australia invaded Afghanistan, seeking to oust the Taliban and find al-Qaeda leader Osama Bin Laden. He was eventually caught by U.S. Navy Seals and killed in May of 2011.

During this decade, the world economy almost doubled in size from U.S. $30.21 trillion in 1999 to $58.23 trillion. The United States retained its position of being the world's largest economy. Additionally, the euro, a common currency for most European Union member states, was established in 1999. This new currency was put into circulation in 2002, and the old currencies were phased out. Only three of the fifteen member *states decided not to join the euro at this time (The U.K., Denmark, and Sweden). By 2004, the E.U. admitted ten new member states, and two more in 2007, thus establishing a union of twenty-seven nations.*

The year 2003 began with the January 16th launch of Space Shuttle Columbia on its last flight, while the last signal was received from NASA's Pioneer 10 spacecraft, which was 7.5 billion miles from Earth. On February 1st, at the conclusion of its mission, Columbia disintegrated during re-entry over Texas, killing all seven astronauts on board. On January 24th, the United States Department of Homeland Security was established. A few days later, on January 29th, Ariel Sharon was elected Prime Minister of Israel. In February, with an ongoing Iraqi disarmament crisis, U.S. Secretary of State Colin Powell addressed the UN Security Council on Iraq. By the end of February, global protests against that war began as more than ten million people protested in over six hundred cities worldwide. On March 19th the Iraq War began with the invasion of Iraq by the United States and allied forces. In mid-April, the Human Genome Project was completed, with 99 percent of the human genome sequenced to 99.99 percent accuracy. In 2004, the Mars Exploration Rover (MER) Mission reached the surface of Mars and sent detailed data and images of the landscape back to Earth. Another rover, Opportunity, discovered evidence that an area of Mars was once covered with water.

In technology, there was a huge jump in broadband Internet usage globally. By the end of the decade, wireless Internet would become prominent, as well as Internet access in devices other than computers, such as mobile phones and gaming consoles. Email became the standard form of interpersonal written communication during this decade with such popular email addresses as Hotmail, AOL, Gmail, and Yahoo! Google became the most used web browser. The USB flash drive replaced the floppy disk for low-capacity mobile data storage. There was a huge boom in music downloading to transfer music over the Internet, thus sparking a rise of portable digital audio players. This caused the entertainment industry to struggle through the decade.

Over this period, Windows 2000, Windows XP, Microsoft Office 2003, and later Windows 7 became industry standards in personal computer software. Toward the end of the decade, Apple slowly gained market share. Digital cameras, flat panel TVs, and DVR devices such as TiVo became popular. DVDs, and subsequently Blu-Ray discs replaced VCR technology as the common standard in homes. High Definition (HD) became popular later in the decade, with a change from analog to digital technology. Mobile phones and text messaging surged in the Western world, and paper mail became known as "snail mail." Social networking sites were enormously popular, allowing people to communicate as long as they had the Internet.

Hybrid cars such as the Toyota Prius and the Ford Escape came to the fore. Automobiles began to further implement computer and other technologies with DVD players, Xenon headlights, keyless start and entry, voice activation, cell phone connectivity, and satellite radio. GPS (Global Positioning System) became very popular in cars, with many offering navigation systems. Portable navigation systems became very popular as well.

The decade saw further expansion of LGBT (Lesbian, Gay, Bi-Sexual, Transgender) rights, with many countries recognizing civil unions and partnerships, and some even extending civil marriage to same-sex couples. Climate change and global warming became household words. It was stated that the 2000s may have been the warmest decade since records began in 1850. The incredibly successful Harry Potter series by J. K. Rowling was concluded in July 2007, having first been published in 1997. In movies, Oscar winners for the decade were: "Gladiator" (2000), "A Beautiful Mind" (2001), "Chicago" (2002), "The Lord of the Rings: The Return of the King" (2003), "Million Dollar Baby" (2004), "Crash" (2005), "The Departed" (2006), "No Country for Old Men" (2007), "Slumdog Millionaire" (2008), and "The Hurt Locker" (2009). In 2009, "Avatar," a sci-fi film written and directed by James Cameron, made extensive use of cutting-edge filming techniques and was released in 3D, as well as traditional viewing. This stereoscopic filmmaking was touted as a breakthrough in cinematic technology.

In music, the Internet had allowed unprecedented access to music. It let artists distribute music freely without label backing. During this era, Hip Hop reached its commercial peak, and the American rapper Eminem sold thirty-two million albums. Other popular Hip Hop artists were Jay Z, Kanye West, OutKast, Cam'ron, Pharrell, Snoop Dogg, 50 Cent, and Nelly. There were various genres such as "Gangsta rap" and "Hyphy". Beyoncé was named the female artist of the decade. On June 25, 2009, Michael Jackson died, creating the largest public mourning since the death of Diana, Princess of Wales, in 1997. A new trend in popular music gave rise to Auto-Tune, a device used to measure and alter pitch in vocal and instrumental recording performances. It was used to disguise, or correct off-key inaccuracies. Towards the end of the decade, electronic dance music dominated western charts and would continue into the next decade. R&B and Hip-Hop accounted for almost every one of the top 20 hits in the 2000s. According to Billboard, the top ten were: "Independent Women Part I" Destiny's Child 2000, "How You Remind Me" Nickelback 2001, "Family Affair" Mary J. Blige 2001, "U Got it Bad" Usher 2002, "Hey Ya!" OutKast 2003, "Yeah!" Usher 2004, "We Belong Together" Mariah Carey 2005, "Gold Digger" Kanye West 2005, "No One" Alicia Keys 2007, "Big Girls Don't Cry" Fergie 2007, "Apologize" Timbaland featuring One Republic 2007, "Bleeding Love" Leona Lewis 2008, "I Gotta Feeling" The Black Eyed Peas 2009, "Boom Boom Pow" The Black Eyed Peas 2009. The only two exceptions from R&B and Hip-Hop were Nickelback's "How You Remind Me" and Timbaland's collaboration with One Republic, "Apologize."

In American television, the 2000s saw a sharp increase in popularity of reality TV. Numerous competition shows such as "American Idol," "Dancing with the Stars," "Survivor," and "The Apprentice" attracted large audiences. There was a steady decline in sitcoms, as crime and medical shows such as "CSI: Crime Scene Investigation," "House M.D.," and "Grey's Anatomy" became well-liked. Paranormal shows such as "Medium," and "Ghost Whisperer," and action/drama shows such as "24" and "Lost" came to the fore. Comedy-dramas became more serious, now dealing with important issues such as drugs, teen pregnancy, and gay rights, and new comedy-dramas such as

"Desperate Housewives," "Ugly Betty," and "Glee" gained popularity. Adult-oriented animated shows also continued a sharp upturn in popularity. "South Park" and "Family Guy," with longtime show "The Simpsons," topping the list. Along with these network shows, there was now a rise in premium cable dramas such as "The Sopranos," "Deadwood," "The Wire," "Battlestar Galactica," "Breaking Bad," and "Mad Men." The PBS series "Mister Rogers' Neighborhood" aired its final episode on August 31, 2001. Two years later, Fred Rogers died from stomach cancer. His work with children's fears remains a long-remembered legacy. Video games reached the 7th Generation in the form of consoles like the Wii, PlayStation 3, and Xbox 360. The number one selling game console of the decade was the PlayStation 2, released in 2000, and still remained popular until the end of the decade, even after PlayStation 3 came out.

In sports, the 2008 Summer Olympics were held in Beijing, and one of the most prominent events was the achievement of Michael Phelps, the American swimmer. He won fourteen Olympic gold medals, the most by any Olympian. This decade saw the rise of digital media as opposed to the use of print as e-readers such as Kindle and Nook became more and more available. Popular books were the "Harry Potter" series, "Twilight," and Dan Brown's Robert Langdon books, including "The Da Vinci Code," "Angels and Demons," and "The Lost Symbol." Vampire, fantasy, and detective fiction, as well as young-adult fiction, in general, were popular.

Fashion trends of the decade drew inspiration from the sixties, seventies, and eighties. Hairstyles includ-

ed bleached and spiked hair for boys and men, and long, straight hair for girls and women. Both men and women highlighted their hair with blonde streaks, and Kelly Clarkson made chunky highlights fashionable in 2002 on "American Idol." Velour tracksuits were worn in the early 2000s. Baggy cargo pants were fashionable for both sexes. Until then, bell bottoms were the dominant pant style, but in 2006, fitted pants started to rise in popularity. Skinny jeans became a staple for young women, and Gap and Levi launched their own skinny jeans lines. Skechers shoes were popular as chunky sneakers were no longer the mode. Hip hop fashion was also popular with clothing and shoe brands such as Rocawear, Phat Farm, G-Unit, Pelle Pelle, Nike, and Air Jordan. Followers wore oversized shorts, a lot of jewelry, NFL and NBA jerseys, pants and T-shirts. By the late 2000s this gave way to more fitted, vibrantly colored clothing, and men now wearing skinny jeans, too.

Generation Y was the name given to the last people of this generation who were born in the early 2000s, while Generation Z were the first people born in the mid 2000s.

Chapter Four

Sacramento, 2003

I was in my junior year in college. Robert and I became engaged last summer, and I often looked down at the pretty little diamond on my finger. I felt so in love it was scary. It was almost time for winter break, and I looked forward to going home. I loved the holidays every year, but this year something different occurred. I made a major, life-changing decision last summer. My fascination with the Jewish faith led me to the moment when I knew I wanted to convert to Judaism. This was not because Robert wanted me to; if anything, he never asked nor expected it of me. But from my first real up-close introduction to the religion from Esther, I was so drawn to the culture, practices, and principles that I needed to explore it further. Over the summer of my sophomore year, I had gone to Temple Beth Israel Judea, a local Reform synagogue, hoping there was a possibility of furthering my knowledge toward an eventual conversion. I was met with more than a bit of resistance by their rabbi, Danny Gottlieb, which I had trouble understanding. I learned that Jews don't proselytize, that is to say, they do not go out of their way to invite converts to the faith.

I learned that choosing a Jewish life meant different things to different people. I knew it would involve a significant investment of time to study, pray, and contemplate. I loved the thought of becoming enmeshed in such an old, rich tradition. It was all so amazing to me, considering I came from a great-grandmother who had practiced Buddhism and then had converted to Presbyterianism, the faith I had been raised in by my parents. Rabbi Gottlieb initially told me to think further about my decision, and to contact him at some later date. I left his office in a state of confusion. As I said, I knew that Jews didn't seek out people to convert, but I was upset by his almost total disinterest. The following week, I returned once again, and again the rabbi was cold and disinterested. I let a few more days go by, then went back to see the rabbi. The two times he had seen me, he'd shown a coldness I found extremely disconcerting.

I did some more reading and found out that Jews believe that, when a gentile keeps the seven *Noachide* laws, he merits a place in the World-to-Come; therefore it isn't imperative for him to become Jewish. So, if like Christians and Moslems, Jews believed that those of other religions are condemned to damnation, then we would desire to convert people. However, they believe that a person can be completely righteous and merit the World-to-Come without conversion, just by adhering to the basic moral laws revealed to *Noach.* It is because of this that they feel no compulsion to convert others. Additionally, I read that since sincerity is one of the criteria for conversion, one way of determining that sincerity is by discouraging the person from converting. If the person persists, and we see it is for the love of Judaism, then that person is accepted with open arms.

On my third visit to the rabbi, he was a lot more welcoming—that's as good a way of putting it as I can. When I got to his office, rather than sitting at his desk facing across from me, he sat in the chair next to me. He said he could understand how I was drawn to the ancient faith, and explained that many felt like they were "coming home," or "finding a new family." He told me it was important to be comfortable, to be honest with myself about the reasons for my choice. I must understand that everyone practices their faith in their own way. This time, he smiled at me, and I knew that he had truly accepted my decision to convert. My parents were supportive. It was my decision, they said, and while they were surprised, they said they had no problem with it. All they wanted was for me to be certain before I began the conversion. I understood that many people wouldn't understand, and I found that as people heard of my decision, I was often questioned. Rabbi Gottlieb repeatedly said there would be times I would have misgivings and doubts. I found the thought of learning Hebrew intimidating, but my plans were to begin my conversion this coming summer. I also planned to study Hebrew at school in my senior year. Robert and I would be home for Hanukkah this year. It began on December 19th, just a few days before Christmas, and I was invited to spend the first night at Robert's home. I was intimidated, yet excited. As always, Robert and I would exchange gifts. This year, though, I would also be bringing presents for Robert's mom and sister.

My finals were done, papers handed in, and as I drove home, all I could think of was how busy I would be this year. Though we were engaged, we decided to hold off on getting married until we both graduated. Hopefully, Robert would be going on to law school, and I was undecided about pursuing my master's degree since I had chosen to convert, and a great deal of my time would be dedicated to accomplishing that.

Traffic was awful, and I calmed myself by singing at the top of my lungs to the music on the radio. I didn't get home until late afternoon and was grabbing a couple of slices of turkey breast out of the fridge when I heard my cell phone ringing. I had forgotten to take it out of my bag when I got in and it was upstairs on my bed along with my suitcase. Racing up the steps, I grabbed it just as it stopped ringing. Robert had called, and I quickly grabbed the house phone to call him back. He was home already, I saw, as the call was from his home number. I tried to be really careful with my cell phone use since I knew it was costing my parents a lot of money.

"Hey!" he answered.

"Hi, I just got in about fifteen minutes ago," I said. "When did you get home?"

"About a half hour ago; there was a lot of traffic," he replied. "I'll come by after dinner if that's good for you," he said.

"Sure, babe, I can't wait," I told him. "My mom's going to be late, so we're planning to just order a pie or something. I'll call you when she gets home, so you'll have an idea of time. Is that good?"

"Absolutely," he responded. "Talk later."

I hung up the phone, and still hungry, I found the usual bagels in the freezer and popping one into the microwave to defrost, I grabbed a bottle of orange juice. The microwave beeped, and I sliced the bagel and threw it into the toaster. I poured myself a glass of juice and sat down at the kitchen counter to wait for my bagel. When it popped, I put some more turkey breast and mayo on it and ate it in front of the TV. I thought that, after I had eaten, I'd unpack and check in with Lisa, who I knew had been home since yesterday.

My dad got in around 6:30 and by then Mom had called saying we shouldn't wait for her for the pizza. She would eat when she got home later. I called Robert and told him to come around 8:00 o'clock unless he wanted to join us for pizza.

"My mom is cooking dinner now so I'll see you later," he told me.

My father and I had a really nice conversation over our pizza and soda. We talked some more about my plans to begin the conversion and I got caught up on family news from him. Over the years, with young people now buying their music and listening to it on headphones, using their various MP3 players, radio was becoming less and less popular. In cars, a lot of people played CDs. Of course, people would always listen to the radio, but there had been a lot of changes.

> *A new form of radio broadcasting called satellite radio had become popular. Signals from satellites were broadcast nationwide, therefore covering a much wider geographical area than regular radio stations. The service was primarily intended for use in motor vehicles. It was available only by subscription, was mostly commercial free, and it offered subscribers a wide variety of programming, from music, to talk radio, to weather and traffic, and sports. Because of this technology, U.S. and Canadian listeners could hear the same stations anywhere in their countries.*

CHAPTER FIVE

DALY CITY, 2003

The holiday break was different this year. I went shopping with the girls, as usual, and spent my very first Hanukkah with Robert's family. I watched his mom and sister light the menorah as they all sang the Hebrew prayer. We ate a delicious meal of brisket, roasted Brussel sprouts, and crispy, salty *latkes*, (potato pancakes), which were wonderful, and were served with a choice of apple sauce or sour cream. I realized that, next year at this time, I might actually be celebrating the holiday and singing with them. It was all so surreal. There is no designated time for Jewish conversion. You're ready when you're ready. I would have to know Hebrew quite well in order to become a Bat Mitzvah, but not necessarily to convert. Christmas with the usual suspects was wonderful, as always. It hit me hard when I realized it was probably the last time I would celebrate the holiday as a Christian. Wow, it was really sinking in now!

My visit with Dr. Saperstein went very well. I had the tests, and all was status quo. I knew Esther would have uttered the words *Baruch Hashem,* which basically means with

God's help. I was in a very good place! Several days later, I kept my appointment with Rabbi Gottlieb. We discussed the particulars of my conversion process this time. We agreed that it would be best to wait until summer to begin my studies. In the interim, he recommended three books that he wanted me to read in preparation for the classes. This period of study would be central to my conversion process, he explained. Not only did I need to familiarize myself with basic beliefs and practices of Judaism, but I would need a chance to become integrated into the local Jewish community. There would be a lot of "internal growing," he explained. There would be a great deal to study and understand. It is truly an educational process, and it was his job to evaluate my progress until the subjective criteria were met. We had already spoken of all the ritual aspects that would be necessary to formalize the conversion, and he once again explained that becoming a Reform Jew would involve not only my course of study, but the necessity for me to participate in worship at the synagogue, and to live as a Jew for a period of time. We discussed that the conversion would take at least a year, maybe more—there was never a specific time frame. I was determined to come home on some weekends to attend services on Saturdays. Of utmost importance, he explained was the convening of a *Beit Din* prior to my immersion in the ritual *mikvah* bath, and the saying of the blessings. This, he described to me in great detail. The *Beit Din* is a Rabbinic Court that is, he explained, an assemblance of two or three additional rabbis who will ask a series of questions about my motivations for converting, my experience studying and practicing Judaism, Jewish holidays, rituals, theology, etc. This would take approximately thirty minutes to an hour. He gave me some additional literature to read but wanted to explain it further as we sat together.

"You will be asked your Hebrew name, and why and how you chose it." He explained that, as with literal newborns, the convert is a spiritual newborn, *k'tinok she'nolad,* and must select a Hebrew name, also adopting Abraham and Sarah as spiritual parents. "What most appeals to you about converting to Judaism? What has been your favorite part of the process? Is there any particular part of Judaism that you are interested in learning more about? Those are just a few of the questions," he explained.

I commented that this examination sounded grueling and difficult. He said that, yes, many found it so. His, and the rest of the committee's job, was to pull apart my conclusions and make me defend my answers.

I left the rabbi's study that day wondering if I was indeed ready for this enormous undertaking. When I got home, I called Esther, but she wasn't home yet, and her mom said she'd have her call me later. Then I called Robert and told him about my visit with Rabbi Gottlieb. He calmed me down immediately.

"Babe, this is what *you* want and no one is talking you into this. You made this decision, but you knew from day one it wouldn't be easy, especially while you're still in college. Are you sure you don't want to wait until after you graduate?" he asked.

"No, no, I'm sure. It's just very overwhelming, but this is definitely what I want, and I want to start as soon as the school year is over."

Chapter Six

Sacramento, 2004

Esther and I became closer friends than ever. I spent time at our school's Hillel chapter, and attended my first and eventually several other Shabbat services on Friday nights. Hillel's mission on college campuses is to "Help enrich the lives of Jewish students at school so that they may continue to enrich Jewish people and the world." I had been driving home every few weekends to attend services at Temple Beth Israel Judea and Rabbi Gottlieb always found time for me to chat afterward.

Spring break was upon us and I went home excited to attend a Passover *seder* at Robert's home. Several extended family members would also be attending. Good Friday and Easter were the same week as Passover. How strange and wonderful it all was, albeit a bit overwhelming! Passover, called *Pesach*, is a very important holiday on the Jewish calendar. Jewish people celebrate it in commemoration of their liberation by G-d from slavery in Egypt and their freedom as a nation under the leadership of Moses. I have learned that some Jews do not write the name God casually, but rather

G-d, rather than running the risk that the written Name might later be defaced, obliterated or destroyed accidentally. Case in point, a computer looks to correct G-d as an error and writes God.

I had offered to go over to Robert's house to help his mom and sister with some of the preparation. Not only would it be helpful to them, but I would actually be involved hands-on in the putting together of the *seder* plate, including the making of the *charoses,* and other items. Of course, between my reading, and my wonderful Esther, I now understood the meaning of the *seder* plate. Robert's family is Ashkenazi, as I have chosen to be since my roots are Chinese, and I have no ancestors from any of the Ashkenazi countries, and some of the traditions differ from the Sephardic ones. Ashkenazi Jews are the Jews of France, Germany, and Eastern Europe. Sephardic Jews are the Jews of Spain, Portugal, North Africa, and the Middle East. Some of the foods and traditions differ, but the beliefs are the same.

> *The seder is a ritual meal, involving the retelling of the story of the liberation of the Israelites from slavery in ancient Egypt. Often, it is a group effort, with one leader calling on participants to read from the Haggadah, which is given to every participant who is old enough to read. Many parts are read as a group and traditional songs are sung. The "Four Questions," "Mah Nishtanah," are recited by the youngest child. Why is this night different from all other nights? On all other nights, we eat leavened bread and on this night only matzo. On all other nights, we eat all vegetables and on this night only bitter herbs. On all other nights, we don't dip our food even once, and on this night we dip twice. On all other nights we eat sitting or reclining, and on this night we only recline.*

Every item on the seder plate and the foods eaten at Passover are also "food for thought." The seder plate abounds in meaning and allusion. The first item is a shank bone, z'roa. It is a piece of roasted meat, often a chicken neck that represents the lamb that was the special Paschal sacrifice on the eve of the exodus from Egypt. A hard-boiled egg, beitzah, is next, to represent the holiday offering brought in the days of the Holy Temple. The meat of this animal, the chicken, often constitutes a main part of the Passover meal. The egg, because of its shape, signifies the circle of life. Next are the bitter herbs, maror, which remind us of the bitterness of slavery. Horseradish is often used. Then there is the charoses, or paste. This is a delicious mixture of apples, nuts, and wine, often seasoned with cinnamon, and resembles the mortar and brick the Hebrews used when they toiled for Pharaoh. There is also the karpas, usually, parsley dipped into salt water, which represents tears and alludes to the back-breaking work of the Jews as slaves. Last is lettuce, chazeret, which symbolizes the bitter enslavement. While romaine leaves are not bitter, the stem left in the ground grows hard and bitter. Endive may be used as well. The sixth symbolic item on the seder table is a plate of three whole matzo, which are stacked and separated from each other by cloths, or napkins. The middle matzo is broken, and half of it is put aside for the afikoman, meaning "that which comes after dessert." It is often hidden by the head of the household for the children to find and receive a reward, usually of money. The top and the other half of the middle matzo is used for the hamotzi, the blessing over bread, and the bottom piece is used to form the korech, a Hillel sandwich. As part of the seder, there is a re-enactment of ancient customs as we read from the Haggadah, the book all seder participants use. We eat matzo, which is a flat bread which symbolizes the yeast-less bread that was eaten by the Jews and baked in haste, with no time for the yeast to rise. Hillel, a famous Jewish leader, is said to have wrapped the Paschal lamb, the matzo, and bitter herbs between two pieces of matzo, to satisfy the statement, "With matzo and maror they shall eat it." Hillel is famous for having said, "If I am not for myself who is for me? And being for my own self, what am I? And if not now, when?" It is also traditional for a bowl of salt water to be placed on the table. Often, hard-boiled eggs in salt water are eaten. After the re-telling of the story, a traditional meal is eaten. Desserts often incorporate honey and apples. Macaroons and pomegranates are also popular.

The *seder* at Robert's home was wonderful. They had gone to cousins for the first *seder* night, as two were celebrated, and this was the second night. I was totally enthralled by the interaction at the table. With Robert's father no longer alive to conduct the seder, their close neighbors, who were dear friends, were at the seder, along with their son and daughter, who was Bonnie's close friend. Jerry, the neighbor, conducted the reading of the *Haggadah*. I thoroughly enjoyed myself. The *charoses* were delicious. I dipped my finger into my wine glass ten times as part of the tradition, and wiped it off on the side of my plate as we recited the ten plagues that G-d had perpetrated upon the Egyptians, including the smiting of the first-born son.

Presbyterianism is a quietly practiced religion. So much of Jewish practice seemed so alive with tradition and meaningfulness. Tonight was a night of joy and family love as I did my best to sing the phonetic lyrics to the song *Dayenu*, meaning "It would have been enough for us" or "It would have been sufficient." It is to thank G-d for all the gifts given to the Hebrew people, including taking them out of slavery. Later, at home, I was aware of a totally corny warm and fuzzy feeling. One more time I felt secure in my decision to convert.

I went back to school after the break, and finished my junior year with a 3.7 GPA. Robert had taken the LSATs (the half-day standardized test necessary for admission into law school), in June. He had completed what's called a BARBRI prep course earlier in the semester and now would wait for his LSATs results prior to his application to law schools in his senior year. He ended school with a 3.9 and passed his LSATs with a more than decent score. I was so proud of what we had both accomplished.

Chapter Seven

Daly City, California, 2004

A beautiful summer passed, and I was very close to finishing my senior year in college. I was busily enmeshed in my Torah studies, the pre-requisite for me to convert to Judaism. I attended classes at the temple once a week on Tuesday nights in addition to my Hebrew course at school. I was doing a lot of driving back and forth. I regularly attended Shabbat services at school, as well. The classes were wonderfully interesting, but I found the Hebrew class I was taking difficult. I hoped to get a good grade. I was exhausted at times, but I was putting my heart into it because I wanted it so badly.

I couldn't believe graduation was almost here! Robert was accepted to McGeorge School of Law, which was part of his school, University of the Pacific. The school was highly ranked in the United States. Having graduated with such a high GPA, he won a partial scholarship, which would make things easier on him and his mom as he was taking huge student loans to attend the school. We knew our marriage would involve years of paying back loans. He had undergrad loans as well. Fortunately, my folks had footed the bill for my B.A.

degree. I knew how very lucky I was. Since he was going to still be local, it would make it easy on our relationship. Fortunately, my senior year workload wasn't huge and not terribly difficult, except for the Hebrew class. I expected to graduate with a more-than-decent GPA. Naturally, our families would be attending both of our graduations, only a few weeks away. I was coming home to continue my studies, but it was easier because I would no longer have the college workload. I continued my Hebrew studies at home through the temple. Rabbi Gottlieb told me I was doing well, and he was very pleased.

Graduation was exciting, and it was an amazing experience. I couldn't believe I had my Bachelor's degree. My parents were quite proud of me. It was hard to say goodbye to the girls and guys I had developed strong friendships with. We all promised to keep in touch. I knew I would continue to be friends with Melissa and with Esther, who was so proud of me. Going home for good felt strange. Yes, it was summer, and I was always home for the summer, but it was different. My future lay ahead of me as I continued my studies in my Jewish education. Now, with my journalism degree, I felt a newfound sense of responsibility. I needed to begin my search for a job. Many of my friends were searching for work as well, and many had had the opportunity to work at internships in the past two years during the summers, while I had studied for my *Beit Din.* Other friends would be starting their workload towards an M.A. or M.S. degree. Robert had been offered a summer internship. It was in marketing in the music field dealing with pop and rock. How coincidental, considering my dad has been in a similar field for a lifetime. It wasn't a well-paid position, but he was excited to get started somewhere.

I emailed my short resume out to many headhunters, hoping to land a job interview. Robert and I planned to live together before we married. Surprisingly, a small art book business showed interest in me, and an interview was arranged. The offices weren't terribly far away—a twelve-fifteen minute ride from where I lived now. I met with an "artsy" type of woman in her late fifties, I guessed. They were looking for someone with either a journalism or art degree. I had no experience in either field, but I had a degree in Journalism, and they liked me. They couldn't pay much of a salary. I would be a receptionist for the most part, but it would involve some proofreading, as well as other simple duties. I could learn on the job, she said. They had preferred an art student for some of the other tasks, but my journalism degree got me the position. I decided to take it, knowing full well that I was lucky to get offered a job on the first shot. Robert and my family were terribly proud of me, and of him. I would have to continue my Jewish studies with evening classes.

I began my new job, and found that I like the small staff very much. I made an appointment to see Dr. Saperstein. Things were the same, and we all gave thanks for the great news. I gave a donation to my temple, called *tzedakah*. In the Jewish faith, it is seen as not quite charity, but as a religious obligation, regardless of how small an amount one can afford to give. All was good. I enjoyed my work, studied hard, and Robert began law school. He found his initial classes challenging. It's known to be the most difficult year of law school. You didn't get to choose your courses for the first year of law school, known as 1L. It was overwhelming, with hundreds of pages of assigned reading. Law school classes were graded on a forced curve, meaning there was only a set number of each grade given out, such as As, A minuses, B pluses, Bs, etc. The majority of grades fell in the B plus/B range. On top of everything else, there were no homework assignments or graded tests. Each student was totally responsible to work on his own. What counted was the final exam. Even grading was blind; the professor saw nothing but the students' ID numbers. Classes included contract and constitutional law. Robert spent hours reading, and as the first semester waned, I hardly saw him, between his and my studying, classes, and job.

I finally completed my studies. My Hebrew was pretty decent and I was very proud of myself. I chose a Hebrew name for myself, Shoshana, which meant lily in Biblical times, but in modern Hebrew it was understood to mean rose. It evolved to become Sue, Susan, Suzanne and other derivatives. In the Song of Songs, the lovely girl is compared to a lily of the valley, a lily among thorns. I have chosen to be that strong, beautiful flower. At last Rabbi Gottlieb told me he felt I was ready for my *beit din*, my formal conversion to Judaism. This authorization by a Jewish court represents, in a manner of speaking, the whole Jewish people. This court of three rabbis may approve or deny my application. As the day drew closer, I found myself apprehensive about the actual questioning process, but never did I have a moment's pause regarding my decision to convert.

On the day of my *beit din,* I dressed carefully in a modest navy blue dress, with my arms covered, and a pair of low-heeled matching pumps. We met in my rabbi's study. There were two other rabbis there. I was introduced to them and invited to sit, whereupon the questioning began. It was held in the form of a conversation, and my heart was beating strongly but I felt prepared with my heartfelt answers regarding my choice to convert to Judaism. It seemed to last forever but finally, once they had ascertained my sincerity, the members of the *beit din* signed a conversion certificate bearing my new Hebrew name, Shoshana. Before all the rituals were completed, I completed the final one, the process of immersion in a *mikvah*. This bath is a rebirth, actually the source of the Christian baptism, not meant to wash away my past life, but rather to offer a beginning and a promise. I dressed for the first time as a Jew and returned to my rabbi, who now had my family and friends with him. I was greeted with applause and those who knew it sang *"Siman Tov U' Mazel Tov,"* which is a song of congratulations. The rest of the family and more friends met us at a restaurant where we celebrated with a wonderful meal, and lovely gifts were pressed upon me. I cannot find the words to express my joy. Robert was beaming, and gave me a beautiful gold Star of David encrusted with tiny diamonds and sapphires on a thin chain. Truly my cup runneth over.

Chapter Eight

Westlake, 2008

Robert graduated from law school, and now it was his turn to seek a job. He was interested in finance, and had sought work with a brokerage house or bank. He never knew how he actually scored on the Bar exam; it was only posted as pass/fail. But, pass he had! I had a B.A. after my name, and he a B.A. and J.D. (Juris Doctor) after his. I changed jobs, finding the art book company job was offering little chance for advancement. I had been writing ads and articles, which garnered me a lot of experience, but I felt exploited as I was working very hard for very little money. A friend had heard that a fabulous magazine was looking for writers. I sent them my resume and they arranged an interview. Two weeks later, I was working there. It was a new, smart, local magazine that afforded me a chance to do research for the various writers, as well as write some articles on my own. Happily, Robert had obtained work with a brokerage firm called Morgan Stanley. His position was in the compliance department, which ensures that all employees and officers of the firm comply with the Securities and Exchange Commission (SEC) and Financial

Industry Regulatory Authority (FINRA) rules. It turned out to be a wonderful opportunity as the following year the company would undergo many changes and a merger that would change their name to Morgan Stanley Smith Barney and become the largest wealth management company in the world.

We had been engaged for five years and living together as well. With our lives finally settled, it was time to get married and we had been working on the plans for quite some time. Our wedding was to be in a month, and we were frantically putting the final touches on everything. Rather than a Chinese/American wedding, it would be a Jewish wedding, complete with a *chuppah* (marriage canopy), and *kippahs* (*yarmulkes*, or skull caps) available to the guests. We weren't kosher, so the food would allow myriads of choices for all to enjoy.

My gown was simple. It was an ivory lace A-line, with a sweetheart neckline and a fingertip-length veil. Attached to the veil was a small headpiece of Swarovski crystals. My color scheme was mauve and ivory and so our invitations and wedding decor were in those colors. Mrs. Roberts, whom I had long ago started calling by her first name, Andrea, and my mom, were wearing long, elegant gowns in shades of mauve. Esther, Melissa, Allison, and Ellen were my bridesmaids and also had long dresses in a deeper shade of mauve. Lisa, my matron of honor, wore a beautiful lace-trimmed gown in a similar shade. She had gotten married two years earlier. Each of the bridesmaids' dresses was a slightly different style, and Esther's dress had long sleeves to accommodate her religious practice that she adhered to in temple. A kosher meal would be provided for Esther and her new husband, Ari, as well as for Rabbi Gottlieb, who was conducting the ceremony, and his wife. Robert had four groomsmen. Lisa's husband Paul was his best man. All were wearing black tuxedos. We had hired a band, chosen our flowers, and all seemed ready to go.

Our wedding was all I could have dreamed of and more. Everything was perfect. We had about one hundred and fifty people, including family and friends from both sides. How my family had grown! It was wonderful to see Joey and Joanie and their kids, Lawrence, Linda, Matt and the twins, and all our dear friends and family. The ceremony was beautiful and traditional as we drank from the *Kiddush* cup and exchanged our vows and rings and the rabbi pronounced us husband and wife. Robert stepped on the glass as a reminder that despite the joy, Jews still mourn the destruction of the Temple of Jerusalem. The crowd yelled "Mazel Tov!" My heart was overflowing with joy.

Epilogue

Pacifica, 2030

Susan and Robert Jacobs, along with their children David, nineteen, and Samantha, sixteen, live in the house with the apple trees in front. Jazzy, the poodle was replaced by Piper, another apricot toy poodle, who also loves apples. Their lives were simple and happy. Robert works for the law firm O'Brian, Johnson, Graber, and Fine, and several years ago became a junior partner. Susan left *C Magazine*, having made the move five years earlier to work for Penguin Random House, one of the largest American multinational publishing companies in the world. She was a creative manager, collaborating with authors to help them find ways to succeed at writing stories that would appeal to audiences worldwide. David was in his second year of college, and Sam was a sophomore in high school. Following family tradition, Susan gave her daughter the journal that their matriarch, Zhang Ling, Sam's great grandmother had written many years ago.

Ling was born in Shanghai in 1905, and wrote in the journal throughout her life. It was passed to each daughter (fortunately, there was a daughter in each of four generations).

At the age of sixteen Samantha was the fourth daughter to receive the journal. The brown leather book had been carefully preserved. Ling had her journal translated into English before she gave it to her daughter Yuming. She had written Chinese characters in the Wu dialect spoken in Shanghai, which Yuming couldn't read. Years later, Yuming gave the book to her daughter, Mina, (who had Americanized her name from Min). She had the journal and translation carefully preserved be placing them in polyethylene jackets, and then stored in artifact boxes. The family photographs, which were collected by Ling throughout her life, were stored in the same way. This was a precious family heirloom, immortalized in print and graphics. At sixteen, Susan, who had received it from her mother Mina, passed the memoir to her daughter Samantha, who was overwhelmed, as were the previous recipients, by the life of this extraordinary woman.

For several years, Susan had been thinking about publishing the journal. Susan worked as a copy editor, having gone back to school to complete a Master's Degree in Publishing years earlier. The process was started by collaborating with various members of different departments at the publishing house. Legal and technical matters were attended to first. The journal then went through the editorial stage. Susan wrote a prologue to the manuscript, paying homage to the author, Zhang Ling. There were no changes in the journal itself other than working with the typographers. The photographs were rich illustrations to the story. Titles and fonts were chosen, and artwork for the cover design was decided upon. In Susan's many years in her field, nothing had prepared her for how publishing this work would touch her heart. Since she began keeping her journal in 1920, at the age of sixteen, here, at last, was the incredible story of "The Journey from Shanghai to Gold Mountain."